Meeting Peg

As I watched, the pool kind of sucked itself up and swirled around and turned into an old bogeywoman. She was short and onion shaped from the layers and layers of ratty, wet skirts and shawls she had on. Her nails were long and black, and her thin gray hair dripped over her head and shoulders like a string mop. She had a round, pale face and round, muddy eyes, and a smile like a row of green knives. That, and the way she was looking at me as if I were a double-dipped chocolate ice cream cone, told me that she rode with the Wild Hunt.

"Hello there, dear. You can call me Peg Powler. I was at your Changing. You were too little to remember me, but I remember you. You, if memory serves, are called Neef."

My first thought was that when Astris found out I'd been talking to Peg Powler of the Wild Hunt, she was going to kill me, or at least put me to sleep for a hundred years.

My second thought was that if I could get myself out of this, she'd never have to know.

FIREBIRD
WHERE FANTASY TAKES FLIGHT™

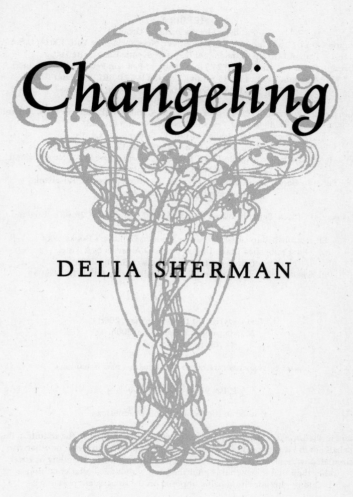

Changeling

DELIA SHERMAN

FIREBIRD

AN IMPRINT OF PENGUIN GROUP (USA) INC.

FIREBIRD
Published by the Penguin Group
Penguin Group (USA) Inc., 345 Hudson Street, New York, New York 10014, U.S.A.
Penguin Group (Canada), 90 Eglinton Avenue East, Suite 700,
Toronto, Ontario, Canada M4P 2Y3 (a division of Pearson Penguin Canada Inc.)
Penguin Books Ltd, 80 Strand, London WC2R 0RL, England
Penguin Ireland, 25 St Stephen's Green, Dublin 2, Ireland
(a division of Penguin Books Ltd)
Penguin Group (Australia), 250 Camberwell Road, Camberwell, Victoria 3124, Australia
(a division of Pearson Australia Group Pty Ltd)
Penguin Books India Pvt Ltd, 11 Community Centre,
Panchsheel Park, New Delhi - 110 017, India
Penguin Group (NZ), 67 Apollo Drive, Rosedale, North Shore 0632, New Zealand
(a division of Pearson New Zealand Ltd)
Penguin Books (South Africa) (Pty) Ltd, 24 Sturdee Avenue, Rosebank,
Johannesburg 2196, South Africa

Registered Offices: Penguin Books Ltd, 80 Strand, London WC2R 0RL, England

First published in Great Britain by Hodden Children's Books, 2006
First published in the United States of America by Viking,
a division of Penguin Young Readers Group, 2006
Published by Firebird, an imprint of Penguin Group (USA) Inc., 2008

1 3 5 7 9 10 8 6 4 2

Text copyright © Delia Sherman, 2006
Map copyright © Sam Kim, 2006
All rights reserved

LIBRARY OF CONGRESS CATALOGING-IN-PUBLICATION DATA IS AVAILABLE

ISBN 978-0-14-241188-9

Printed in the United States of America

FOR
Masako Katagiri, Ellen Kushner,
and Ophelia Goss
Who were, are, and will be

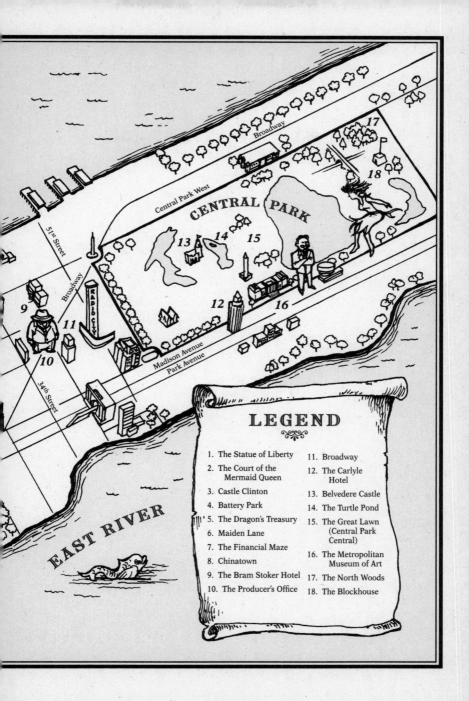

LEGEND

1. The Statue of Liberty
2. The Court of the Mermaid Queen
3. Castle Clinton
4. Battery Park
5. The Dragon's Treasury
6. Maiden Lane
7. The Financial Maze
8. Chinatown
9. The Bram Stoker Hotel
10. The Producer's Office
11. Broadway
12. The Carlyle Hotel
13. Belvedere Castle
14. The Turtle Pond
15. The Great Lawn (Central Park Central)
16. The Metropolitan Museum of Art
17. The North Woods
18. The Blockhouse

CHANGELING

CHAPTER
1

FAIRY GODMOTHERS ARE ALWAYS RIGHT.

Neef's Rules for Changelings

"Wake up, Neef. Spring cleaning today. Cobwebs to sweep, mice to relocate, turtles to wake up and polish. And you have to clean your room."

I groaned and put the pillow over my head.

A cold, wet nose touched my forehead and flipped the pillow away.

"None of that, now," Astris said. "If you don't get cracking, the bogles will come visit, and then where will you be?"

"Asleep," I said. "Go away, Astris."

The covers slithered off my shoulders. I made a grab for them, caught something long and whiplike instead, let it go again. Fast. I haven't pulled her tail on purpose since I was very little. Astris hates having her tail pulled even more than I hate waking up. She says it's not respectful to pull my fairy godmother's tail.

Astris is a white rat and very beautiful. She has fur like a powder-puff, eyes like polished rubies, and long, delicate whiskers. I swear she says as much with her whiskers as she does with words.

"Finally," she said, as I sat up and yawned. "Come right down as soon as you've dressed and had breakfast. I want to get a start on those turtles." She surveyed my room, her whiskers severe. "This place looks like a hooraw's nest. We'll have to get the Blockhouse brownie in to help you organize it. Again."

I knew my room was a mess. It always is. It's hard to keep a place neat when the only furniture is a curtained bed and an old chest. The walls are mostly taken up by pointy stone windows, so there's nowhere except the floor to keep my leaf collection and my rocks, not to mention the mortal magazines and papers and stuff I've picked up in the Park.

Astris hopped off my bed and disappeared down the stairs. I got up and sifted through the chest looking for something I could wear. Everything I had was suddenly too tight, too short, or both. Much as I hated spring cleaning, at least it meant I'd be getting new clothes. I wiggled into some green leggings and a shirt that used to be floppy, tried to drag a comb through my frizzy hair, gave up, and dug around until I found my silver knife and fork. Then I took Satchel down from its hook and climbed back onto my bed.

"Toast and jam, please," I told it. "Apricot jam. And apple juice."

Satchel is my magic bag. It's brown leather and has brass buckles and its own ideas about a proper breakfast for spring cleaning day. When I lifted its flap, I found a glass of orange juice (I hate orange juice) and a plate of eggs and sausage, which I wasn't in the mood for. But I ate it anyway. In the New York I live in, mortals don't call the shots. The Fairy Folk do.

Ordinary mortals think New York Outside is the only one there is. They're wrong. There are at least two New Yorks, and probably more, sharing the same space, but not exactly the same reality. I live in New York Between.

Things that are invisible Outside are visible Between. Every tall building, for instance, has its mountain spirit that Outsiders can't see. But we can. Our bridges and tunnels are swarming with trolls and demons of all sizes and colors. Our streets are crowded with sidhe from Ireland, kitsune and tanuki from Japan, devi from India, and an assortment of giants and demons and frost spirits and will-o'-the-wisps from all over the world. Some of the more human-looking Folk cross to New York Outside for fun and adventures, but ordinary mortals can't come to New York Between unless the Folk bring them.

This happens more often than you'd think. Mostly the

visiting mortals don't remember much. I remember—but then, I live here.

I'm a changeling. A Kid-napper from the Bureau of Changeling Affairs brought me here when I was little, leaving a fairy that looked just like me behind in my bed. It's a great honor to be the Central Park changeling. Other neighborhoods in New York Between have a bunch of mortal changelings, but Park Folk aren't all that comfortable with mortals and only take a changeling because it's traditional. So I was the only mortal around.

I've spent a lot of time thinking about why I was stolen and brought to Central Park. Before I was big enough to understand that questions were against the rules, I used to pester Astris about it. Her answers were either silly ("Because you have curly hair"; "Because you like cookies") or too vague to be useful ("Because you're good for us"; "Because we can"). Finally I got the message and stopped asking.

After I'd finished my eggs, I went down the spiral stair to the kitchen, where Astris had a row of what looked like mud-covered rocks lined up on the floor. Every once in a while, one would poke out a wrinkled head, blink, yawn, and retreat again. I knew how it felt.

"Hand me down the turtle wax," Astris said. "And fetch some water. I swear, they're even muddier than usual this year."

There's no running water in Belvedere Castle. Hauling it from the Turtle Pond is my main chore. It's no joke, especially on bath day. The bucket is wooden, and heavy even when it's empty. I have to lug it across the terrace to the edge of the cliff overlooking the Pond, attach the bucket to the rope, drop it into the water, and pull it up again without spilling. Plus, I have to be careful not to disturb the fish, or I'll get in trouble with the Water Rat.

The Water Rat is a Fictional Character. A writer made him up, but he was so real that he took on a life of his own. He loves messing about in boats, and spends the whole summer either fixing his rowboat or sculling it around the pond having picnics and talking to the fish and the turtles and insulting the ducks that nest in the reeds.

Today, he had the boat turned upside down on the grassy bank and was painting the bottom sky blue.

"Hullo there, youngster," he called up to me. His white polo shirt and baggy chinos were neat as always, but he had a streak of blue paint across his muzzle. "You haven't picked up any fish in that bucket of yours, by any chance? Spring cleaning or no spring cleaning, I don't like my fish disturbed in spawning season."

"No, Mr. Rat," I called back politely.

"That's a good girl," he said. "Busy time of year, isn't it? When things have calmed down a bit, look me out and I'll take you for a nice row. We'll pack a basket, trade stories. Have I told you about the time Mole and Toad and Badger and I turfed the Wild Wooders out of Toad Hall, back in the Old Country?"

"Yes, Mr. Rat. But I'd like to hear it again."

"Excellent," he said cheerfully. "Come when you like. Bring Astris. A few of those wonderful golden biscuits of hers would be very welcome. And a new story, if you have one."

All Folk love stories. They love to hear them nearly as much as they love to tell them. I've heard stories from Japan, Brazil, Ireland, Russia, Kenya, Jamaica—just about every country in the world whose Folk have followed the mortal immigrants to New York. Astris, who is a native New Yorker, specializes in New York stories like "The Sewer Maintenance-Worker's Wife" and "Little Red Baseball Cap." The stories are as different as the Folk who tell them, but the one thing they have in common is morals. "Don't be greedy" is a popular one, and "Don't ask too many questions," and "Don't be too curious," and most important of all, "Don't break the rules."

I love the stories, but I could live without the morals. They all boil down to *Don't*. Don't do this. Don't talk to that. Don't turn around and look when you hear a strange noise. Don't turn over stones to see what's under them. Don't swim in Harlem Meer or walk on Sheep's Meadow without a Shepherd. Don't ride on any black animal with flaming eyes. Because if you do, you'll be sorry, sorry, sorry, sorry. Once I asked Astris what happened to all the mortals who hadn't disobeyed all those Don'ts and she just looked at me, her whiskers confused.

"I don't know," she said. "I never thought about it. Perhaps they went straight to living happily ever after."

Well, I thought about it. And what I thought was that nothing happened to those mortals—nothing at all.

Which was what was happening to me. Like Radiatorella with no ball to go to, I was stuck fetching water and cleaning my room forever and ever.

The Water Rat went back to his painting and I hauled the bucket, sloshing, back across the courtyard. When I got to the kitchen, Astris had brushed the worst of the mud off the turtles.

"Thank you, pet," she said, dipping her scrub brush into the water. "There's more to do today than I'd thought. I've been talking to the mice. There are *six* families to pack and move to the Shakespeare Garden, and the ghosts in the basement are stuck in the cobwebs again, and the squirrels need help getting those nutshells out of the attic. I can't spare the time to go to the Blockhouse. We'll have to leave your room until tomorrow."

This is the kind of news that sounds better than it actually is. No brownie didn't just mean not cleaning my room today. It meant entertaining baby mice and calming hysterical ghosts or, if I was really lucky, shoveling nutshells out of the attic. And I'd still have to clean my room tomorrow.

"Why don't I go get the brownie by myself?" I said.

"No," said Astris, scrubbing briskly. "Unsupervised adventures are for big girls."

"But I *am* big, Astris. Just look at me!"

She looked. Her whiskers expressed a familiar combination of impatience and worry, moving into surprise as she took in my too-short leggings and my too-tight shirt.

"So you are," she said slowly. "Still, the North Woods. It's not safe up there. Maybe the Pooka can go with you."

On any other day, this would have been fine. The Pooka is a lot more fun to be around than Astris, who tends to turn everything into a lesson on Folk lore. He's a trickster and a shapeshifter. When he's not being a man, he's being one of those flaming-eyed animals it's dangerous for mortals to ride. But he's my fairy godfather, so I can ride him whenever I want.

Today, though, I was feeling itchy and restless. I wanted to be somewhere I didn't always go, doing something I didn't always do. I wanted an adventure.

"It's spring cleaning day," I said. "He's probably busy. *Please* can I go alone? It's not like the Blockhouse is hard to find. All I have to do is follow the brownie's path up to the crest of the hill, and I'm there."

"Well . . ." said Astris. Her eyes darted from me to the turtles to the swarm of excited mice piling candle stubs and candy wrappers and moldy bread by the kitchen door. "All right. But go straight there and come right back. Keep on the main path to the Blockhouse. Don't look to the left, don't look to the right . . ."

"And whatever I do, don't wander from the path," I finished for her. "Do I look like Little Red Baseball Cap?"

Astris fixed me with her ruby eyes. "The North Woods

are dangerous, Neef. The Wild Hunt lives in the North Woods. Just because the Hunt doesn't ride by daylight doesn't mean all the Hunters are asleep."

I was about ready to jump out of my skin with impatience. "I *know*, Astris. I can take care of myself. You taught me how to say 'I am under the protection of the Genius of Central Park' in about a million languages, remember?"

"So I did," Astris said. "But the Genius's protection only covers you from consumption and grievous bodily harm. There are other ways the Hunt can hurt you. Don't talk to anyone you don't know. And if you meet a stranger, call the Pooka immediately. Do you have the hair to summon him with? Do you have Satchel in case you get hungry? Oh, dear. Maybe I should come with you after all."

"Don't worry," I said. "I'll be fine. Bye!" And I was out of there before she could change her mind.

The stones of the courtyard were warm under my bare feet, and the air smelled of damp soil and green things growing. The big mulberry tree in the Shakespeare Garden was bright with tightly furled buds. Down by its roots, the fairies Mustardseed and Peaseblossom were trying to talk some primroses into unfolding early so they could have new skirts. I waved and shouted, but they didn't even hear me.

The shortest way to the North Woods lies straight across Central Park Central. On warm, bright days, the huge lawn is usually thick with Folk playing complicated games or spreading their wings to the sun. Today it was deserted except for a team of corn spirits drifting slowly along the grass, combing it smooth with their long fingers. Hoping they were too focused on their work to see me, I tried to sneak across behind them, but as soon as my foot touched the grass, they yelled at me to get off.

One of the things I hate about Folk is that they notice you when you don't want them to.

The path took me east to the Obelisk, then turned north toward the Metropolitan Museum. Some adventure. This was the path I walked nearly every day on my way to the Museum to learn art and mortal languages. Sometimes I went on to the nearby Reservoir to swim with the nixies and undines. I'd never been allowed to go further north than that, not alone.

Today, the Reservoir embankment showed signs of spring cleaning, all draped with waterweed airing in the sun. I scrambled up and threw a pebble into the water. A sleek-headed nixie surfaced and shook her long green hair out of her eyes.

"What do you want?" she snapped.

"Hi, Algae," I said. "I'm going to the North Woods to fetch the Blockhouse brownie. By myself."

"You nearly brained me with a rock to tell me *that*? Go away! Some people have work to do." Algae flicked her tail and disappeared.

Folk are like that. Bother them when they're busy, and they'll bite your head off. The nasty ones do it literally.

Beyond the Reservoir is the East Meadow. From here, the most direct route to the North Woods is by way of the Mount. It is not, however, the safest way to go. The Mount is surrounded by woods and haunted by ghosts and forest demons and ogres and enchanted snakes. Even under today's bright sunshine, the trees looked extra dark and gnarly, totally un-spring-cleanable.

I decided that Astris would want me to take the long way around.

It was a long walk. By the time I got to Harlem Meer, my feet were like lumps of hot tar. I got an apple from Satchel and cooled my toes in the water while I ate it. It just wasn't fair. At the very least, I should have met an old woman at the crossroads or a magic bluebird or a fairy musician offering to sell his fiddle in exchange for something I shouldn't give up. The most exciting things I'd seen today were teams of veelas and squirrels and dryads cleaning the dead wood out of the trees and encouraging the baby leaves to grow. Boring.

Something rustled in the reeds, and my heart beat a little faster. A pair of ducks appeared from behind a rock, herding a clutch of puffball ducklings out toward open water. I threw my apple core at them, got up, and trudged on toward the North Woods.

As Astris said, the North Woods are wild. South of

Central Park Central, the dryads and hamadryads keep the trees and bushes groomed and neat. In the North Woods, they don't bother. The Wild Hunt lives in the North Woods, and the Wild Hunt acknowledges no authority—except, sometimes, the Genius of Central Park.

For anybody who doesn't know, Genius is short for *genius loci*, which (I know from my Latin lessons) means "the spirit of the place." Important New York places—Wall Street, Broadway, Grand Central Station, the New York Public Library, the Village—have Geniuses. Some are really, really old, like the Mermaid Queen of New York Harbor. Some are practically brand-new, like the Conductor of Lincoln Center. But each Genius rules its territory absolutely.

The Green Lady of Central Park is the original Genius of the Island of Manhattan. We Park Folk are very proud of her. During the Genius Wars, she fought the newer, younger city Geniuses for territory, losing acre after acre of woodland to their buildings. Eventually, they made a treaty. Central Park was separated from the rest of the city and the Lady got some of her land back. Now she's the queen of all the green places in New York, and the Wild Hunt owes her allegiance. Mostly, she lets them do what they want, which is why the North Woods are so dark and tangled and dangerous.

The path to the Blockhouse is easy to find, because the brownie keeps it clean and clear of brambles and rocks and old dead branches. I stomped along it, getting hotter and crabbier by the step, until I got to the massive stone stair that leads to the top of the hill. I wiped my sweaty face on my sleeve. Heroes in stories have magic shoes and things that help them through the boring parts of their adventures. So I wasn't a real hero, or this wasn't a real adventure. Which I'd already figured out, but I didn't like having my nose rubbed in it.

I tripped on the third step and landed sprawling. Sitting up, I licked my scraped palm and checked out the rip in my leggings.

And then I noticed a second path branching off the steps to the right, a path I swear hadn't been there before.

Scrambling to my feet, I peered into the shadows. It looked as if the path climbed the hill in a gentle spiral, longer but not nearly as steep as the brownie's stair. The path itself was narrow and rocky and weedy underfoot, and the branches of the trees wove together above it to make a cool, green, murmuring tunnel.

I knew what I *should* do, of course. I *should* turn away from that tempting path and climb straight to the Blockhouse as Astris had told me to. But if I did that, there'd be no adventure. Every story I'd ever heard started with the hero breaking a rule, sometimes by accident, sometimes on purpose. Either way, they lived happily ever after.

Stairs or path? A fake adventure or a real one? It was up to me.

Who cared about Little Red Baseball Cap? She was an idiot who couldn't tell the difference between an old lady and a wolf in a nightgown. I'd heard a lot of fairy tales, and I remembered what I'd heard. If the stories warned me against getting into trouble, they also showed me ways of getting out of it again.

I took a deep breath and stepped onto the rocky path.

CHAPTER
2

STICKS AND STONES MAY BREAK YOUR BONES,
BUT WORDS CAN GET YOU IN A LOT OF TROUBLE.

Neef's Rules for Changelings

After its gentle beginning, the path curved steeply up over boulders and knobbly tree roots. I squashed the thought that the stairs would have been easier and scrambled on. The path narrowed, twisted up along the side of a particularly craggy rock, plunged down a slope thick with slippery pine needles, and finally trickled out into a swampy green pool at the foot of a gigantic, half-rotten willow tree.

I flopped down on a stump and looked around. Behind the pool and the willow, the woods made a solid wall of green and brown. The path had totally disappeared.

My heart thumped painfully. What lived in swamps? Water-horses and vodyanoi, mostly. I knew how to deal with them. Or there could be a demon living in the willow. Whatever it was, I was ready for it.

"What have we here, my dear, a-wandering in the woods? Is it tender? Is it delicious?"

The voice seemed to come from the pool. It sounded like sharp teeth and hunger. The hair on my neck prickled with excitement.

"Peace be upon you, good Folk," I said, maybe louder than I needed to. "I am under the protection of the Genius of Central Park."

"Awwww," a second voice said. It was as hungry as the first, but higher and whinier. "It knows the words."

"Of course it does," the toothy voice said. "It's a clever little changeling girl, isn't it, dear? And it's been well taught. What's your name, little changeling?"

Here's where I should have kept my mouth shut and called the Pooka to come get me. But I should have stayed on the main path, too, and there's not much point in choosing to have a real adventure if you're going to scream for rescue as soon as anything interesting happens. It wasn't like I was in any real danger or anything, I reminded myself—not as long as I didn't tell the voice my name. You'd have to be dumber than Little Red Baseball Cap to tell anybody your real name in New York Between. It gives them too much power over you.

"I'll tell you mine if you tell me yours," I said.

"There, dear," said the voice. "Didn't I say she was clever?"

The second voice sighed. "This is boring. What say we leave her here until she's dead, dead, dead, and *then* we eat her? The Lady couldn't get us for that, could she?"

"It may be an idea, dear," the first voice said. "But it's a very stupid one. Don't be frightened, little changeling," it went on soothingly. "Blueberry here was only joking. We wouldn't dream of hurting a hair on your little head."

It hadn't sounded like Blueberry was joking to me, but I laughed anyway, to show that I wasn't scared. And I wasn't. Really. I was just thinking that this adventure wasn't going anywhere, and I might as well leave. But when I turned around, the path had disappeared behind a thicket of thorny brambles.

I started to feel just a little nervous. "Ha-ha," I said. "Very funny. Could you put the path back, please? Astris of Belvedere Castle is expecting me back soon, and if I don't show up, she'll come looking for me. You wouldn't like that."

"Oh, no," the voice bubbled. "We're old friends, Astris and I. I was at your Changing, you know. Let me take a closer look at you."

As I watched, the pool kind of sucked itself up and swirled around and turned into an old bogeywoman. She was short and onion-shaped from the layers and layers of ratty, wet skirts and shawls she had on. Her nails were long and black, and her thin gray hair dripped over her head and shoulders like a string mop. She had a round, pale face and round, muddy eyes, and a smile like a row of green knives. That, and the way she was looking at me as if I were a double-dipped chocolate ice-cream cone, told me that she rode with the Wild Hunt.

"Hello there, dear. You can call me Peg Powler. My, how you've grown! But then, you would, wouldn't you? Being a mortal child and all. Let me see, what did Astris call you? Oh, I remember now. Neef."

My first thought was that when Astris found out I'd talked to Peg Powler of the Wild Hunt, she was going to kill me, or at least put me to sleep for a hundred years.

My second thought was that if I could get out of this by myself, she'd never have to know.

Peg spread herself comfortably on a stone like a huge and very ugly toad. "It's too beautiful a day to be running errands for a rat, even a fairy one. Sit down, dear, and let's have a chat. Blueberry, will you join us?"

"No," said the second voice sulkily. "I'm hungry."

Peg grinned greenly at me. "Blueberry's just shy. It'll come out when it's ready. Now. What shall we talk about? Oh, I know. We'll talk about dancing. Do you like to dance, dear?"

As it happens, I do. When I was little, Astris had sent me to the peri Iolanthe for dancing lessons, and I really got into it. I always went to the full-moon dances on Gathering Nights, although someone always made me stop dancing just when I was starting to have fun. But I wasn't about to talk about that with Peg Powler. I shrugged. "It's okay."

"Oh, I think you like it more than *that*, dear. I've seen you at the Gatherings, kicking up your mortal heels in the fairy ring just as if you'd been born to it."

"Why ask me if you already know the answer? Yes, I like to dance. So what? I like hamburgers, too, and chocolate and those mortal magazines I find in the Park. Have you ever seen *Glamour* or *Macworld*? They're awesome."

Peg ignored this. "I was just wondering, dear, seeing how good a dancer you are and how much you enjoy it, why we never see you at the Solstice Dance?"

When Peg said "Solstice Dance," the trees cracked overhead, the air thickened, and my skin prickled all over. I felt as if the whole Park was listening for my answer. The embarrassing thing was, I didn't have one.

"I don't know," I said. "What's the Solstice Dance?"

The feeling of waiting and listening swelled suddenly and popped. Peg's smile grew until the ends disappeared behind her ears.

"You don't know about the Solstice Dance? You're pulling Old Peg's leg, dear. Everyone dances at the Solstice Dance. The ghosts dance and the ghouls dance. The veela dance and the vampires dance. The dragons and the griffins and shapeshifters dance. Even the Geniuses dance at the Solstice Dance, dear. Even the changelings."

Now that was weird, because I'd never met another mortal changeling in the Park. In fact, I'd never met another mortal changeling at all. I couldn't be sure that I hadn't *seen* one, especially at the Museum, where Folk come from all over the City to play with the exhibits. But there are so many Supernaturals who can look like mortals that it's impossible to tell who's what without getting close enough to check out their feet or their ears or how long their fingers are or whether their shadows match their shapes. And the guards and docents didn't approve of me talking to tourists, so I couldn't ask.

"Mortals aren't allowed in the Park," I told Peg Powler.

Peg raised her claws in the air. "Astris never told you that, dear! Not in so many words: That would be a lie. Far be it from me to speak ill of your godmother, but rumor has it that poor Astris has a bad history with changelings. Oh my, yes. There was the one that drowned in the Reservoir and the one that fell off the top of Belvedere Castle and that other one that came to grief on Sheep's Meadow. Quite by accident, of course—they weren't watching where they were going. But still. And then we had a feast." She licked her lipless mouth.

I went cold all over. "That's a lie! Astris is the best fairy godmother in New York!"

"Is she, dear? Well, we'll see. When you get back to that drafty Castle of yours, just tell her what I've said, and see what her reaction is."

"Okay," I said. "I will. She'll say that you're making it all up."

"Oh no, dear, I'm not making it up. Old Peg's got her little ways, but she doesn't invent things. She can't. Astris lost those changelings before they were full grown. Everyone knows it. Everyone knows about the Solstice Dance, too. There are two, you know, one at Midwinter and one at Midsummer. Winter is the longest, but summer is best. The trees dance in the summer, dear, and the fire Folk dance fireworks in the sky. But you won't see it, will you, dear? You won't be there."

The willow leaves rustled and a demon appeared, swinging from a slender branch. It was blue, with purple tusks, and it was grinning from ear to pointed ear. "Poor little changeling," it cooed. "Can't come to the dance. It's not Folk, it's not fowl, and it's not good red herring. I bet it tastes good, though."

That did it. This adventure was officially out of control. I needed rescuing and I needed it fast. Groping in my pocket for the hair from the Pooka's tail, I brought it to my mouth, blew on it, and whispered:

> *By thy oath and by thy faith,*
> *Come thou quickly by me.*
> *Gallop, gallop to my aid;*
> *Danger draweth nigh me.*

Before I'd finished, I heard something crashing around in Peg's bramble thicket.

"Over here, Pooka!" I shouted. "I'm over here, by the big willow!"

Peg Powler laughed. "Did I frighten you, dear? Or was it Blueberry? What a pity, when we were having such a nice chat." She heaved herself to her feet. "Say hello to Astris for me, dear. Peg Powler. Don't forget. Tootle-bye!"

"Tootle-bye!" echoed the blue demon and, sticking out a tongue like a raspberry Popsicle, it vanished. All that was left was the swaying willow and the bright stream and the stony path and a pony with flaming yellow eyes and bramble scratches on his glossy black sides.

I ran to the pony and threw my arms around his neck. "Oh, Pooka. Am I ever glad to see you."

The Pooka shook himself free. "I can't entirely return the sentiment," he said, "seeing as how I'd rather be where I was when you called me, and you in no danger that I can see."

"Well, I'm not in danger *now*," I said. "It went away when it heard you."

"Taking the brambles with it, the creature," the Pooka said. "Do you know who it was, at all?"

This was not a conversation I wanted to have. At best, it was going to lead to a lecture on talking to strangers. At worst, the Pooka would tell Astris I'd disobeyed her and I'd get locked up in my tower room with only Satchel for company until I'd sorted a pile of seeds by size or something equally lame.

"Some fat old bogeywoman and her demon friend," I said. "I didn't like her teeth."

The Pooka shook his mane thoughtfully. "Teeth, is it? A Wild Hunter, without a doubt. Did you speak with her?"

"I gave her the words," I said, which was true as far as it went.

"It could be worse," the Pooka said. "Using the words was almost as clever as leaving the path in the first place was foolish. Where were you going, then, all on your own-some in the North Woods? Running away from spring cleaning, were you?"

Relieved to be on firmer ground, I told him about the mice and the turtles and the ghosts and the squirrels and what a mess my room was and how Astris had decided that I was big enough to fetch the Blockhouse brownie by myself.

The Pooka's black sides rounded in a windy sigh. "Then I'd best take you to the Blockhouse and carry the pair of you back to the Castle. Not that you don't deserve to walk."

"I know, Pooka," I said. "Thank you, Pooka." And I scrambled up onto his back.

On the way up to the Blockhouse, I persuaded him not to tell Astris about my adventure in the North Woods. It wasn't hard. The Pooka may be my fairy godfather, but he's still a trickster.

CHAPTER
3

**HE WHO WISHES TO FLY THROUGH THE AIR
CAN END UP IN A DRAGON'S CLAWS.**

Neef's Rules for Changelings

By the time the Pooka dropped the brownie and me off at the Castle, Astris had the turtles gleaming and the mice nearly packed and ready to move to their summer quarters. Eldritch shrieking from the basement told me that the ghosts were still tangled in the cobwebs.

Astris didn't look at me, but her whiskers let me know she was not happy I'd been gone so long. All she actually said was, "Be welcome to this house, brownie. Please excuse the mess. You know how it is when you're in the middle of cleaning—it always looks worse before it looks better." The brownie nodded sympathetically. "I've got things down here pretty well under control, but Neef's room is a wreck. We won't get it clean this side of Midsummer without your help. Do you mind?"

Like the brownie had a choice. Cleaning is what brownies do, if you ask, until you give them some old clothes, which makes them go away. That was my fairy godmother: as good as she was beautiful and always considerate. It was possible she hadn't told me about the changelings who died because she didn't want to freak me out.

I felt a tug on my shirttail. "Earth to Neef!" Astris said. "Show the brownie your room and explain to it why your magazine collection isn't trash. Don't give it your old clothes until the place is spick-and-span—by my standards, not yours. And go straight to bed when you're done. You look exhausted."

Which showed how distracted she was, because Astris is usually good at telling when I'm upset. Which I was. Very. In fact, when the brownie wanted to throw out my rocks and my leaf collection as well as my magazines, I yelled at it not to touch my stuff.

I apologized right away, of course—insulted brownies can do a lot of damage. The brownie sighed deeply, then used the rocks and magazines to build a kind of bench under the south-facing window. It decorated the walls with the leaves, it polished my silverware, and it cleaned the glass. To make up for yelling, I swept the stone floor and sprinkled it with rosemary.

When the room was as tidy as it was going to get, I bundled all my too-small clothes into the brownie's spindly arms. "Here you go," I said. "Thank you for organizing everything."

The brownie shrugged and vanished.

I wasn't even slightly sleepy, so I perched on my new window seat and looked south, toward Midtown. Evening was drawing in. The shadows were taking over the Park and the trees of the Ramble rustled and murmured to one another below my window. A hazy light pulsed in a thicket—a will-o'-the-wisp waiting for a traveler it could lead astray. Brighter lights began to wink on in the buildings beyond the Park. Everything in Central Park was peaceful and ordinary. Except me.

I knew about the Solstice, of course. There were, as Peg Powler had reminded me, two: one on the longest night of the year and one on the shortest. Astris had taught me that the Solstices were big juju, with lots of magic floating around. Everybody went a little wild, she'd said, and then she'd done that thing with her whiskers that meant, "Don't ask questions, because I won't answer." I didn't actually remember her saying mortals were banned, but she certainly let me believe it. Which made sense: Astris's big thing was keeping me safe. Mortals, she always said, are fragile and hard to fix when they break.

But I had to wonder: What was the point of letting me think that other mortals weren't even allowed to visit the Park? And why keep me from even knowing that every creature in New York Between spent Solstice Nights dancing their brains out while I was—what? Under a forgetting spell? Turned into a rock?

And why hadn't anyone else mentioned it?

It's not like Astris and the Pooka are the only Folk I

hang around with. There's my dancing teacher Iolanthe and a fairy called Bugle and the undines and nixies and water nymphs in the Lake and the Reservoir, not to mention the fictional characters like the Shakespeare Fairies and the Water Rat and Stuart Little, who lives at the Boat Pond. I couldn't believe there was some huge conspiracy to make me the only changeling in New York who wasn't invited to the Solstice Dance. Even if there was, why would Peg Powler tell me about it? Not because she cared about my social life. And all that stuff about Astris and her bad luck with changelings—why would she tell me *that*? To warn me? Peg Powler?

I didn't know what to think.

The trees of the Ramble and the lights of the City beyond got kind of blurry. I wiped my eyes and told myself that the waitresses in Astris's stories didn't get to be debutantes by being all weepy and sorry for themselves. No, they figured out what they had to do and they found magical helpers and talismans and things to help them do it. Plus, they mostly lived Outside, where magical helpers aren't all that easy to find.

I was lucky, really. In Central Park, you can hardly take two steps without bumping into a magic animal or a wish-granting fairy of some kind. If I wandered around the Ramble for a while going "Alas and alack" and "Woe is me" to show that I was unhappy, I'd soon be surrounded by moss women asking what they could do for me. Moss women hate for anyone to be unhappy, which is why more mortals don't get lost in the Ramble forever.

By now, the moon was hanging over the City like half a silver apple. I asked Satchel for a snack (it gave me an orange and a handful of nuts), and then I went to bed, feeling a little less awful. It was good to have a plan.

I woke to a beautiful day and a new pair of jeans and a T-shirt draped over my clothes chest. The T-shirt had a winged cat on it. I put it on, wondering why I felt so crabby. And then I remembered yesterday's adventure.

Come on, I told myself. Who are you going to trust? Astris, who brought you up? Or some bogeywoman you've never met before?

That should have settled it. But as I ate the oatmeal Satchel gave me, I couldn't stop thinking about the dance and how one of Astris's changelings had fallen off Belvedere Castle. Finally I decided it wouldn't hurt anything to find out what somebody besides Peg Powler said about it all. So I slung Satchel over my shoulder, put the Pooka's tail hair into my pocket, and went downstairs.

If Astris had been home, she would have noticed right away how weird I was acting. But the kitchen was empty except for a round, golden cookie on the table and a note in Astris's scratchy handwriting telling me that she was having lunch with the werebears in the Zoo.

I can't live on fairy food, because I'd starve to death if I tried, but Astris's sun cookies are my favorite snacks. Just one makes everything look brighter. It says something about how confused I was that I left the cookie where it was and headed straight to the Ramble.

The Ramble is not as wild as the North Woods, but it's still a very tricksy place. The paths shift and hide themselves, and the trees get their kicks out of sticking their roots under your feet so you'll trip and fall. It's where the Pooka took me for lessons in basic questing and wish-making. I also learned the Riddle Game from him, plus bargaining with supernaturals, fairy-tale patterns for all purposes, and fairy law. Tricksters, oddly enough, are experts on rules. The Pooka always says you can't break a rule properly unless you really understand it.

Once I was good and lost, I started to call out "Alas and alack" and "Woe is me." For all the good it did, I might as well have been crying "Hot cross buns." After a while, I got frustrated.

"Alas, alack, and woe!" I shouted. "Hey! I'm unhappy here. *Really* unhappy."

At this point, I tripped over a root that hadn't been there a minute before and fell on a rock and skinned my knee.

"*Now* you're unhappy," a gentle voice said. "Before, you were mostly pretending. I can't help you if you're pretending."

The voice came from a clump of twigs that looked like a nest built by a bird who wasn't very good at nest-building. It was perched unsteadily on the root I'd tripped over.

"That's a nasty scrape," the moss woman said sympathetically. "You want me to put a bit of spiderweb on it? Or a burdock leaf? There's nothing more cooling than a burdock leaf."

"No, thank you," I said as patiently as I could.

The moss woman blinked. "You're the mortal changeling, aren't you?"

"Uh-huh." There was something about the way she'd said it that made me uncomfortable. It almost sounded like she was sorry for me.

"Oh, my goodness. You really *are* unhappy." The moss woman stood up, which made her look like a nest propped up on twigs, and got into wish-granting position. "Okay, shoot."

I bit my lip. Of my two questions, the one that was bothering me the most was what had really happened to Astris's other mortal changelings. But I was having trouble phrasing it as a wish. "I wish I knew if Astris was a murderess"? I just couldn't! The second question was a lot simpler.

"I wish I could go to the Solstice Dance," I said.

The moss woman's twigs turned a pale beige. "Do you know what you're asking?"

As a matter of fact, I didn't, but I wasn't going to admit that. "Sure I do. I want to go to the ball, like Radiatorella. What's the big deal?"

"OdearOdear," the moss woman muttered. "What to

do? What to do? She's very unhappy—miserable, in fact. It's coming off of her in waves. Most unpleasant. I have to fix it. But I can't tell her about . . . O dear. OdearOdearOdear!"

As she muttered, her voice got higher and faster and her twigs rattled furiously. Afraid she'd fall apart completely, I told her I withdrew the wish.

The moss woman settled her twigs with a nervous clack. "Are you sure?"

"I'm sure."

"How about another wish? I'd do anything—almost—to make you happy. How about a nice puppy?"

"I don't want a puppy," I said crossly.

"O dear. I'm sorry, I really am, but I *can't*, you see. It's a geas. You do know what a geas is, don't you?"

Geases are a Folk lore basic. "It's when you're not allowed to do a certain thing, and if you do it, something really bad happens to you."

"That's right," she said. "And I'm under one. About the—what you said. So is everybody else around here. Please don't mention it again. Wish for something else instead. How about a nice new dress?"

This would have been the time to ask her about Astris, but I still couldn't find a good way to put it. And I did want to go to the Solstice Dance instead of just sleeping through it.

"I wish I had an antisleeping charm," I said.

"An antisleeping charm?" The moss woman sounded surprised. "I don't know any antisleeping charms. Let me think."

She settled back down to her nest-on-a-root mode and closed her eyes. I waited and waited and waited. You can't rush Folk. The trees rustled peevishly and a toad with a ruby in its head hopped over my foot. I waited some more.

Finally the moss woman stood up. "Okay. I got it. You know the kazna peri over by Huddlestone Bridge?"

"Not personally, no."

"That doesn't matter—you'll know it when you see it. It has a nose you could roll a marble down. Gray, I think—the kazna peri, not the marble. But I could be wrong. It's tending a silver pot over a blue fire. Ask it for some of what's in the pot. Bye."

And the moss woman was gone before I could ask for anything else. I had to find another moss woman to show me the way out of the Ramble.

Huddlestone Bridge is tucked away on the southwest edge of the North Woods. Yesterday, I wouldn't have gone to the Reservoir without telling Astris, much less gone way out-of-bounds looking for a supernatural whose name I recognized from my lesson on minor-league devils and demons. Today, I would have done worse than that if it meant getting one of my questions answered.

It was hot under the trees and I couldn't find anything that even resembled a path. I crashed around in the bushes for a while, grumpy and lost, on the theory that if I looked long enough, I'd surely find *something.*

What I found was a smell. It was toasty, sharp, and sneeze-making, unlike anything I'd ever smelled before, and it led me to a rough stone bridge over a swift, deep stream.

This time, I knew better than to rush into a trap without checking it out first. Crawling cautiously to the side of the bridge, I peered down into the clearing below, trying to look as much like a lump of granite as possible. A small, grayish devil was poking at a fire under a pot. The pot was silver, the fire was blue, and the devil's nose poked out of the darker tangle of its beard and eyebrows like a long gray carrot. I'd found the kazna peri.

I slithered down into the clearing and marched up to the fire, looking, I hoped, more heroic than I felt. The kazna peri gaped up at me, its mouth a black ring studded with sharp teeth.

"Good afternoon, kazna peri," I said. "I am a changeling under the protection of the Green Lady and I've come to ask a boon."

The kazna peri grinned. "And you think this comes as news to me? Would you be here if you didn't want something? Let me guess: You want the magic treasure I'm cooking here in my silver pot."

"Yes, please," I said. "I don't need all of it, though. A mouthful's fine."

"Well, you can't have any at all. You're too young. It'll

stunt your growth. It'll grow hair on your chest. It'll keep you awake for days. It'll give you ulcers, a sour stomach, the shakes. I live on the stuff from the Feast of St. Michael to Midsummer Eve. I know. You want to end up like this?"

The kazna peri stuck out its leathery claw; it shook like a leaf in a high wind.

This might have put me off, if I'd believed it. Maybe the Folk can't make things up, but they can exaggerate. "I can handle it," I said. "Will you give me some, please?"

"'Will you give me some? Will you give me some?'" the kazna peri mocked. "This isn't just any ordinary treasure, you know. It's pure black gold. Why should I give it to you just because you say please? What's in it for me?"

Life among the Folk is all about getting what you need without giving up a pot of gold or an arm and a leg or your firstborn child in exchange. The Pooka had spent a lot of time dinning the principles of bargaining into me, and I was sure he would have been proud of how I talked the kazna peri down from a pint of my heart's blood and my little-finger bone to a dead pigeon I'd seen lying at the edge of the North Meadow. When I brought it back, wrapped in a chestnut leaf, the kazna peri was so happy that it threw in a stone flask to keep the potion in at no extra charge.

I picked up the flask and sniffed gingerly. The smell that had led me to the kazna peri's clearing curled around my nose—toasty, sharp, exciting. My mouth watered, and I lifted the flask to my lips.

"You don't want to do that," said the kazna peri around a mouthful of pigeon feathers.

"Why not?"

The kazna peri swallowed. "Drink it now, you won't have it when you want it. And why I'm telling you this instead of letting you waste it, I don't know. I must be getting soft in my old age. New York's not what it used to be, either. In the old days," it went on wistfully, "my treasure was molten gold, distilled from sunbeams. But you can't get decent sunbeams any more: too much soot." It sighed and spat out a wing bone. "You can go away now."

It chomped into the pigeon again, getting feathers and blood and stuff all over its beard.

"Thank you," I said respectfully, and ran.

CHAPTER
4

To MAKE A BIG OMELET, YOU HAVE TO BREAK A BIG EGG.
Neef's Rules for Changelings

I hid the kazna peri's stone flask among the magazines in the window seat. At first, I kept taking it out and shaking it so I could hear the keep-awake sloshing inside, then unstoppering it and sniffing. After a few days, the potion didn't smell as good as it had at first—not bad, exactly, but kind of metallic. There wasn't anybody I could ask whether it could go rotten except the kazna peri, and I wasn't about to do that. So I tried not to think about it.

Instead, I thought about the Solstice Dance, and I thought about how the other mortal changelings got to attend it and I didn't. I thought about how when I'd complained to Astris about how hard it was to be the only mortal around, all she'd said was that I should be glad I was special. And I thought about the "special" Park changelings who had come before me, the ones she'd had such bad luck with.

With all these questions buzzing around in my head, I hardly dared to talk to Astris for fear I'd blurt out the wrong thing. I spent more and more time away from the Castle, hanging out at the Dairy and sitting for hours in Willow Bay with my feet in the Lake. My daily lessons in Folk lore were not as much fun as they used to be.

"Neef, what's wrong?" Astris asked me one morning when things had gone worse than usual.

"Wrong?" I asked, my heart thudding uncomfortably. "I can only remember two ways of outwitting a piskie, that's all. Why do I need to learn three ways anyway? Isn't one enough?"

Astris's whiskers were severe. "Not if the moon's full. And it's not just that. You left three of the most important storm spirits off this list of destructive nature spirits. I haven't seen you this distracted since you were very small." She fixed me with her ruby eyes, her whiskers quivering with worry. "Whatever's on your mind, pet, you can tell me."

When I was little, I learned that when I cried, it made the Folk fall over laughing, even Astris. Needless to say, I didn't cry much. Lately, however, I'd been choking up over nothing. Mortified, I got up and went to the kitchen window so I could dry my tears and come up with a story that would answer Astris's question and get me out of the Castle.

"I've got a date with Puck and Ariel," I said. "They're

going to race around the earth. I'm supposed to judge who gets back to the mulberry tree first. They're waiting for me. That's why I'm distracted."

I didn't really expect Astris to fall for this. Maybe she didn't. Maybe her whiskers were suspicious, but I didn't look at them. I just stood there with my back to her until she said, "Very well, Neef. Go ahead and meet your friends. But I'll expect you to spend the evening on your piskie lore and reviewing the storm spirits as well as the six signs of a demon and the short list of traditional bogeymen. You need to know these things."

"I know, Astris," I said. "Thanks." And I pelted out of the kitchen and across the courtyard as if the Wild Hunt was on my heels. Then I climbed the mulberry tree and stayed there the rest of the day, feeling awful.

After that, Astris pretty much handed over my education to the Pooka. I thought this would be better. He never made me memorize lists or write essays comparing and contrasting the protective spirits from three different Folk lore traditions. He was more into the fun stuff, like catching leprechauns and tricking demons. But he wasn't nearly as patient as Astris, plus I pitched so many fits at him that he threatened to take back his tail hair.

All in all, it was a good thing that the Solstice was getting nearer. The days grew gradually longer and the Folk grew busier and more excited—the way, I realized, they always did twice each year. The water nymphs went on and on about the fancy gowns they were making out of waterweed and leaves. The leprechauns were snowed under with orders for dancing shoes. The clincher was when I saw Folk lined up outside Iolanthe's door, waiting for dancing lessons. One evening I even saw her twirling with an ogre in sweatpants, dodging his clawed feet and yelling, "Lightly, I said. Trip *lightly*."

When I asked them what was doing, they all pretended they were too busy to talk to me.

Finally it was the day before the Solstice. I still didn't know how Astris put me to sleep every year, and I wasn't completely sure the keep-awake hadn't gone bad. Astris had exploded when I knocked her bowl of cookie dough onto her newly scrubbed floor and threw me out of the Castle until bedtime. I was sitting on the rock overlooking the Turtle Pond, trying to read a rain-swollen copy of a book I'd found under a bush.

It was about all these weird kids who get to be friends because the popular kids hate them, which kind of reminded me of me and the Folk, only without any other changelings to make friends with.

The book stopped suddenly, in the middle of a sentence, leaving all the weird kids' problems unsolved.

I threw the book into the pond, propped my chin on my hands, and watched the sunset gild the windows of the Metropolitan Museum across the meadow. My eye caught a flutter of scarlet crossing Central Park Central toward me. *Oh*, I said to myself. *There's the sandman*.

And then I got it.

The sandman isn't Park Folk. He lives in the City, where his job is to go out into the mortal world every night to put little children to sleep. He and Astris were old friends, and he always visited at Solstice. Being a mortal child, I pretty much fell asleep as soon as I said hello to him and never woke up until morning. I couldn't believe I hadn't figured it out sooner.

There was no time to waste. I jumped up and tore across the courtyard into the Castle and up the spiral stair to my room, where I dug the flask of keep-awake out of the window seat.

The kazna peri's keep-awake potion was cold and oily and tasted like safety pins and old socks. It was all I could do not to spit it out, but I managed to swallow.

The potion hit my stomach like a lighted candle. One minute, I was an ordinary changeling. The next, I was Super Changeling, smarter than your average Genius and very, very, very wide awake.

Just in time, too. Astris was calling me. "Neef. Neef! The sandman's here. Come down and say hello."

I was tempted to yell down to her that I so didn't care and see what happened next. But now was not the time to start acting weirder than usual. So I yelled, "Coming!" instead.

The next part was a lot harder than I thought it would be. I felt like I could cartwheel all the way down the stairs and into the kitchen, but I didn't want to make Astris suspicious. *One step at a time,* I told myself. *Don't rush.*

"What's wrong with you?" Astris said when she saw me dragging my feet from step to step. "You look like you're about to fall over."

I thought fast. Really fast. "Tag with the leshii," I said. "This afternoon. He turns himself into a wolf. I'm pooped."

Astris gave me a doubtful look. "You'd better go straight to bed, then. But say hello to the sandman first."

The sandman spread his scarlet cloak with both arms, unveiling baggy turquoise pants and a gold shirt. The colors made my eyes hurt.

He smiled at me sleepily. "Happy Solstice, Neef."

With the keep-awake fizzing in my head, it took all my self-control to say, "Happy Solstice to you, Sandman," and allow him to fold the scarlet cloak around me like a tent.

Dream sand settled into my eyes and mouth. I yawned and rubbed my eyes. With that much dream sand around, you just have to yawn, keep-awake or no keep-awake. It wasn't hard to stumble up the stairs, fall on my bed, and curl up with my eyes closed. What *was* hard was keeping them closed and breathing evenly when Astris jumped up on the bed to make sure I was really asleep.

I felt her whiskers twitch across my nose. I couldn't help giving a little snort, but I might have done that even if I had been sleeping.

"Out like a light," she said. "I thought I smelled coffee on her breath, but I must have been imagining it."

"Coffee?" The sandman sounded shocked. "Not our little Neef!"

"Not so little anymore," Astris said. "She's growing up, Morpheus. I know the signs. Soon she's going to do something she shouldn't, and things will get ugly."

"Well, it hasn't happened yet," the sandman said cheerfully. "Come on, Astris. I can hear the trees tuning up. We don't want to be late."

Just to make sure they were really gone, I stayed on the bed with my eyes closed, twitching as the keep-awake threw off the dream sand, listening to the fairy music drifting through my open window, counting as slowly as I could to two hundred.

At about seventy-five, the music pulled me out of bed and over to the nearest window.

With dusk blue among the trees, the dance was just getting started. Folk of all shapes and sizes were dancing on the paths, on the rocks, even up in the sky, where tiny winged fairies and peris floated like dandelion fluff among the Oriental dragons and bright-winged garudas. Fairy lights glittered off polished tusks and scales and horns and jewels. I saw a pair of squirrels prance past, their tails brushed to fluffy boas. A huge black kelpie flashed its gilded hooves. Red Cap's red cap was shiny with fresh blood, and the swan maidens from Lincoln Center wore their swan skins over their white shoulders like feathery cloaks.

The music came from everywhere: fiddles and pipes and quick-beating drums. I leaned out my window so far I almost fell out. I couldn't wait to be down there with the rest of them, do-si-doing with dwarves, cavorting with kobolds, pirouetting with piskies, waltzing with were-bears. Maybe—my heart beat faster—maybe even capering with changelings.

I skinned out of my jeans and T-shirt and into my only dress. It was green spidersilk with a floaty skirt and leaves and flowers woven into it, and I'd found it a few days earlier, laid out on a bench in the Shakespeare Garden. I had an idea that the moss woman must have left it for me because of not being able to grant my real wish. It smelled a little of damp leaf mold, but it was the prettiest thing I'd ever worn in my life.

Downstairs, I paused to check myself out in the hall mirror. My hair was its usual explosion of frizzy curls, I was definitely round in the middle, and my legs and feet were not as clean as Astris would have liked. But the spidersilk dress turned me into a woodsy Park fairy.

I ran out into the courtyard. The Shakespeare fairies were dancing gavottes in lace ruffs and doublets and stiff, drum-shaped skirts. Puck winked at me, then whirled away. Had he recognized me, or was he just being Puck? Who cared? I was going to dance in Central Park Central, and nothing was going to stop me.

I edged past the revelers and made it down the steps to the foot of the cliff. I was almost past the Turtle Pond when something caught my leg and hung on tight. Looking down, I saw the Water Rat, almost unrecognizable himself in a black dinner jacket and a red bow tie.

"What are you doing, Mr. Rat?"

"What are *you* doing?"

"Joining the dance," I said. "Or I will be, if you'll just let go."

The Water Rat tightened his grip. "Oh, you don't want to do that, youngster. Central Park Central's full of tourists at Midsummer. Giants. Wyverns. Vampires. Much better to observe from a distance. I understand there's an excellent view from the Castle. Shall I take you up?"

"No way," I said. "This is my first Solstice, and I want to dance."

"Oh, I'm sure you wouldn't like that at all."

I was tempted to kick the Water Rat away, but I wasn't that crazy, quite. "Why not?"

"You are a mortal," he said carefully. "Mortals are delicate, and the Folk get wild as the night wears on. I didn't like to mention it before, but unsupervised mortals can dance themselves to death at a Solstice Dance. You wouldn't want that to happen, would you? Think how upset Astris would be."

Everything seemed to click into place: the sandman, Astris hiding the dance from me, even the fate of the other Park changelings. It was like the story of the Sleeping Debutante, where the mayor passed a law against books because an evil fairy had said that his daughter would die of a paper cut. Those Park changelings must have done something stupid and got themselves killed, so Astris had decided to keep me away from the dance entirely. Didn't she trust me? Didn't she know I could take care of myself?

"I know what you're trying to do, Mr. Rat, but really, it's okay. I'm not a complete idiot, and I won't dance myself to death. I'm going to look for other mortal changelings. I'll be fine."

The Rat's whiskers weren't as expressive as Astris's, but I could tell he wasn't convinced. "Why should you want to do that? They won't know anything about the Park, you know. What would you talk about? And what if they hurt you? Mortals don't always get along with other mortals, I hear. No, it would be best all around if you returned to the Castle."

"With all this going on? Are you nuts? Listen, Mr. Rat. I appreciate the warning and everything, but you're not my fairy godfather. Just butt out, okay?"

The Water Rat looked grave. "Listen here, Neef. I'm just trying to keep you from making an awful ass of yourself. But if you're determined, you're determined, and I can't change your mind. It might be wise, however, for you to watch for a while before joining in. The Solstice Dance is powerful magic, and you need to understand the pattern or there may be serious consequences. Besides," he said practically, "you'll never find a changeling by leaping into a huge, moving crowd and hoping to bump into one."

Even hopped-up on music and keep-awake, I had to admit that the Water Rat had a point. In the end, I promised that I'd climb a tree and watch from above until I was sure I saw the pattern, and then he let me go. I was a little hurt that he waited until I'd found a suitable tree before he joined the dance himself. I may not like rules, but I do keep my promises.

I swung myself up to a nice sturdy branch at about giant's eye-level and put my back against the trunk. The music ran through me like keep-awake. Water Rat hadn't said anything about sitting still, so I bounced until the whole tree creaked and shook.

"Stop that," rustled the tree angrily. "I shouldn't have to put up with this kind of nonsense, not on Solstice Night. Keep it up, and I'll snap."

I said I was sorry and stopped bouncing. I couldn't keep my feet still, though, no matter how hard I tried. The music was like a thousand instruments from a hundred different musical traditions all playing at once. It didn't have anything that even remotely resembled a tune and I couldn't quite catch the beat, but I had to move anyway or bust. So I swung my legs and twitched my shoulders and studied the dance for some clue to its pattern.

There had to be one; the Water Rat couldn't lie. But I couldn't figure it out. For all I could tell, the Solstice Dance was nothing but a bunch of Folk prancing around at random, waving their arms or flippers or tails or horns however they felt like it. For a long time, I watched a bunch of leprechauns with emerald-green Mohawks bop-

ping up and down in a tight cluster, but I still couldn't
make any sense of it.

Then I saw Peg Powler.

She was spinning, her green rags waving like rotten
lettuce leaves. As she turned, she looked up and showed
me every pointy tooth in her head. My heart thumped
uncomfortably under my spidersilk dress, but I grinned
right back at her.

Peg circled away, grinning like a goon, and I returned
to studying the dance. I noticed an odd kind of ripple
moving through the crowd. The ripple came nearer,
turning into a line of heads bobbing slightly out of sync
with the beat. I wondered what kind of Folk they were.
They might have been elves or shapeshifters, except
for being red-faced and kind of heavy looking. As they
danced past my tree, I noticed that they were panting
and gleaming with sweat. A woman tripped, and a man
stumbled over her.

Folk don't trip. Folk don't sweat. Folk don't get tired.
I'd found the mortal changelings.

CHAPTER
5

SPIDERS AREN'T TRAPPED BY THEIR OWN WEBS.
Neef's Rules for Changelings

I was out of that tree before I knew it. I felt like I was flying, but I couldn't have been: Mortals don't fly, either. I landed on a big furry something that roared and grabbed at me. But I was too quick for it.

The moment my feet hit the grass, the music caught me up like a newspaper in the wind.

The knot of mortals was just on the other side of a garland of nymphs, but I couldn't get to them. My feet had developed a mind of their own. For about a heartbeat, I swear I caught the beat. Everything—the trees, the grass, the stones, the stars, the City, the Folk, the mortals Outside—was part of the same dance, and it never ended. What had been and what was to be were the same as now, and always would be. I forgot about the changelings; I forgot that I'd ever been lonely or angry or even mortal.

And then it all fell apart. Suddenly I had two left feet, and neither of them had the beat. The mortal changelings were nowhere in sight. I bumped into dwarves and elbowed trolls and stepped on a blue demon who might have been Peg's friend Blueberry. Werebears growled at me as I stumbled in front of them. Fox spirits barked and snapped. I wished as hard as I could to be home asleep in bed with the curtains drawn, but like all wishes made when it's too late, it didn't come true. All I could do was grimly keep on dancing and hope I didn't get trampled.

And then I found myself face-to-face with the Green Lady.

When she's happy, the Green Lady of Central Park is as beautiful as the most beautiful thing you can imagine. She has greeny-brown skin, long dark-green ropes of hair, and deep-set eyes the color of new leaves after a rain. But she can change shape, and not all of her shapes are beautiful.

As soon as she saw me, her dreadlocks lifted and began to weave around her head and hiss like snakes. Emerald fire smoldered in her eyes, and her lips lifted over teeth that had grown suddenly needlelike.

"Can the music, boys," she yelled. "We have a situation here."

The music fell silent and everyone stopped dancing, just like that. All I could hear was the panicked thumping of my own heart and some noisy panting that was probably the mortal changelings.

The Lady said, "Do you know what you have done?"

She used the voice the Folk use to ask ritual questions, magic questions, questions you'd better answer carefully or you're history. Questions asked in this voice are never as simple as they sound. I licked my lips nervously. "Um. Could you repeat the question?"

"A question is not an answer," the Green Lady said, the snakes weaving around her head. "You must say yes or no."

"The thing is," I said, "it's not that simple. I mean, I know what I *did*, but I don't know why it's a big deal. If that's what you're asking."

The Green Lady burst into howls of nasty laughter that were echoed by what sounded like every supernatural in New York. It was a horrible sound, full of the promise of blood and crunching bones. I looked around for Astris or the Pooka or the Water Rat or even a friendly moss woman to rescue me, but I was surrounded by open mouths and pointed teeth, tongues of red and blue and purple and black, eyes like red sparks and eyes like soup plates, all of them hungry, hungry, hungry.

"You're a pistol, kid," the Green Lady said at last. "You *knew* you were doing something wrong, right?"

Another trick question? I wrenched my mind from the hungry eyes and tried to concentrate. Sure, every benevolent supernatural in the Park had warned me away from the Solstice Dance. But I'd never thought about whether I might actually be breaking a rule. So I'd be lying a little whether I said yes or no. I thought it might be safest if I shrugged.

The Lady's hair snakes all twisted around to get a good look at me. My stomach turned over. "I didn't *mean* to do anything wrong," I explained.

"Geddouttahere," the Lady snapped. "You think I was born yesterday? The squirrels tell me you've been breaking rules right, left, and center since spring cleaning day. Besides, it doesn't matter what you meant. It only matters what you did."

"But what did I do?" I meant to yell, but it came out more like a sob.

"*What did you do?*" the Green Lady echoed back at me. "You just broke the geas I laid upon you at your Changing, that's all."

I felt like I'd opened a door and gotten bonked by a brick. All I could think was *It's not fair* and *I want Astris*.

Something cold and wet touched my hand. I jumped about a mile and screeched. The Green Lady and the Wild Hunt howled with laughter.

Astris patted my knee with a small pink paw. "Hush, pet. It's only me. I did my best to keep this from happening, but mortals are so *curious*. Didn't I warn you that curiosity killed the cat?"

Her voice was brisk, but her whiskers were worried. I let my legs fold and put my arms around her.

The Green Lady smiled graciously at us. "What a good fairy godmother you are, Astris. Aren't you going to fill your changeling in on what's going down here?"

Astris's whiskers twitched angrily. "Perhaps the Lady will recall that she laid a geas on me, too."

"Not to speak of Neef's geas in her hearing," the Lady said helpfully. "Too bad you remembered. The Hunt would have had a ball with the pair of you." She turned her leaf-green eyes to me. "Okay, kid, here's the scoop. The Hunt loves to hunt mortals. But mortal changelings are under my protection. So we have a deal. I put a geas on every mortal changeling that comes to the Park, and when—er, *if*—they break it, the Hunt gets a crack at them."

I couldn't believe I'd heard her right. "Are you telling me that the Wild Hunt is going to chase me down for breaking a geas nobody was allowed to tell me about?"

"Technically," the Lady said, "breaking the geas only removes you from my protection. But since my protection is the only thing keeping the Wild Hunt off you, yeah, that's about the size of it."

The Wild Hunt cheered. My throat felt tight. Astris pressed against me, warm and furry and solid. The Hunt loves the taste of fear, I reminded myself. Freaking out would just bring them down on me faster. I swallowed hard.

"Get up," the Green Lady said, and I did, shakily. She lifted her slender hand, and her voice rolled like a bell over the mob of New York Folk. "The changeling Neef, having broken the geas laid upon her at her Changing, is no longer under my protection. She is without home, without sponsorship, and all the paths of the Park are closed to her. And this I swear by my name and hers."

At the last word, she disappeared, taking Astris with her.

The Wild Hunt began to circle widdershins, from right to left. No surprise: It's an unlucky direction. With every rotation, the Hunters got a little closer to me and I got a little closer to breaking down and running until they'd worked up an appetite.

Another circuit, and I could smell their blood-breath, hear their eager, hungry whines. My jaw hurt from clenching it; my legs trembled. I couldn't stand it anymore. I opened my mouth and took a breath so I could scream and get it over with.

And that was when a big black *thing* came swooping down, grabbed my shoulders in strong, sharp claws, and carried me away.

That did it: I screamed like a banshee. The Hunt leaped up after me, but whatever had nabbed me rose even faster. We spiraled smoothly up and up, neatly avoiding the dragons and garudas and pigeons and other winged Folk who had been dancing in the air. Soon we were so high that I could see the whole Park spread out below me with the buildings of the City clustered around it like a stone forest around a green lake.

I screamed some more.

The whatever-it-was plunged down through the center

of the Hunt, leaving my stomach behind. It wheeled and flew east over the Metropolitan Museum, and suddenly it dawned on me that maybe I was being rescued.

I stopped screaming, but I didn't relax. How could I? I was about twenty stories up, dangling from a pair of really sharp claws that belonged to something that might be taking me home so it wouldn't have to share. Not to mention that I was heading out into the City. For me, the City was something to look at, not visit; for me, the City was even more dangerous than the North Woods.

We swooped down toward a pale building crowned with glittering gold. I closed my eyes, and waited for the crash. But there wasn't one. I touched solid ground with my feet, the claws released my shoulders, and I collapsed, shaking all over. Then I was scooped up, in somebody's arms this time, carried a little way, and dropped onto something soft.

We were there. Wherever "there" was. And I was still alive.

CHAPTER
6

MANNERS ARE ALWAYS IMPORTANT.

Neef's Rules for Changelings

I lay where I'd been dumped. I didn't have the strength to move. I didn't want to open my eyes. With any luck, whatever had snatched me from the Park would think I'd fainted and leave me alone.

Fat chance. Something poked me in the side. Hard.

"Ow," I said.

Ah, you are *awake.* The voice was in my head, not my ears, which was icky. *Sit up and let me see you.*

This didn't sound like I was about to be eaten. So why had I been snatched? Witches sometimes stole mortals to comb their hair and fetch water in sieves, but witches didn't talk in your head. Could it be a dragon, maybe, wanting someone to clean his cave? Only one way to find out. I sat up and opened my eyes.

A man-shaped supernatural was sitting cross-legged

on a cushion, his hands on his knees and his head tipped to one side like a bird.

Here's where mortal curiosity comes in handy. Instead of pitching a fairy fit, like normal Folk presented with something they didn't recognize, I studied him. Bright black eyes, long, straight black hair tied back in a ponytail, bare feet, black pants under a black turtleneck. No wings or claws now, which meant he must be a shapechanger. His nose was the giveaway, though. It was about a mile long, red, and pointed like a needle.

Long nose, bare feet, mind-speaker, shapechanger. Put it all together, it spells tengu. Japanese mountain spirit, trickster, thief. Hates priests, likes gold. There was something else, too, but I couldn't remember what.

Wonderful, the tengu buzzed in my head. *I don't suppose she's ever combed her hair in her life, or washed her feet. And that look of sulky suspicion! Perfect! Simply perfect!*

"Thank you," I said, and yes, I sounded suspicious. I *was* suspicious. Also puzzled.

Sarcasm! Wonderful! The tengu rubbed its long hands together. *Snatching you was a risk, but I'm glad I did it. Just think. The naughtiest child in New York, and she's mine, mine, mine!*

"The naughtiest child in New York?" I echoed stupidly.

You don't agree? Consider: You strayed from the path, you talked to strangers, you lied to your godmother, you ingested a forbidden substance, you stayed up past your bedtime, you broke a promise. . . .

The sheer unfairness of this blew my mind. "That wasn't the way it was at all!" I shouted. "You don't know anything about it, you, you long-nosed creep!"

I shut my mouth hard, but it was too late. The tengu's head got small and feathery, his nose developed a sharp point, his beady eyes got even beadier. In a breath, I was facing a man with a raven's head. His beak dropped open and he let out a bunch of little caws. After a terrifying moment, I realized he was laughing.

Perfect! he cawed joyfully. *Such exquisite rudeness! And after I saved your life! The award is mine!*

"Award?" I asked blankly.

The Eloise Award for the Naughtiest Child in New York. Such a wonderful coincidence that you should come along just now, right when I needed you. Mortal child, you are going to make me the most famous bogeyman in New York City!

He told me to call him Carlyle.

Country mountain spirits are called after the mountains they live on; New York mountain spirits are called after their buildings. Carlyle lived in the golden spire on top of the Carlyle Hotel. He'd modeled his nest on a traditional Japanese room, with rice straw mats on the floor and paper walls. It was sparsely furnished with a lacquered chest, a low wooden table, a scroll painting of a mountain in the clouds, and a lacquer shelf that held a peony in an iron vase and a very beautiful blue-and-green china horse. I saw no windows to escape out of and no visible doors.

The thing I'd forgotten about tengus, of course, was that they collect naughty children. From Carlyle's point of view, he hadn't been rescuing me from the Wild Hunt at all. He'd been bagging a prize specimen.

Well, I wasn't anybody's specimen. I was the official mortal changeling of Central Park, and I needed to get back there and straighten things out. Sure, the Green Lady had exiled me, but I knew there had to be some way around it. In the story of the Hippie Chick, for instance, the wicked witch had locked this girl with superlong hair in a penthouse with no door. When the girl found a boyfriend anyway, the witch cut off her hair and blinded her boyfriend and sent her into the suburbs to be a single mom. But the Hippie Chick still managed to get back to the City and live happily ever after. If she could do that, plus restore her boyfriend's sight, I figured I could live in Central Park again under the Lady's protection.

First I needed to get away from the tengu.

It wouldn't be too hard to escape from a room with paper walls. All I had to do was wait until Carlyle went to sleep or something, rip open a door, find the stairs, and walk west until I got to the Park. In the meantime, I realized I was starving.

And then I realized that I'd left Satchel behind in my room.

It was like taking a step that wasn't there. I closed

my eyes tight and breathed very slowly through my nose. Satchel was more than a portable pantry. Satchel was the only magic I had. And I was still hungry.

Carlyle gave an anxious squawk. *You're not going to faint or anything, are you? I hate it when my naughty children faint or throw up. Such a mess, and no fun at all, not like crying and screaming.*

There's nothing like being annoyed to stop you from wanting to cry. "I'm hungry," I said. "Do you starve your naughty children, or just torture them?"

Naughty children get sent to bed without supper, he buzzed primly.

"In that case, I'll faint for sure and probably never wake up again."

Carlyle slid open one of the paper walls, darted through the opening, and slid it shut behind him, squawking crabbily. I rushed to the opposite wall and hit it as hard as I could. It gave a little, but it didn't come close to tearing. I couldn't kick through it, either, or slide it. I worked my way around the nest, poking, punching, pushing. Nothing budged, not even the panel the tengu had used.

I was frustrated, but I wasn't discouraged. Escaping from a bogeyman wasn't supposed to be easy. Naughty children from Outside exist for bogeymen to torture. But most naughty children don't have my training. *I* knew somewhere in here there had to be a charm or an enchanted cockroach or a trail of breadcrumbs that would help me find the way out. I just had to keep my eyes open and be ready to seize the opportunity when it came.

The wall slid open and Carlyle stalked in carrying a bowl of rice covered with shiny brown strips.

Grilled eel, he buzzed in my head. *Very good for you. Do you know how to use chopsticks?*

He was obviously hoping that I hated grilled eel, or at the very least that I'd have to eat it with my fingers. Smugly, I picked up the chopsticks, arranged them in my right hand, and dug enthusiastically into the brown mess. I'd had grilled eel before—it was a favorite with the tanuki who tutored me in Japanese Folk lore, language, and culture. I liked it okay if it was a little crispy and the sauce wasn't too sweet.

This eel was soggy and much too sweet, but I ate it anyway. Carlyle looked irritated and began to yatter on about the other bogeymen and how awful the contest was going to be—trying to get me to cry and scream, I guess. Since his voice was in my head, I couldn't exactly ignore him, but I managed not to react until he mentioned the name Eloise.

The eel caught in my throat. Eloise is the Genius of the Plaza Hotel and official Patroness of Spoiled Brats everywhere. According to Astris, she was ten times more destructive than a boggart—in other words, nobody I really wanted to meet.

Carlyle's nose twitched happily. *Oh, you've heard of Eloise, have you? Then you won't be surprised when you*

meet her, but never mind: I have another surprise for you.
I love surprises. Don't you?

"No," I said.

This is a good *surprise. You'll like it.* He smiled unpleasantly. *Would you like to see it now?*

"I'm not finished eating." I snatched up the bowl and
stuffed more eel into my mouth. I wished for the Pooka
to rescue me, but it was an empty wish: His tail hair was
in my jeans back at the Castle.

Don't think about the Pooka, I told myself. *Think about*
escape. Maybe if I could persuade Carlyle that I wasn't as
naughty as he thought, he'd let me go.

I swallowed my mouthful, put the bowl on the straw
matting with the chopsticks laid carefully across it, and
bowed deeply, as the tanuki had taught me.

"Honorable tengu," I said in my politest Japanese, "I
am ashamed. My words and actions toward one who has
so generously saved my miserable life and given me delicious grilled eel have been nothing less than criminal."

This speech did not have the effect I was aiming for.
Carlyle screamed a curse that raised a blister on the back
of my neck. *Horrible child! I don't have time for tricks,* he
screeched in my head. *There are three hundred bogeymen*
and their naughty children coming. I have preparations to
make, plans to lay. I need to find filet mignon for Eloise
and raisins for her turtle, Skipperdee. If you won't cooper-
ate, I might as well just take you back where I found you. I

don't think the Wild Hunt will care if you're a bit late.

"I was just kidding," I said hastily. "I'm bad. Look, I'll prove it." I grabbed the china horse and heaved it at Carlyle's head. Flexing its wings, it soared past him and landed, prancing, on the lacquer cabinet.

Ha! Carlyle cawed triumphantly. *Now you show your true colors! I expect you thought you were being clever. All naughty children think that way. But you can't outsmart me, young lady, any more than you could outsmart the Genius of Central Park. Did you actually think you were going to break your geas and get away with it?*

It was time to set the record straight. "It wasn't my fault," I said. "I didn't know I was under a geas. I didn't even know about the dance until Peg Powler told me about it. She set me up. I didn't know I was doing anything wrong."

Carlyle rubbed his long hands together. *Perfect! Classic! Denies responsibility, displaces blame, regrets only getting caught!* He bounced up onto his bare feet. *Well, I've got an awards ceremony to prepare for. And you've got a surprise waiting for you. Follow me.*

If there had been anywhere to go, I would have run. If there had been any point in fighting him, I would have fought. But there wasn't. I let the tengu drag me to the paper wall. He pulled open a panel, shoved me stumbling into a foul-smelling darkness, and slid the wall shut behind me.

CHAPTER
7

A ROSE BY ANY OTHER NAME IS A LOT SAFER.
Neef's Rules for Changelings

The smell was the first thing I noticed. Foul, cold, and unnatural, it made my eyes water and caught at the back of my throat. I'd never smelled anything quite like it, not even when a squirrel died in the Castle basement. I coughed and breathed through my mouth until I got used to it enough to notice other things. Like the cold. And the dark. And the humming.

Soft and even, it vibrated in my skull, buzzing a little, like a snore. I quickly started to run through the ten identifying signs of a closet monster, but couldn't remember any further than number six (the smell of old socks).

Well, whatever it was, it was better for me to find it than for it to find me first.

I began to explore. The floor was hard and cold. The wall at my back was clammy. Over my head, I found a row of hooks with cloths and wooden poles hanging from them. One pole had bristles on the end: a broom. Another pole ended in damp, sour-smelling ropes that made my hands feel greasy and dirty: a mop. I groped along the wall to a corner and came to a smooth, cold tublike thing with damp, greasy rags hung over the lip. As soon as I touched them, I knew just where the stink was coming from.

I stepped backwards, gagging. Something gave unpleasantly under my foot, then jerked sharply away. I lost my balance, falling onto something squishy and lumpy that screeched angrily. I hastily scrambled away from it as far as I could get, which wasn't very far.

"You stepped on me!" the closet monster yelled. "That hurt!"

Given the size of its closet, it had to be a small monster, but that didn't mean it wasn't dangerous. Boggarts are small; so are many devils. It's not a good idea to annoy either one. "I'm sorry," I said hastily. "I didn't mean to."

"You stepped on my hand," it accused. Its voice was loud and flat. "You should watch where you are going."

"I can't see in the dark," I said apologetically.

"Then you should be more careful."

The monster still sounded angry, but it hadn't mentioned grinding my bones to make its bread yet, which was a good sign.

The humming got suddenly more intense.

"Is that you?" I asked.

Silence, except for the humming and a rustle that I read as the monster making itself comfortable. "I believe," it said thoughtfully, "that is the compressor of the central air-conditioning unit."

"Oh," I said. "Is that some kind of dragon or something?"

There was another silence. "You are teasing me," the monster said reproachfully. "I do not like being teased. Teasing is not nice."

Now, I've spent my whole life learning how to talk to different kinds of Folk. Nixies are interested in fish and cute boys. Leprechauns love shoes and gold. Brownies are into household hints. Tricksters like practical jokes. Demons like contests. All the Folk I knew about told stories, traded gossip, granted wishes, played games. They never, ever said things like "teasing is not nice."

But if Carlyle's surprise wasn't a supernatural, then what was it?

"I've never heard of a compressor," I said cautiously. "What's its magic? Is it dangerous?"

More silence. "Is this a test?" the surprise asked.

"No. I really don't know. And I don't like not knowing things."

"Neither do I," the surprise said. "Insufficient data can lead to unfortunate mishaps."

"Right," I said, which I figured was a safe thing to say. "Will you tell me about the compressor beast, please?"

"Very well," the voice said. And it proceeded to give

me an explanation in which the words "and," "the," "chill," and "air" were the only ones that made sense. As the voice went on and on about flower-carbons and cold-producing poisonous magic insects called "refriger-ants," I realized something.

Carlyle's surprise was a mortal child.

Park Folk can be pretty nasty on the subject of mortals, but Astris had always told me that most mortals were perfectly nice. Changelings were mortal, after all. Mortals from Outside were fine, too, as long as they stayed where they belonged. Wild mortals in New York, though, were nothing but trouble. They didn't know the rules, and even when they knew them, they usually broke them.

Secretly, I'd always thought it might be fun to meet someone where I didn't know what they were going to say before they opened their mouth. And now, here I was, talking to a genuine wild mortal. Or rather, it was talking to me.

Too excited to keep quiet, I broke into the stream of strange words. "Are you really, you know, a"—I couldn't call it a "wild mortal" to its face—"a human being?"

The ugly voice stopped short. Silence filled the darkness—the thick kind that happens when someone is really mad at you.

"Have I got that wrong?" I said uncertainly. "I read it in a magazine. I'm a human being, too—a mortal changeling. I didn't mean to offend you."

Silence. I babbled on nervously. "I guess it's a silly

question, huh? If you weren't a mortal child, Carlyle wouldn't have stolen you."

"Carlyle did not steal me," the mortal child said sulkily. "The Carlyle is a hotel. I can see it from my bedroom window."

"It's also the home of the tengu who brought you here."

"You mean the man with the long nose?"

"The Japanese mountain spirit," I corrected. "Yes."

The mortal ignored me. "He said I was a naughty child," it complained. "That is not an accurate description of my behavior. Sometimes it is difficult for me to tell whether my behavior is appropriate or not, but I am not naughty."

"Why did he *think* you were naughty, then?"

The mortal child was silent awhile. "It may have had something to do with taking my father's computer apart," it said at last. "I remember that he was very angry when I dismantled his cell phone last summer. However, the situations were not parallel. I dismantled the cell phone out of curiosity. I dismantled his computer so that I could repair it."

"Your father has a computer? Cool!"

I'd never seen a mortal computer, of course, but I'd read *Macworld* from front to back three times, so I knew more about them than magic computers, which were the realm of Tech Folk anyway.

"My father is a software designer," the mortal said.

"He was the one who taught me to install memory. He should have known that I would not attempt to repair his motherboard if I had not been confident of success. I still do not understand why he was so angry."

"I got in trouble for doing something I didn't know was wrong, too," I said. "It's so unfair. You were just trying to help your father and I just wanted to go to a dance, and now we're stuck in a broom closet, waiting to find out if a bunch of bogeymen vote us the naughtiest children in New York."

"You are teasing me again," the mortal child said reproachfully. "Bogeymen do not exist. Michiko made them up. And I am twelve years old. I am a preadolescent, not a child."

I sat up in the darkness. "What do you mean, bogeymen don't exist? What's Carlyle, then?"

"Carlyle is a nightmare."

"Nightmares are horses," I explained. "Carlyle is a bogeyman. They're not alike at all. Who is Michiko?"

"Michiko looks after me. She is from Japan. She says that the Funny Man who lives on top of the Carlyle Hotel will come get me if I do not go to bed when she tells me to, whether I am sleepy or not."

"Well, Michiko was right. That's exactly what he did."

"I *told* you," the mortal said. "The Funny Man is a figment of Michiko's imagination. I am having a bad dream because Michiko shouted at me. I do not like people to shout at me."

I was beginning to understand why Michiko had shouted. "Are all mortals like you?" I asked.

"No," the mortal said. "I am very intelligent, but I have difficulty relating to people. When I was younger, I had a therapist who helped me develop social skills. For instance, when I meet someone, I am supposed to say, 'How do you do? My name is Jennifer Goldhirsch.'"

The last two words hit me like a wave of freezing water. "Don't *say* that!"

"What did I say?"

"Your name."

The mortal was quiet for a moment. "Why not?" she asked at last.

"Somebody might be listening."

"What would be wrong with that?"

I tried to imagine explaining the most important rule of survival in New York Between to a mortal child who didn't believe bogeymen were real. "Never mind. Just never say that name out loud again. Ever."

"I do not understand," the mortal child said. "I like my name. It creates a pleasing image. Jennifer means 'white wave,' and Goldhirsch means 'golden stag.'"

I didn't care what the mortal's name meant. I just never wanted to hear it again.

Not because I didn't like it. I did. It was my name, too—my true name, almost the only thing I remembered from before I came to live with Astris. It was a horrible coincidence that another mortal had it, too. I knew names worked differently Outside: Probably there were hundreds of Jennifers and even Goldhirsches, so the power got diluted. But in New York Between, I was it.

"Pretty," I said, thinking furiously how I could keep this other Jennifer from blabbing our name all over the place. "Listen. You said this was a dream, right?"

"I believe it is," said the mortal. "Yes."

"Well, you know how in dreams, the rules are different from when you're awake?"

She considered this. "Yes."

"In the dream, the rule about names is that you don't tell them to anybody at all."

"Why not?"

"Bad things will happen."

"What kind of bad things? Do you go to jail?"

I didn't ask what jail was. "Worse. Anyway, you can't use your real name. For example, everyone calls me Neef. It's my dream name. See?"

"Neef is a silly name," she said.

I gritted my teeth. "Neef is not my *name*," I said as patiently as I could. "It's what you can *call* me. You need a dream name, too."

"Are you referring to a nickname? I already have a nickname. Mom calls me Jenny."

I shivered as if refriger-ants were crawling up my back. "That's not made-up enough. What color is your hair?"

"Brown."

So was mine. "That's no good. I can't call you Brownie if you aren't one. Let me think. What about Closet?"

"Closet is not a name."

I thought up a couple more names, but she nixed all of them. We were arguing over MC (for "mortal child") when the wall behind us opened. Carlyle appeared, all dressed up in a formal kimono, his long nose twitching with eagerness.

"And now, here it is," he projected over his shoulder. *"The moment you've all been waiting for! I present to you— the naughtiest children in New York!*

"Come on, you two. It's showtime!"

CHAPTER

8

Carlyle dragged us out of the closet and into a riot of screaming and wailing like a banshee family reunion. I shut my eyes and clamped my hands over my ears. It didn't help. Besides, I couldn't stand not knowing what I was facing.

I peeked through my eyelashes at sea of bogeymen. They were every color of the rainbow and then some, bristling with horns and antennae and spines and spikes and teeth.

I closed my eyes again. Okay, it's important to know what you're dealing with. But sometimes the problem is too big to look at all at once.

Ladies and gentlemen. Honored patron of brats, buzzed Carlyle, his mind-voice smug and confident. *Let me tell you a little something about my candidates for this year's Eloise Awards.*

When he wasn't talking directly to me, I could tune the tengu out and think about other things. Like how he couldn't possibly fit three hundred bogeymen into his nest. We must be somewhere else—somewhere big, maybe with exits I could see. I forced my eyes open a second time and studied my surroundings.

I was standing on a raised stage at one end of an immense hall lit by giant chandeliers like sculpted ice. Carlyle stood between me and the blur of color that had to be the unluckily named mortal child. Garlands of flower fairies draped the mirrored panels along the walls; a couple of long tables piled high with fairy food and balloons stood waiting in the back. I didn't see any windows or doors.

The bogeymen laughed hideously at something Carlyle said, and a chorus of panic-stricken screaming swelled to a fever pitch behind me. Turning, I saw a seething mass of scarlet faces and roaring mouths, grabbing hands and squirming bodies. It took me a breath or two to realize that they belonged to the naughty children, penned up in a big brass cage at the back of the platform.

The bogeymen were less terrifying.

Carlyle pulled me around again, but not before I noticed that there was a space between the cage and the back wall.

As you can see, Carlyle buzzed, *they're a pair of hooligans. Disgustingly dirty, of course, but that's the least of it. This one* (he shoved the mortal child forward) *is driving her parents to the edge of madness. She is stubborn. She is disobedient. She is destructive. She is incredibly rude. She throws tantrums, and she never says she's sorry. This one* (he shoved me up beside her) *is even worse. She broke the geas set on her by the Genius of Central Park and disrupted the Solstice Dance. And she's not sorry either. Just look at that sullen pout. Have you ever seen a more hardened case?*

Three hundred pairs of yellow, poison-green, and scarlet eyes fixed themselves on me. I blinked hard and glared back. I wasn't some stupid wild mortal who didn't know what was what. I was the Central Park changeling, and I wasn't going to cry.

I came pretty close, though. What saved me was a small brown turtle. I felt something tickling my foot, and when I looked, there it was, clambering purposefully across my toes. There was a stir among the bogeymen. A hand appeared from nowhere and grabbed the turtle by its shell.

"Gotcha!" said the hand's owner. "Bad Skipperdee, skittling off like that. Do you want to get squished flat?"

It was Eloise. Her hair was like dried grass, and her belly hung out over the waistband of her pleated black skirt. Except for the red bow in her hair and the pink undies that showed whenever she bent over, she was paper white outlined in black, with sketched-in features. I'd never seen anything like her before, and I hoped I never did again.

Eloise scrambled to her feet and skewered me with a beady black glare.

"Here's what I like," she announced. "Playing with turtles." She stuck Skipperdee's nose against mine, so I was looking cross-eyed into its little turtley face. It opened and shut its mouth unhappily and retreated into its shell.

"Here's what I hate. Being bored. Being bored is not allowed. A lettuce leaf makes a nice hat."

She spun around and collapsed at the edge of the stage with her black-and-white legs sprawling and tossed Skipperdee from hand to hand. I knew how he must feel.

See, Carlyle projected triumphantly, *Eloise likes them.*

"Eloise is bored out of her mind," shouted a bogeyman in the back. "And so am I. One of them is rude? Don't make me laugh, birdman. That's wuss stuff. My kid would eat her for breakfast!"

"Yeah," shouted another. "You got nothing, Carlyle. You hear me? Nothing."

On the contrary, Carlyle objected. *I have a great deal. I have the girl who broke up the Solstice Dance single-handedly,* and *I have her exact twin, who may not be an actual juvenile delinquent, but is, I think you'll agree, undeniably naughty. And what do you have, pray tell? A boy who tied his sister to a tree and forgot about her. I rest my case.*

Her exact twin?

I turned and looked, really looked, at Carlyle's surprise.

She was staring at the nearest chandelier as if it was the only thing in the room. Her body was roundish and so was her face. Her eyes were hazel and her mouth kind of tucked in at the corners. Her hair sprang in wild brown corkscrews around her head. It looked uncombed and unkempt, and it would look that way no matter what. I know. I have the same hair. And the same face and eyes and mouth. If she'd been barefoot and wearing a spidersilk dress instead of sandals, a long blue skirt, and a jacket embroidered all over with flowers, even I couldn't have told us apart.

Carlyle's surprise wasn't a mortal child at all; she was a fairy changeling. My fairy changeling.

I'd always known how I'd come to live in New York Between. Astris had often told me the story of how a Kidnapper from the Bureau of Changeling Affairs had chosen me out of all the little girls in New York Outside to be the official changeling of Central Park. She hadn't said a word about the fairy changeling left behind in my place, and I hadn't asked. I was more interested in hearing about me.

Carlyle's mind-voice broke into my shock.

Just look at them, he was saying. *Like two peas in a*

pod. What are the chances, do you think, of finding them in two different realities and bringing them together? I should get points just for that.

"You should be disqualified, you mean," yelled a bogeyman in the front. He was kind of mauve, with huge red eyes and the usual mouthful of nasty teeth. He wasn't on any of the lists I'd learned. Someone must have made him up.

"Yeah," a dog-headed bogeyman said. "That one on the right, she's not even mortal."

Not mortal? Carlyle scoffed. *She smells mortal. Her parents treat her like a mortal. She's growing up and getting older. That's what mortals do, isn't it?*

The bogeymen weren't impressed. There were cries of "Cheat!" and "Not fair!" and "What does Eloise say?"

Eloise scrambled to her feet and stood on the tips of her little black Mary Janes, holding Skipperdee over her head with both hands. "Here's what I say," she screeched. "BEAR PILE!"

And she dove into the crowd of bogeymen headfirst.

A bright green bogeyman unhinged his jaw and roared. Carlyle shifted into a raven and flew at him, scaly claws spread.

This seemed like a perfect time to escape—if only I could find the way out.

"I do not like this dream."

My fairy twin had transferred her attention from the chandelier to the storm-tossed sea of bogeymen. Her arms were crossed and her head was sort of tucked down in the collar of her jacket, like Skipperdee in his shell. I could hardly stand to look at her. Was my face really that round and piggy? And was my voice really that ugly? I mean, next to the silver music of most fairy voices, I knew my voice was flat and coarse, but inside my head it didn't sound nearly as bad as hers.

A small red bogeyman came hurtling over my head, bounced against the cage of naughty children, and flew back into the scrimmage.

"There's got to be a door," I said. "Bogeymen can't walk through walls."

"Bogeymen do not exist."

"Then we've got nothing to worry about, do we?"

"My therapist says that dreams, however subjectively frightening, have no objective reality. It would be irrational to be frightened."

I glared at her. She didn't notice. I walked to the back of the stage. Just as I had thought, the little space behind the cage of naughty children was big enough to squeeze through. Once I got past them, I could jump down off the stage and crawl along the wall, checking the mirrors as I went to see if any of them opened or transported me somewhere. It wasn't the best idea in the world, but it was the best one I could come up with.

The fairy changeling appeared beside me. "Can you read kanji?"

"Can I read *what*?"

"Kanji." She pointed to one of the mirrors. "There is a sign over that door, but I cannot read it. It is Japanese, or possibly Chinese. Japanese is written in Chinese characters called kanji."

She started to tell me more about kanji, but I interrupted her. "You can see *doors*?"

"Yes. There are three, one in the center of each wall."

I believed her, of course. If she said she saw a door, there was a door. Without being able to see the sign, I didn't know where it led, but anywhere was better than where I was. Unfortunately, I was going to have to bring her with me.

"Listen," I said. "We're going to move very slowly to the side of the stage and then we're going to slip behind that cage and crawl along the wall to the nearest door and then we're going to go through it."

"Then will I wake up?"

"Maybe," I said cautiously. "You can't tell until you've tried."

I was surprised at how calm I sounded. I envied the fairy changeling her belief that the biting, scratching, screaming bogeymen were just a bad dream.

We edged nearer the naughty children. When we got close, the ones by the bars started grabbing at us and begging us to rescue them.

It was horrible. If my dress hadn't been magic, they would have torn it right off me. Their hands were hot and sticky against my arms and face, and I had to keep pinching them to make them let go. The fairy changeling went into a panic, scratching and slapping and screeching, "Do not touch me! I do not like to be touched!" at the top of her lungs. Luckily, the naughty children were already making so much noise that the bogeymen didn't hear her.

Breaking free from the last of the clutching hands, I jumped down from the stage and crouched panting against the wall. Eloise's bear pile was a lot more terrifying when you were right down in it. A lot more dangerous, too. A barbed tail whipped at my shoulder. A clawed hand nicked my knee. I was too scared to move.

With one last "Do not *touch* me!" the fairy changeling tumbled from the stage, picked herself up, and scurried off along the wall like a frightened squirrel. I ran after her, dodging fighting bogeymen and a hail of dried-out raisins, toward a strange glimmer—not a sign, exactly, but something like the shadow of a sign. I was almost even with it when I cannoned into a large, warty, chartreuse-green bogeyman.

"Hey, you guys, look!" the bogeyman shouted. "The naughty children are escaping!"

The noise got, if possible, louder. Carlyle's mind-voice exploded in my head: *Stop them! Stop them!* I leapt for one of the mirrored panels and pushed. It swung open onto a whistling darkness.

The fairy changeling was behind me, her hands over her face, screaming. I grabbed her wrist.

"Do not touch me!" she wailed, and wrenched herself free.

A lot of Folk don't like to be touched—leprechauns, for instance, who have to give up their gold if you catch them. The Pooka, who had made a study of catching things that don't want to be caught, told me you have to grab Folk from behind, pinning their arms if possible.

This isn't as easy as it sounds, particularly when you're in a hurry and scared out of your mind, but I managed to get a grip and drag my fairy twin backwards through the door. I could see the kanji sign now, and under it, another sign that read, "Carlyle Hotel/Madison Avenue." We were on a narrow platform beside a formless roar. It took me a breath to realize that we were in a Betweenway station.

I'd never ridden the Betweenways.

As I hesitated on the platform, I could hear a ruckus that sounded a lot like three hundred bogeymen, plus Eloise, trying to get through a narrow door at once. Nothing ventured, as the Pooka often said, nothing gained.

I stepped backwards onto the Betweenways, pulling the changeling with me.

CHAPTER
9

SOMETIMES THE LONG WAY AROUND IS THE BEST WAY HOME.

Neef's Rules for Changelings

The Betweenways are a magic transportation system the Folk use to get around New York. Astris had always told me that they were dangerous for mortals and it took a long time to learn to use them safely. Folk always know exactly where they want to go and can't be distracted. But mortals have to concentrate very hard on their destination to keep from riding around forever or until they starve to death and blow away, whichever comes first. She'd promised to take me for my first lesson after Midsummer. I'd really been looking forward to it.

Now that I was actually on one, I hated it. The noise was boneshaking. I felt like I was smooshed up in the middle of a crowd, but I couldn't actually see anyone or anything but ads (STORMS BY HOWLAA: THUNDERBOOMERS OUR SPECIALTY) suspended in the air above me. The Betweenways aren't dark, exactly. It's more like they're always on their way somewhere else, so they're not really *there*.

Plus, I didn't have the first idea where I was trying to go.

The fairy changeling wiggled and kicked and screeched.

"Ow!" I yelled as her sandal hit a bruise on my leg. "Do you *want* to be the Ghost of the Betweenways? Shut up and let me think!"

She elbowed me in the stomach.

I wanted to let her go. In fact, if she hadn't just basically rescued me from Carlyle and his bogey friends, I would have. But only oldest sons and wicked stepsisters abandon Folk who help them out of tight spots.

Following the Pooka's rules for subduing hysterical supernaturals, I wrapped my arms more tightly around her. She jerked a few times and screeched almost louder than the Betweenways. But she stopped struggling just enough for me to be able to consider the options.

Where I wanted to go, of course, was home. I wanted Central Park so badly that the station sign blinked past us over and over like a fairy flying in tight circles. But Central Park wasn't home anymore, was it? Hadn't the Green Lady said its paths were closed to me? And wouldn't the Wild Hunt be all over me as soon as I set foot there?

Not in the daylight, it wouldn't. The Hunt only rode at night.

I guess the Betweenways took that as a decision, because the next thing I knew, it spat us out onto a platform.

In front of us was a sign that said CENTRAL PARK and an arch that framed a familiar scene of trees and bushes. I was home.

I released the fairy changeling and stepped out into the Park. Morning light slanted along a path winding through a grove of linden trees. I knew those trees. Central Park Central lay beyond them, and the Turtle Pond and Belvedere Castle. And Satchel and my safe, curtained bed. And Astris.

I swiped at my eyes and blew my nose on the hem of my spidersilk dress. There was no point in crying now. Soon I would be in the kitchen at Belvedere Castle, dumping all my problems into Astris's white, furry lap.

But not right away. My biggest problem had collapsed under the arch in a full-scale fairy fit.

You can't talk a supernatural out of a fairy fit, or comfort it, or tease it. All you can do is wait it out. I looked up to check the sun. Midmorning. Plenty of time before I needed to worry about the Hunt.

I sat down on a rock in the sun and wondered what Satchel would give me for dinner and whether Astris might have baked some cookies and what kind of adventure this was going to be. Maybe the Pooka would trick the Green Lady into lifting her ban. Maybe the Pooka and Astris and I would all go on a quest together. Maybe Astris would find a prince for me to marry.

I hoped it wouldn't come to that.

While I was wondering, the fairy changeling continued to melt down. I'd seen plenty of fairy fits, but this one was harder to watch than most. I think it was because her face was all red and squinched out of shape, and her nose was running. If that was how I looked when I cried, it was no wonder the Folk laughed themselves into fits. Their idea of crying (when they do cry) is to allow two perfect crystal drops to fall from their eyes.

I sat and watched her until the sun left my stone, and then I got up and paced.

I started to worry about how long the fairy changeling could keep this up. Maybe I could just leave her and come back later. Would that make it my fault if she got into trouble? What if she was rude to something dangerous and got eaten? What if she forgot and told our true name to somebody like Peg Powler? I wasn't certain whether knowing our name would give Peg power over the fairy changeling, but I was sure it would give her power over me.

Figuring out how to Folk-proof somebody who didn't believe in magic occupied me long enough for the changeling to calm down a little. By the time I'd worked out a plan, she'd collected a bunch of pebbles and twigs from the path around her and was sorting them into piles. In the sunlight, the embroidery on her jacket glowed bright as a flower garden. Her face had smoothed, and she was humming: three notes up and three notes down, over and over again, kind of like the compressor-beast in the broom closet.

"I'm going to tell you a story," I said. "It's about your dream. It has all kinds of made-up things in it, like fairies and bogeymen and magic animals. Those things don't exist when you're awake, but they're real in your dream. The rule is: If it talks, then it's real, and you have to be polite to it."

The fairy changeling began to arrange her pebbles and twigs in a pattern of neat, interlocking rows. She didn't look up from her task, but she did stop humming. I decided this meant she was listening.

"Once upon a time," I said, "a girl dreamed she was kidnapped by a tengu and brought to a place called New York Between. In the dream, she met another girl, called Neef. Together, they escaped from a bunch of scary bogeymen and rode the Betweenways to Central Park Central. Are you with me so far?"

The fairy changeling added a pebble to the pattern. I checked the sun. The morning was passing.

I took a deep breath to steady myself. "In this dream, if somebody knows your name, they can use it to hurt you. So Neef gave the girl a special made-up name. She called her"—I hesitated—"Changeling."

I held my breath, waiting for my fairy twin to object, but she only poked a twig more perfectly straight.

I went on. "When Neef and Changeling got to Central Park Central, they went to see Neef's fairy godmother, who was called Astris. She was kind and beautiful, with eyes like rubies and a coat of soft, white fur."

Changeling wrapped her arms across her chest and clutched her elbows. "People with fur coats are bad," she said. "It is wrong to kill an animal just so you can wear its skin."

"Do mortals do that? Just like ogres. Ick. No, it's nothing like that. Astris *is* an animal, see, a white rat. She talks. Remember what I said about things that talk?"

"You said they were real," Changeling said dubiously. "But . . ."

"No buts," I said. "They *are* real."

Changeling fingered the embroidery on her sleeve. "I am not a big fan of rats," she said. "Rats are dirty. They carry diseases."

Suddenly I was so mad I could hardly see. "Not here, they don't. And where do you get off, calling anybody dirty?"

Changeling pulled the flowery collar of her jacket up around her ears and started humming again. A breath ago, I'd wanted to kick her. Now I wanted to kick myself. Folk only understand their own rules. Unless they're tricksters, they don't *mean* to drive you crazy. They just can't help it. Yelling at them makes it worse. I knew that. It would have been easier to be patient with her if she didn't look so much like me.

"I'm sorry, Changeling," I said formally. "I keep forgetting you don't know the rules here. There are lots of them, and I think I know them all. I know the Words of Protection and the Seven Signs of a Shapechanger. I know where Monkey keeps his heart and Lion keeps his courage. So you don't have to worry. Stick with me, and you'll be okay."

Changeling stopped humming and lifted her head. "You promise?"

I didn't answer right away. I couldn't. Words are power in New York Between. A promise is a Promise, and breaking it is even worse than breaking a geas because you've taken it on of your own free will. If I promised Changeling I'd keep her safe, I'd have to do it, even if I could hardly stand to look at her.

The sun was moving up the sky. We needed to get a move on. "All right," I said. "I promise. Can we go now?"

Changeling got up. "Which way do we go?"

That's when I found out what the Lady had meant about the paths of the Park being closed to me.

I'd grown up in Central Park. I'd walked on its grass and played hide-and-seek in its groves and ridden all over it on the Pooka's back. Belvedere Castle was my home, and I could almost see it from where we were standing. But I couldn't get there.

It was like one of those dreams where I'm in the Museum and I'm looking for Early Roman Art and I keep ending up in Eighteenth-Century Furniture instead. I'd take three steps toward Central Park Central and find myself heading uptown or crossing the bridge to the Lake or veering off toward the Museum, which at least was in the right direction, if the next step hadn't taken us to the ravine where I'd found the kazna peri.

I stamped my foot and carefully did not swear. I was in enough trouble without swearing.

Changeling was starting to look frayed around the edges. "Where is the talking rat?" she demanded. "Are you lost?"

"No," I said through my teeth. "I know just exactly where I am. It's getting where I want to be that's the problem."

Picking a path and closing my eyes didn't work. Concentrating on Astris didn't work. I was very close to melting down myself. Then I took another step, and—we found ourselves standing at the edge of Central Park Central, looking across the meadow at Belvedere Castle.

Our shadows streamed out to the left. I looked west. The sun was perched on the pointed tower of a tall building like a giant yellow pompom. We'd been wandering around the Park all afternoon.

"Why are you going around in circles?" Changeling asked. "Is this some kind of a game?"

"Yes," I said. "It's a game. Unfortunately, nobody told me the rules."

It was then that my brain, which I'd thought was completely out of ideas, came up with another one. "There's one move I haven't tried yet," I said slowly. "The only thing is, we'll have to hold hands."

She thrust hers deep into her pockets. "I told you. I do not like to be touched."

"To win this game, you have to lead me to that castle over there. How can you do that if you don't touch me?"

Changeling scowled thoughtfully, then grabbed a handful of my spidersilk skirt. "I will lead you like this," she said.

"That'll work," I said. "Okay, I'm going to close my eyes and you're going to take me to the castle. Straight there, okay? Don't step either to the right or to the left. And don't stop until we get to the door."

"You can trust me," she said proudly. "I am very good at staying on task."

"Fine. I've got my eyes closed now. Onward and up-ward."

Changeling took off at a trot. Following her would have been easier if I could see my feet, but I didn't dare peek. Central Park Central seemed to have grown very big, and somebody had been planting sharp rocks in it. By the time we got to the Castle stairs, my toes were throbbing. I stumbled upwards, wincing at every step. When we got to the courtyard, the sun-warmed pavement was like fire under my feet.

"I believe we have arrived," Changeling said, and stopped.

I pried my eyes open. The Castle door was about an inch from my nose. Light-headed with relief, I shouted

for Astris, who popped out the door as if she'd been waiting for me.

"Neef!" she said, her whiskers twitching nervously.
"What a surprise. I didn't expect to see you."

"Changeling brought me," I said. "She's—"

"I know what she is. You realize, of course, that as
soon as the sun's below the horizon, the Wild Hunt's going to come for you. My guess is they'll be even happier
hunting two changelings than one."

"I know," I said miserably. "What are you going to do?"

"*You*," Astris said, "are going to get out of the Park."

I stared at her. "Aren't you coming with me?"

"And have the Lady's ban fall on me, too? What good
would that do? I'm Park Folk, Neef. I don't have power
anywhere else."

"I'm Park Folk, too!"

"No, you're not; you're a mortal. Mortals are supposed
to leave home and seek their fortunes. You're just a little
ahead of schedule, that's all."

"But I don't *want* to leave home. I'm not *ready* to seek
my fortune. Where am I supposed to start?"

"The Metropolitan Museum, of course."

I thought about this. I'd been a Museum member as
long as I could remember, and had a lot of friends among
the docents and exhibits. The Museum wasn't home, but
it was close.

"That makes sense," I said. "Only, how am I supposed

to get there? I can't take a step now without getting totally lost."

"That's why I summoned the Pooka," Astris said.

I heard a busy clicking behind me, and a big black dog dashed up, yellow eyes flaming and feathery tail whipping the air. I threw my arms around his furry black neck, but had to let go when he shifted into his pony shape.

"Up with you, then," the Pooka said. "The sun's sinking fast."

I climbed up on his back. Changeling was backed up against the Castle wall, as far from the Pooka as she could get. She'd retreated into her jacket again. I couldn't hear, but I guessed she was humming, three notes up and three notes down.

"Changeling?" I called. "We have to go."

"Leave the creature be," the Pooka said. "What's the harm in it if the Hunt eats her?"

"She comes, too," I said.

"I ask again, what's the harm? For all she's your living spit, she's no kith nor kin of yours. She's neither full fay nor mortal child, and not a particle of use to man nor beast."

There wasn't time to argue. I leaned down, grabbed Changeling's shoulder, and tried to haul her up onto the Pooka's back. Bad idea. As soon as I touched her, she hit me. I would have had to leave her if she hadn't suddenly shot up into the air and landed square on the Pooka's hindquarters. I looked down to see Astris brushing sparkling dust from her front paws.

"I knew I'd been saving that fairy dust for something." She held a familiar brown leather bag up to me. "Here's Satchel. Don't let it out of your hands again. Obey the rules and keep your mortal wits about you. Be careful. Find your fortune. And remember that I'll be waiting for you to come back and tell me all about it."

I hardly had time to sling Satchel across my back before the Pooka spun around on his hind legs and sprang over the wall and down off Castle Rock. Changeling clamped her arms around my waist. I whooped with excitement. Now that I was on my fairy godfather's back, running from the Wild Hunt seemed less like a nightmare and more like an adventure.

We landed on the far shore of the Turtle Pond with a thump that knocked the breath out of me. To the west, the sky flamed red and gold. Over the clop of the Pooka's hooves, I thought I heard a distant howling.

The Hunt was awake.

CHAPTER
10

HE WHO HESITATES IS LOST; LOOK BEFORE YOU LEAP.

Neef's Rules for Changelings

The Pooka raced across Central Park Central like a wind-blown cloud. In three strides, we were past the Obelisk and almost to the Museum. I felt a small, perverse pang of disappointment. Our escape was too easy.

Then the Pooka swerved north and galloped up the path that led to the Reservoir.

Startled, I grabbed the Pooka's mane and yanked for all I was worth. I expected a quick and undignified trip to the ground, but he only tossed his head and ran faster.

The light faded as the Pooka ran. Branches caught in my hair and plucked at my skirt. I clung to the Pooka's back, and Changeling clung to me, doing her banshee impersonation in my ear. I tried to tell her that she couldn't fall off unless the Pooka dumped her, but I don't think she heard me.

Halfway around Harlem Meer, I lay forward on the Pooka's neck—not an easy move, with Changeling stuck to my back like a baby monkey—and yelled, "Hey Pooka, what do you think you're doing?"

His ear twitched irritably. "Riding you through the Park, of course."

"Why?"

"I'm the Pooka," he said unhelpfully. "When a mortal gets on my back, I take her on a wild ride. That's what a Pooka does. I have no choice in the matter."

I wanted to kick him, but I didn't. "You do too have a choice. You're my *fairy godfather*. What about your oath to protect and aid me?"

"I'm not at all easy in my mind about it," the Pooka admitted.

"Oh, that makes it all right, then."

"It's a fierce dilemma," the Pooka said, sounding hurt. "There's the Lady's geas and my oath to you; there's my heart that bids me help you and my nature that bids me gallop the stranger on my back until sunrise. Throw the fairy changeling to the Hunt, and I'll take you to safety before a faun can scratch his ear."

I thought about it—not very hard, and not very long. But I did think about it. "I can't," I said. "I promised Changeling I wouldn't let anything hurt her."

The Pooka tossed his head and slowed to a rough trot. "Do you say so?"

"I do," I said. "I owe her a life debt. She helped me

escape from a tengu and three hundred bogeymen, plus Eloise and a bunch of screaming kids."

"She outwitted the Genius of the Plaza Hotel?" The Pooka was impressed.

"Kind of. Plus, she shares my true name, Pooka. If you save me, you have to save her, too."

A low-hanging branch raked across my back like grasping claws. Changeling, who had settled into a steady moaning, shrieked with terror.

"Idiot," the Pooka said.

"Thanks a lot," I said bitterly.

"Not you," he said. "Me. Hang on tight."

He veered suddenly. I heard a snap that sounded horribly like sharp teeth missing my head. A deep voice bayed behind us in the undergrowth: "They're getting away!"

The Wild Hunt had found us.

The Pooka crashed through a stand of trees and barreled down the East Meadow, the Hunt surging up at his heels. A dead-meat smell choked my nose; wings and claws and snapping mouths haunted the edges of my vision.

I bent low over the Pooka's neck. Through his whipping mane, I saw the shadow of the Reservoir embankment and the glimmer of an early moon reflected in the Museum's glass wall. We were almost there.

I grinned with relief. And then I remembered that the Museum's entrance was all the way around the building on Fifth Avenue.

The Pooka gathered his hind legs under him and leapt up and up and up the glass wall, leaving my stomach behind. He cleared the hedge around the roof garden and landed with a tooth-jarring thump. As I rolled off his back, the Hunt appeared in the air above us, yipping and bellowing triumphantly. I scrambled under the nearest wooden bench and curled up hopelessly, waiting for the Hunt to find me.

Nothing happened. No claws ripped the bench away. No meaty breath seared the back of my neck. After a while, I peered around the bench. The Wild Hunt was boiling like a frustrated thunderstorm a tall giant's height above the Roof Garden.

"What's with them?" I asked weakly.

The Pooka had shifted into a black goat, and was huddled in the stony folds of an abstract sculpture. "I haven't a notion," he said. "Perhaps they have no tickets, the creatures."

"Neither do you," I said.

"Hush. Maybe no one will notice."

The Hunt obviously hadn't given up on their dinner. Claws out, they swooped toward us, only to bounce away when they hit the Museum's invisible barrier. Then they landed on it and tried digging through it. Something about their shrieks and their ugly, screaming faces reminded me of the naughty children in Carlyle's cage.

Giggling, I stood up, stuck my thumbs in my ears, and gave the Wild Hunt my best booga-booga.

"Don't be playing the fool, Neef," the Pooka bleated. "We're not out of the woods yet. They're likely playing with us, the creatures."

I stared at him. I'd never known the Pooka to be afraid before, or out of bright ideas, but then, I'd never seen him deal with a mess that wasn't his idea in the first place. "It's okay, Pooka," I said. "The Museum's on our side."

"But I haven't a ticket," he said nervously.

I thought for a moment. "I'm a life member. You can get in as my guest."

"And the fairy girl? What of her?"

I couldn't believe I'd forgotten Changeling. "I don't know. I'll think of something. Just get under the trellis, okay? That's where the door is."

The Pooka scrambled to his feet and trotted over to a long trellis next to the glass building that housed the elevator.

I looked around for Changeling. She was lying a little distance away, with the back of her jacket pulled up over her head like a flowery turtle shell. I gave her a gentle nudge with my foot to get her attention. "We're going inside, Changeling, where it's quieter. See that statue under the trellisy thing? The three droopy guys with the long arms? That's Rodin's *Shades*. It's a door guard. It'll protect you."

There was a pause, and then she rolled up onto her hands and knees and scuttled toward the trellis.

As we joined the Pooka by the door, Rodin's *Shades* raised its three drooping heads. "This is not an entrance," its three hollow voices chorused. "If you wish to visit the Museum, you must use the main entrance on Fifth Avenue."

"We can't," I said. "The Wild Hunt is in the way."

The statue sighed. "Is that what all the noise is about? The Curator will be very displeased."

"In that case," the Pooka piped up, "he should be informed immediately, so he can deal with them. We'll be glad to oblige, if you're busy at all."

"This is not an entrance," Rodin's *Shades* repeated.

"Looks like one to me," I said, and banged on the door as hard as I could.

The Curator appeared almost at once. He looked from us to the Wild Hunt wheeling overhead and opened the door.

"What on earth is going on here?" he asked crossly. "All Hallows' Eve isn't for months."

If the Green Lady of Central Park is all about wildness and growing things, the Curator of the Metropolitan Museum is all about collecting and conserving and keeping things safe. He's got a neat brown beard and little oval gold-rimmed spectacles clipped to his nose, and he tends to look at you as if he's judging your authenticity. Right now, he was examining the three of us like puzzling fragments of Mesopotamian pottery.

"Fascinating," the Curator said. "It's not often I see an original and a forgery side by side. Not to mention the Wild Hunt. Is that pooka with them, Neef, or with you?"

"*The* Pooka," I said. "He's my fairy godfather."

"*The* Pooka. Of course. Well. It's very irregular, but under the circumstances, we'd better talk about it inside."

He opened the door wider and we trooped in. The Pooka held his curling horns high, but I could see he was still feeling shaky. Changeling's hair was so matted with leaves and twigs that she looked like one of the untidier moss women. She headed straight for a potted palm in the corner, rolled herself behind it, and hid her head in her arms.

"That's better," the Curator said, closing the door. "Now. The forgery is welcome as long as she observes the Museum rules. The Pooka, however, poses a problem. He is not a member nor even a copy of a member. In fact, he has no more right of entry than those unspeakable hooligans outside. I don't know what the Museum was thinking of, letting him land here."

"He's my godfather," I said. "He was saving me. Plus, I'm a life member. I get to bring guests."

The Curator frowned. "One guest. In this case, the forgery."

I thought fast. "But Changeling *isn't* a forgery. She's me. We're both originals, like two editions of a print. We count as one person. The Pooka is our guest. It's all completely legal. It must be. You said yourself that the Museum let him land."

I held my breath while the Curator stroked his beard. "A neatly circular argument," he said, and I let it out. "Still, allowing a trickster into the Museum is likely to lead to shenanigans. I do not approve of shenanigans. They upset the exhibits. I will only let the Pooka enter if you pledge your word that he will abide by the Museum rules while he is here."

I looked at the Pooka, who looked back, his yellow eyes unreadable. Another promise; another responsibility I didn't want. Tricksters are tricky, after all. They're better at wiggling out of bargains than nixies are at swimming. But if I didn't agree, the Pooka would have to go out and face the Wild Hunt alone.

"I promise," I said.

The Pooka looked sarcastic—but then, goats always look sarcastic.

"Good," said the Curator. "Perhaps you'd like to start by informing him that goats are not welcome in my Museum."

I knelt and looked the Pooka in the eye. "You heard the Curator," I said pleadingly. "I've promised you'll be good, and I'd really, really appreciate it if you didn't make a liar out of me."

The Pooka lifted his bearded chin. "It's sore grieved I am," he said, his brogue thick enough to spread on bread, "to know that my own godchild should be having so little faith, when I'm after saving her hide at sore risk to my own."

"Come on, Pooka. You know I'm grateful. You saved my life. But I'm not a total idiot, either."

The Pooka slid his eyes sideways, then nodded. "I promise to try, then," he said. "And you can't be asking for more than that, for you won't get it."

I patted his cheek. "Good enough," I said. "Let's shake on it."

To shake, of course, the Pooka had to take his man shape. As a man, everything about him was long: feet, hands, hair, and body. He was so tall that the Curator only came up to his nose, and the top of my head was about even with his chest. His yellow eyes were deep-set and slanted under eyebrows like birds' wings. He wore black jeans, red high-top sneakers, and a black T-shirt with THE OYSTER BAND stamped across the chest in faded red Celtic scrollwork.

He tossed his long black hair out of his eyes and held out his hand. "Since you ask so nicely," he said.

"Thank you," I said, and shook. He still smelled like a goat.

The Curator nodded. "That's settled, then. Good. Now to get this riffraff out of my air space." He clapped his hands. "Guard!"

The elevator clunked, the double doors whooshed open, and the Assyrian Winged Lion stalked out.

The Pooka put his hand over his heart and bowed almost double. Even I was impressed, and the Lion and I were old friends. But he looked a lot bigger here than he did hanging out in Ancient Near Eastern Art. His golden horned cap brushed the ceiling as he bent his kingly head to the Curator.

"The Wild Hunt is making a disturbance," the Curator said. "Please encourage them to make it elsewhere."

The Wild Hunt, all teeth and claws and hunger, is as old as the forests of the Old Country and as strong as fear. But the Assyrian Lion has been protecting mortals against evil spirits since the beginnings of human civilization. He paced through the glass wall as though it didn't exist, unfurled endless wings as bright as rainbows, and reared up onto his three back legs. He tossed his gleaming horns, opened his bearded lips, and roared until the building rattled around us.

The Wild Hunt tumbled up and away from him like a tattered wave, wailing with terror.

"That should settle them," the Curator said placidly. "Now, if you're quite sure there's no one else trying to eat you, I need to get back to work. Enjoy your visit."

CHAPTER
11

NEVER LET THE TRUTH INTERFERE WITH A GOOD STORY.
Neef's Rules for Changelings

The elevator hall seemed very empty without the Curator and the Assyrian Lion. "That was thirsty work," said the Pooka. "Do you know if there's such a thing as a Guinness about the place, at all?"

"I don't know," I said. "What's a Guinness?"

"It's a soothing potion for overwrought Pookas is what it is, and I'll be wanting a good deal of it very soon, if it's quite convenient."

He was looking at me with one flying eyebrow raised, waiting for an answer I didn't have. I shrugged.

"You *must* know," he said severely. "I am clean out of my element, Neef. My nature tells me to wreak whatever havoc may suggest itself. If I can't follow my nature, I must follow you."

I looked from him to Changeling, balled up behind the

potted palm. I'd hoped someone else would take charge now, but it obviously wasn't going to happen. I sighed.

"I don't know what Guinness is," I told the Pooka, "so Satchel probably won't either. We'll have to go to the cafeteria in the Fountain Court. Pooka, you call the elevator, and I'll get Changeling."

"Right you are," said the Pooka. "What is an elevator, for all love, and how does the creature like to be called?"

On the ground floor, we were greeted by a small green-black cat, who leaped in as the elevator door opened and wound herself around my ankles.

The Museum guide lists Bastet as an ancient Egyptian bronze coffin for a sacred cat. She insists she's really a goddess, and I guess she ought to know. She's got a narrow, elegant face and bat ears, and I was so glad to see her that I would have picked her up and kissed her if I'd thought she would let me.

"Don't think I've missed you," she purred, "or care what's been going on or why everybody's talking about you. I'm just here to keep the Old Market Woman company."

The Old Market Woman was waiting for us out in the hall, her face twisted in a furious snarl. It didn't mean she was angry—that was just how she'd been carved. She's a docent, someone who conducts tours of the Museum. Her specialty is Greek and Roman statuary. She is also my Ancient Greek and Latin teacher.

"*Ave*, Neef," she said. "*Quo vadis?*"

"To the cafeteria," I answered. "We're hungry and tired, and the Pooka wants a Guinness. Do you know what a Guinness is?"

The Old Market Woman glared at me, but her voice was calm. "Some kind of barbaric alcoholic drink, I think."

"I heard the Wild Hunt's in the Museum air space," Bastet said, popping up between us. "Did you bring it? And what's a pooka doing in the Museum, and why are you wearing a spidersilk dress, and where did the forgery come from, and why did you bring her here?"

I glanced at the corner by the elevator, where Changeling stood stroking the embroidered flowers on her sleeve and humming three notes up, three notes down. I chewed my lip. "I had to. I owe her a life debt."

"You do?" Bastet's tail quivered eagerly. "Tell! Tell!"

"I'm too hungry."

"Come eat, then," the Old Market Woman said. "The Pooka and the forgery, too, of course."

I'd thought Changeling was still too freaked to be listening, but I was wrong. "I am not a forgery," she declared. "I am a preadolescent girl."

Bastet tapped over to her and sat down with her bronze tail around her paws. "You are not a girl," she told Changeling. "You were made a fairy, but you're not one now—at least, not entirely."

"That is nonsense," Changeling said. "People are not made, they are born. And fairies do not exist, except in this dream. You are teasing me, and I do not like it."

The Old Market Woman turned to me. "Has no one told this changeling what she is?"

"I've *tried*," I said. "Is it my fault if she doesn't believe me? Can we go eat now? And Bastet—Changeling is under my protection. Could you just please be nice to her?"

"I am a goddess," Bastet said with dignity. "I don't need to be nice. But I will try to be polite."

According to the Old Market Woman, the Fountain Court is based on the atrium of an ancient Roman house. There are slender columns holding up a vaulted ceiling, and between them is a long, shallow pool. Comma-shaped bronze dolphins dance on the surface of the water, ridden by cheerful bronze boys who tootle softly on double flutes. Art-loving Folk from all over the City sit at little round tables, refreshing themselves with maiden's tears, fresh milk, and other Folk favorites. Astris says the Museum fairy cakes are stale, but I love them anyway.

Today, the Court was almost deserted. The Museum is always open, but on a fine summer night, most Folk have things they'd rather do than play with mortal art.

I found a place to sit. The Pooka drifted off, I suppose to see about the Guinness. Feeling light-headed, I unslung

Satchel and asked it politely for a hamburger, medium, with ketchup and no tomato. I got it, too, although Satchel added mushrooms and forgot the ketchup. I took a big bite. And then I realized that I'd lost Changeling again.

I checked out the corners, then thought of looking under the table, and there she was, curled around the pedestal like a plump, flowery dragon. "Are you hungry?" I asked.

"Yes."

"What do you want to eat?"

"Macaroni and cheese."

I considered asking her what macaroni and cheese was, decided that might provoke another fairy fit, and told her I'd do my best. The Pooka wandered up with a bowl of Irish stew and a glass of black stuff with foam on top (the Guinness, I guess—it looked nasty), sat down, and devoted himself to making it go away as quickly as possible.

Without much hope, I asked Satchel for macaroni and cheese. It made me wait for a long time, and then it gave me a wedge of cheddar and a hunk of bread and a golden apple. I explained to Changeling that Satchel didn't do macaroni and cheese, and would she settle for cheese and bread?

"I usually have a cheese sandwich for lunch on Monday," Changeling said. "Is today Monday?"

"What's Monday?"

Changeling stared at me resentfully, then took the cheese, careful not to touch my hand. She sniffed, then nibbled it like a mouse, starting with the pointy end of the wedge. I laid the bread and apple on the floor beside her and went back to my hamburger.

Bastet flowed up onto the table and assumed her favorite pose, tail-around-paws. "I'm ready for your story now," she said.

"I'm eating, Bastet. Give me a break."

"You wanted to eat; you are eating. I want a story; I'm listening."

I took another bite. Bastet watched, unblinking, while I chewed it.

"Story," she said.

I knew Bastet. She wasn't going to stop pestering me until I did what she wanted. And she wasn't the only one. While I was feeding Changeling, the Old Market Woman had appeared behind me. Also the Assyrian Lion, a Suit of Seventeenth-Century Parade Armor, a Bodhisattva of Infinite Compassion, and a dozen other docents from various periods of art history, all staring at me eagerly.

The Curator seated himself across the table from me.

"I am not at all pleased with having the Wild Hunt infesting my air space," he said. "They worry the exhibits. They put off visitors to the Museum. I have given you and your curious protégés asylum. You owe me—you owe all of us—an explanation."

I swallowed the last bite of my hamburger and started to talk.

Usually I like telling stories. I know all the patterns and the traditional plots that tell you what kinds of events usually go between "Once upon a time" and "They lived happily ever after." But the story of how I brought the Pooka and Changeling to the Metropolitan Museum was full of extra things that tales like "The Twelve Dancing Debutantes" don't have, and no happy ending in sight.

Still, I did my best to make it all fit a fairy-tale pattern. I told my audience how once upon a time, I'd gone to the North Woods on an errand for my godmother and met an old woman under a willow. The old woman, as old women will, revealed forbidden knowledge to me: in this case, the existence of the Solstice Dance. I told how I wanted to go to the dance more than anything in the world, and how I'd bargained with the kazna peri for a keep-awake charm and how I'd fooled Astris and the sandman and how I'd climbed a tree and watched the Folk of New York Between dance under the stars.

When I got to how I saw the other mortal changelings and joined the dance, I glanced over at the Curator. He was shaking his head like he couldn't believe what he was hearing.

"What?" I said. "You asked what happened, and I'm telling you. It's not my fault I broke the geas. The Green Lady set me up."

"You were curious," the Curator said sternly. "Mortals can subdue their curiosity through force of will, although they seldom choose to do so. You knew that what you were doing was, at the very least, unwise."

Overwhelmed by a number of feelings, all of them uncomfortable, I put my head in my hands. There was a little silence, and then Bastet said, "So, what happened next?"

The next part was harder, because it was a different kind of story-pattern from the first part. Besides, I was getting sleepy.

I told them about how Carlyle snatched me. "Then he told me he had a surprise for me and put me in a broom closet. At first, I thought the surprise was a mortal child, and then I realized she was a fairy raised by mortals—a fairy changeling. My twin." My throat closed up. I coughed and plunged on.

"Fascinating," the Curator said when I stopped talking.

"You left out a lot," Bastet complained.

"I'm too tired to talk anymore," I said. "And my throat's sore. *I'm* not made of bronze, you know."

The Curator stood up. "Come and rest, then," he said. "I forget how fragile mortals are."

Changeling was fast asleep under the table, the last of the bread clutched in her hand. The Assyrian Lion offered to carry us both, so the Pooka hoisted her onto the Lion's back, and I climbed up behind.

The Curator led us to the bedroom of the Palazzo Sagredo, which is one of my favorite rooms in the Museum. All that green brocade and those gilded curlicues always remind me of the Park in summer, with the sun shining down through the leaves. Unfortunately, it's infested with pudgy little boys wearing tiny wings and nothing else. They're called amorini, but I can think of lots of better names for them. Airheads. Motormouths. Busybodies.

I could hear their squeals all the way down the hall.

"Is that the *Assyrian Lion*?"

"Oh, it *is*. Cool!"

"What's *he* doing in this part of the Museum?"

"What's that on his back?"

"That's Neef, you dork. She comes here all the time."

"Look, guys. Someone's copied her!"

"Cool! Are they going to sell it in the Museum Shop?"

When we got to the door, the Curator held up a hand. "Silence, all of you, and listen well; I have an important task for you. This mortal and her companions are weary. You will watch over them as they sleep."

"Like guards, you mean? In case anybody tries to get in and steal them?"

"In case any of them tries to get out," the Curator answered dryly. "Especially the Pooka."

I waited for the Pooka to make some sarcastic comment, but he was already stretched out in the middle of the rose brocade bed, with Changeling curled beside him like a flower-covered rock. I flopped down on my stomach and hid my face in my crossed arms so I didn't have to watch the amorini watching me. And then I fell gratefully asleep.

CHAPTER 12

YOU CAN'T TEACH OLD FOLK NEW TRICKS.
Neef's Rules for Changelings

I didn't sleep long.

As it turned out, when the Assyrian Lion chased the Wild Hunt out of the Museum's air space, it flew straight to the Green Lady. What was the good of her putting bans on people, the Hunt wanted to know, if the ban didn't hold? Twice the Hunt had chased me, and twice I'd gotten away scot-free, leaving them without so much as a toe to nibble on and laughing at the Lady as I went.

Which is why I was pulled out of a dreamless sleep by the Old Market Woman's husky voice in my ear. "The Green Lady's here," she murmured. "The Curator has sent for you."

I groaned. "I'm asleep. Can't the Assyrian Lion deal with her?"

"The Curator's waiting," the Old Market Woman said

severely. She poked my shoulder with her marble basket until I got up, and then she made me finger-comb the leaves out of my hair and brush down the skirt of my spidersilk dress. When I was done, the gold-framed mirror by the door informed me that the dress looked a lot better than I did.

The Old Market Woman glared at the amorini. "If the Pooka or the copy wakes, call a guard. Otherwise, not a peep out of you. Come on, Neef."

We paused at a Renaissance fountain and I splashed my face in it, hoping the cold water would clear my head. It made me feel better, but not nearly good enough to face the Green Lady in a fury.

When we got to the Great Hall, I noticed right away that she'd grown about three times as tall as she usually was, and very pointy about the teeth and nails. I was glad to see the Curator was there, too, with a good dozen of the most powerful guards behind him.

The Old Market Woman gave me a gentle shove forward. "Hail, Lady," I croaked.

The Lady said something that made my hair crackle and my toes tingle.

The Curator made a clucking noise. "Remember, Lady, that you are a guest in my domain."

"*You* remember that you're harboring a fugitive from justice. *My* justice." The Green Lady pointed a green claw at me. "You're busted, kid. I suppose you think you're pretty smart, escaping the Wild Hunt and enlisting the

Pooka and generally blowing off my geas. Well, you're not. You can't laugh at a Genius and get away with it. So I've decided to throw you out of New York."

Her words hit me like freezing water. I gasped, and the Green Lady smiled at me. Her smile was a Wild Hunter's smile, wide and toothy and cruel.

"The Genius of Central Park is bluffing," the Curator said briskly. "In my Museum, on my territory, she can't raise a breeze without my consent. Which she doesn't have."

The Green Lady turned her smile on the Curator, and then she began to change. First she grew taller and then she grew thinner. Her arms and legs flowed into her body and her head kind of collapsed and reshaped itself. In the space of two breaths, she'd turned into a humongous green serpent with brown markings like leaves all down her back and the Lady's narrow green eyes glaring out of the snaky face.

I tried to hide behind the Old Market Woman, which was like a troll trying to hide behind a piskie.

The Curator made a *tsk, tsk* noise and clapped his hands.

Nobody moved. *Even the guards are scared of her*, I thought.

I heard the faint scraping of terra-cotta skirts as the Minoan Priestess glided purposefully across the marble floor, a sacred snake clutched in each fist. As an ancient priestess of the Snake Goddess, she was certainly the right guard for the job, but I would have felt better if she'd been more than six inches high.

"You don't really want to fight us," the Priestess said. Her voice was a lot bigger than she was, low and calm and firm.

The Lady-serpent flicked her forked scarlet tongue. "Oh, yes I do," she hissed. "I want to strike and sear and squeeze."

"That would be most unwise of you," the Priestess said. "This is the Curator's territory. Here, he is stronger than you are."

The great serpent's mouth opened wider than I believed possible. Two gracefully curving fangs swung down and locked into place. The Minoan Priestess's tiny snakes hissed like radiators. For a quivering moment, I was sure there was going to be a battle. Then the serpent's fangs retracted. Her great head dipped, and she began to sway slowly.

"That's more like it," the Priestess said. "Now, if you shift into something more comfortable, you can talk this over calmly with the Curator. What do you think?"

In answer, the serpent gave a long shiver. By the time the shiver reached her tail, she was the Lady again, still a little larger and toothier than usual, but not nearly as scary as she had been. I came out from behind the Old Market Woman, trying to look as if I'd never moved.

"Thank you," said the Curator. "Really, Green Lady, I don't know why you're so upset with Neef. If I didn't know better, I'd swear she was a new kind of trickster. In fact, you should be proud of her. She hardly acts like a mortal at all."

The Lady pouted. "She's broken every rule in the book. She has to be punished. That's the way it works."

"Of course it is. But a Genius as ancient and powerful as you are can think of something more imaginative than simply feeding her to the Hunt."

The Green Lady tapped her teeth thoughtfully with one green nail. "I'm guessing you're not going to let me cut off her hands or her ears or anything fun like that."

"Your guess is correct."

"No blood, no bones, no close encounters with demons?"

"I am a conservator, Madam. I cannot accept physical damage of any kind."

The Lady started to swell again. "You 'cannot accept'? Well, *I* cannot accept some snotty-nosed mortal brat tromping through my Park without my permission. I've got to make her suffer somehow, or it'll be all over town that the Green Lady of Central Park is going soft."

The Curator said, "Hmm," like he thought she might have a point.

I opened my mouth to object. Loudly.

"Don't you dare," the Old Market Woman muttered.

"But I've already suffered. Plenty."

"Not everything is about you, Neef. You don't know what's at stake here. If the other Geniuses think the Lady's getting weak, the Genius Wars could start all over again."

"They couldn't break the treaty—they wouldn't dare!"

"You broke your geas."

I was about to point out that it wasn't the same thing at all when a new voice broke into the debate.

"What if my Lady had the Magical Magnifying Mirror of the Mermaid Queen?"

Everybody turned around, and there was the Pooka at the top of the Grand Staircase, looking very sleek in a green velvet coat and silver-buckled shoes from the Costume Institute. His black hair was pulled back neatly, and his eyes were glittering yellow slits.

"What's he doing here?" the Old Market Woman muttered. "I'll clip those amorini's wings for them, you just see if I don't."

The Green Lady glared at the Pooka. "What do you know about the Magical Magnifying Mirror of the Mermaid Queen?"

"I know that it knows all and sees all. I know it would be very useful to any Genius who owned it."

The Green Lady frowned. "It sure would. And old scaly-tail's as likely to give me her eyeteeth for earrings."

The Pooka sauntered down the stair and across the hall, and took up a position between the Green Lady and the Curator. He spread his long hands as if gathering up everybody's attention.

"To be sure, my Lady. Which is why you'll be needing

a champion to get it for you—a mortal hero of one sort or another. In return for a boon, of course."

The Lady looked thoughtful. I was confused. Champion? Mortal hero?

The Suit of Seventeenth-Century Parade Armor raised a mailed fist. "I object," it boomed. "It is improper for a young female of tender years to go a-questing."

The Green Lady rolled her eyes. "Sheesh. Get with the program, will ya? This is the twenty-first century. Okay," she said to the Pooka. "The kid brings me the Magnifying Mirror, she can stay in New York. But I won't let her back into the Park. That's asking too much."

Things were moving a little too fast. I'd never heard of the Magical Magnifying Mirror of the Mermaid Queen or been to New York Harbor. Sure I knew a lot of Folk lore, but I'd never actually done much with it except bargain with a kazna peri, which wasn't in the same league as bargaining with a Genius for a major magical talisman. What if I tried to steal it and got caught? And what good would it do me to stay in New York Between if I couldn't go home? Where was I supposed to live if I couldn't live in the Park?

I looked from the Lady to the Pooka to the Curator, who was nodding.

"Um, excuse me," I said. "I don't think . . ."

Bastet butted her head into my ankle, hard. "Hush, mortal. The Pooka's still talking."

"Well then," said the Pooka, "what if she brings you a ticket to *Peter Pan* as well?"

The Green Lady scratched among her dreadlocks. "It's an idea. I've been wanting to see *Peter Pan*, and the Producer hasn't spoken to me since the Hunt ate that vampire. Okay. The kid gets me a seat for *Peter Pan*—a good one, in the orchestra, with the original Tinkerbell— I'll open the paths of the Park to her. But she can forget the protection thing. One measly ticket to *Peter Pan* isn't worth the grief the Wild Hunt's going to give me over this."

This was getting worse and worse. Did the Pooka think he was helping me out? Just how was I supposed to get this ticket? And say I did get it, then what? I might be able to visit Astris, but I'd still be looking over my shoulder for the Wild Hunt at sunset.

"Third time pays for all," said the Pooka. "What if we added the Scales of the Dragon of Wall Street?"

The Green Lady's mouth dropped open. So did the Curator's. So did mine.

Everybody in New York Between has heard of the Scales of the Dragon of Wall Street. They're a pair of magic balances that turn paper into gold. You put paper in one side and gold appears on the other. When you take the gold off, the paper disappears. Sometimes the gold disappears, too, but the Dragon's Scales are still definitely worth having.

"The Dragon's Scales," said the Green Lady happily. "He'd hate that, wouldn't he? And with all that gold, maybe I could buy some of my old land back. Wow. Yeah. The kid brings me the Dragon's Scales, I'll restore my protection, no strings attached."

The Pooka bowed. "Thank you, Lady. You'll not be regretting this night's work."

"I better not." The Lady fixed him with a green glare. "I already got one serious beef with you, Pooka. You did your fairy godfather bit when you helped the kid escape the Hunt. She's going to have to do this hero thing without you. What's more, you're banished from the Park until she's done it. I want you to hang out here at the Museum behaving yourself until your heroic little goddaughter comes back with my treasures and bails you out."

The Pooka put his hand over his heart and bowed low. I couldn't see his face, so I couldn't tell how he felt. Speaking for myself, I felt sick.

The Old Market Woman gave me a sharp nudge with her marble basket. "Did you understand what the Lady said?"

"Yeah."

"You accept the Green Lady's offer, then?" the Curator asked me, his spectacles glittering severely.

I searched my brain for options, but I couldn't come up with any. It was the Pooka's bargain or exile Outside. "Yeah," I said weakly. "I guess."

The Curator turned to the Lady. "Let's get this clear.

The Magical Magnifying Mirror of the Mermaid Queen, a ticket for *Peter Pan,* and the Scales of the Dragon of Wall Street in exchange for removing your decree of banishment and restoring the freedom of the Park and your protection from the hunger of the Hunt. Is that correct?"

The Lady nodded. "Yep. It's a pretty good deal, too, considering."

I thought it was a terrible deal. I was dead. No doubt about it. If the Mermaid Queen didn't drown me, the Dragon would eat me. I wasn't sure what the Producer of Broadway would do. Make me dance in red-hot tap shoes until my feet fell off?

Out of the corner of my eye, I saw the Pooka staring off into space. He looked extremely sarcastic. Staying in the Museum, I realized, was going to be as hard on him as the quest was going to be on me. Harder. Supernaturals had been teaching me about questing ever since I could remember. Nobody had ever taught the Pooka how to behave himself.

I stood up as tall as I could and tried to look heroic. "Okay," I said. "When do I leave?"

CHAPTER
13

Neef's Rules for Changelings

The Green Lady thought I should leave right away. The Curator thought I should wait until I had gone to the New York Public Library and reviewed all the available literature on mermaids, dragons, and the history of Broadway. Since it was my quest, I thought they should let me decide, but when I said so, they just stared at me and went back to arguing.

At last the Pooka said, "Begging your pardon, Geniuses both, for speaking up when maybe I'm not needed, but in the Old Country, a quest always begins at daybreak."

"Does it?" asked the Curator. "Fascinating."

The Green Lady scowled. "This is the New Country, buddy, in case you hadn't noticed."

"In the absence of any other rule," the Pooka said firmly, "a quest starts at daybreak. It's traditional."

The Lady glared at him. "How would you like me to make your exile permanent, trickster? Come to think of it, it might be permanent anyway, if your mortal hero doesn't come back."

For a minute, I really thought I might explode. My face was icy, my ears buzzed, and little black sparkles danced before my eyes like gnats. "The quest's off," I said, my voice shaky with fury. "No Mirror, no ticket, no Dragon's Scales. I won't go unless you let the Pooka go home even if I get eaten."

As soon as it was out of my mouth, I regretted it, but the Green Lady shrugged. "Deal," she said. "You die, the Pooka comes home." She gave me a remarkably friendly smile. "I gotta hand it to you, kid—you're one tough cookie. And loyal. Good luck."

And that was it. The Green Lady left, the Curator and the guards went back to work, and a few docents and curious tourists who'd gathered to watch the show drifted off again. I retreated to the inmost chamber of the Tomb of Perneb, which is just about the quietest place in the Museum, and slumped down against the wall. After a while, Bastet came in and butted my hip with her hard little head.

"That's enough of that," she said.

I wiped my eyes and stroked her cool, smooth back. "I'm fine."

Bastet shook off my hand and started to clean her paws. "Your copy," she said between licks, "is fine, too.

She's in the Temple of Dendur, counting the bricks."

Changeling. I'd forgotten all about her. I put my forehead back on my knees. At least she'd be okay. Nobody was going to bother her in the Museum, and if she was one of those Folk who count things, she'd have plenty to keep her busy while I was gone. Maybe looking after her would keep the Pooka out of mischief.

"Don't even think of leaving her here," said Bastet, looking up from her bath. "You promised to take care of her. She's your responsibility."

You don't argue with a goddess.

I found Changeling sitting cross-legged under the temple gate with her face to the wall. She was muttering to herself.

"Hi, Changeling."

No answer, unless "2051, 2052, 2053" is an answer.

"I'm going on a quest, Changeling. You want to come with?"

"2054, 2055, 2056," she said. "This is not just a bad dream, is it?"

It took me a moment to figure out what she was talking about. "No, Changeling. It's not a dream."

"I have been reviewing the data. In the past two days, I have been frightened and hurt and hungry. I have fallen from a great height and the fall did not wake me. Sherlock Holmes says that when you have eliminated the impossible, whatever remains, however improbable, must be the truth. In a dream, I always wake up when I fall from a great height. Ergo, this is not a dream."

"Sherlock Holmes knows what he's talking about."

"If I am not dreaming, where am I?"

I told her a little about New York Between, stressing the importance of following the rules. I had to talk to her back because she wouldn't turn around, and I wasn't totally sure she was even listening to me. After a while, I kind of trailed off and we sat in silence until she said, "I want to go home."

"I want to go home, too," I said. "That's what this is quest is all about."

Long pause. Then, "If I go on this quest with you, then can I go home?"

I started to tell her that it beat me, but I didn't. That, I suspected, would lead to a freaked-out companion who would be even harder to deal with than she was already. On the other hand, if I told Changeling that this quest was her ticket home, I'd be lying. On the *other* other hand, what choice did I have?

And there was always the chance that I might find a way to get her back Outside after all.

"Let's put it this way," I said. "If you come with me, your chances of going home are a lot better than if you don't."

"Very well, then," Changeling said. "I will come with you. Perhaps I may be of some use."

I doubted that, but I thanked her anyway. Then I went to the Sagredo bedroom, where I picked up Satchel, told the amorini exactly what I thought of them, and went back to the temple. We had some bread and cheese and Changeling fell asleep. Amazingly, so did I, right there on the sandstone floor of the Temple of Dendur.

The next thing I knew, the Pooka was shaking me, and Bastet was meowing in Changeling's ear. I grabbed Satchel, made sure Changeling was on her feet, and stumbled into the hall. It was full of docents, who hurried us along, taking turns pelting me with advice I was way too sleepy to take in. When we got to the Betweenways station, they wished Changeling and me good luck and left us alone with the Curator on the platform.

The Curator cleared his throat. "Your first task, Neef, is to acquire the Magical Magnifying Mirror of the Mermaid Queen. The closest Betweenways stop to New York Harbor is Ferry. Can you remember that? Ferry. Perhaps I should write it down for you."

To my surprise, Changeling piped up. "I will remember," she said. "I have an unusually good memory."

"Good luck," the Curator said, and disappeared. No pat on the head, no special gift to help me on my way. Not that I really expected anything, but a magic sword or even an enchanted pencil would have made me feel a lot better.

I took a deep breath and turned to Changeling, who was doing her turtle impersonation again. "Okay," I said. "The rule for the Betweenway is that we have to stay connected. Is it okay with you if I hold on to your skirt?"

Her chin dipped deeper into her flowery collar. Taking that as a yes, I grabbed a fold of her long blue skirt and we stepped onto the Betweenway together.

The Betweenways were easier this time. They still weren't my idea of fun, and the noise was terrible, but at least I knew what to expect. Changeling turned mushroom-color, scrunched her eyes tight, and folded herself deeper into her jacket. I saw her mouth shaping the word "ferry" over and over again. I did it, too—*ferryferryferryferryferry*—until it stopped being a word and turned into a scurrying noise in my head.

After what seemed like a very long time, I saw a black sign with squiggly blue lines under it. FERRY, it said. I pulled Changeling through a crowd of something leathery—djinn? Giant bats?—and then we were standing on a platform with the Betweenway screeching behind us, facing a gate that opened to admit two kappa in white karate suits. I bowed to them, which is the right thing to do when you meet a kappa, and towed Changeling out of the station.

I know it sounds strange, but until I actually saw Battery Park, I hadn't really understood that going on a quest meant going out into the City. Maybe it was the name. Battery Park was a park, right? Trees, rocks, grass, squirrels, nature spirits? Buildings in the distance, far enough away to be mysterious? Wrong.

The buildings were right there beside the station, a jagged wall of many-windowed towers that blocked out the sun. The park was a flat open space dotted with a few pitiful trees and a low stone fortress that lay beside the Harbor like a gray stone doughnut. Gulls screamed and chuckled overhead, riding a wind that smelled like salt and seaweed.

Suddenly I felt like running. "Hey, Changeling!" I shouted. "I'll race you to the water. Ready? *Go!*"

Running felt wonderful. If I'd had the breath, I would have shouted aloud. I spread out my arms like seagull wings and tried to run faster.

Finally I got a stitch in my side and had to stop and wrap my arms around my belly. *Just like Changeling*, I thought, and hastily unwrapped myself. *I'm not at all like Changeling*, I told myself. *I don't have fairy fits. I'm not afraid of new things. I know more Folk lore than most real Folk do. I'm a hero and a champion and I'm on a quest for the Genius of Central Park.*

Changeling stumped up behind me, her face stony. "You took me by surprise," she said. "I do not like surprises."

I was in no mood to deal with fairy nerves. "Well, you're just going to have to get used to them."

"Why?"

"We're on a quest, that's why. There's going to be surprises, and things jumping out of bushes, and all kinds of things you don't like. If you melt down every time that happens, we're dead. And I mean that literally."

Her mouth set in a grim line. "I am afraid. I want to go home."

"Me, too. Remember what I told you back at the Museum? We have to finish the quest first."

Changeling hummed. I tapped my foot. "Very well," she said at last. "I will do my best to expect the unexpected, and I will try not to have a meltdown. It is only fair to warn you that I am not always in control of them."

She sounded so like the Pooka promising to try and behave that my irritation vanished. "And I'll do my best to explain things when I can." I tried to recall what Astris had taught me about New York geography. "For instance, that water over there is New York Harbor," I said. "That round building is Castle Clinton, and that"—pointing to a huge green lady standing on an island a little way out— "has to be the Statue of Liberty."

"I know what the Statue of Liberty is," Changeling said scornfully. "What shall we do next?"

"I'll tell you just as soon as I figure it out."

We walked down to the pier. The Harbor was dark and oily looking, not at all like the sparking water in the Park. It bustled with boats, from rowboats and skin canoes to tall, graceful, white-sailed ships and heavy freighters. The

Statue of Liberty greeted them all in a voice that carried over the water like a bell.

I sat down with my feet dangling above the water.

The Mermaid Queen probably kept her Mirror with her all the time, right? So the first thing I had to do was find the Mermaid Queen. Who lived in the Harbor, underwater, where I couldn't breathe. So really the first thing I had to do was find some serious magical help. A magic fish seemed like a good bet, if I could catch one without a hook or a net.

I asked Satchel for some bread, which I tore into pieces and threw into the water.

While I waited for something useful to rise to my bait, I thought about mermaids. Astris had taught me the basics, of course: half woman, half fish, control New York Harbor, collect stuff out of sunken ships, have power over the waves. But all I knew of their habits was a story a nixie had told me once, about a mermaid who had pulled a sailor into the depths of the sea so she could make a table out of his bones and a goblet out of his skull.

"Mermaids," I muttered. "I need to know more about mermaids."

Changeling was sitting beside me, looking at the horizon. "'Mermaid' means 'maiden of the sea,'" she said. "Mermaids have long hair and fish tails instead of legs. They like music. Ignorant people confuse them with sirens. Sirens are water sprites who sing so beautifully that sailors used to jump out of their ships to get close to them and drown." She frowned. "I do not think sirens have fish tails, but I am not sure."

I gaped at her. "You know about *mermaids*?"

"I am far from an expert on the subject. I saw a movie once called *The Little Mermaid*. I found it quite silly, but it made me curious about mermaids, so I looked them up online. There is a surprising number of sites. I saw many pictures that depicted mermaids combing their hair while sitting on rocks and looking in mirrors. Often they were wearing pearl necklaces."

I should be used to being lectured by Folk. But when the lecture comes from a fairy changeling who knows nothing about the rules and looks just like me—well, it was hard to take. "That's real useful," I sneered. "If I happened to have a pearl necklace in my pocket."

Changeling didn't seem to notice the sneer. "Data is always useful," she said.

That was, somehow, just too much. "Well, here's some data for you," I said. "I know the Folk and you don't. The Mermaid Queen is the Genius of New York Harbor. From where I'm sitting, that looks like a big job. Just a guess, but I really, really doubt that she sits around a lot singing to herself and combing her hair."

Changeling turtled into her jacket again and began her three-note hum. Part of me was sorry I'd upset her. Part of me was ready to scream.

Before I'd settled on which part to go with, somebody pushed us both into New York Harbor.

~ ~ ~ ~ ~ ~ ~ ~

I kicked back to the surface, sputtering and spitting New York Harbor water. It tasted different from the water in Central Park Lake—oily and salty and nasty. Beside me, Changeling was a pair of splashing hands and a fast-sinking head. Back on the shore, a tanuki rolled on the pavement like a furry barrel, holding its sides and hooting with laughter.

Tricksters. You gotta hate them.

I managed to get a grip on Changeling and haul her up so her face was out of the water. She started churning her arms like an eggbeater, and we both went under. The whole world was white foam and stinging water up my nose. I held my breath as long as I could, but finally had to breathe or burst. I gasped, expecting a lungful of choking water. To my astonishment, I got air instead. It stank of stale magic, but I could breathe.

As my eyes cleared, I saw Changeling thrashing around an arm's-length away. Her mouth was square with panic, her eyes were slits, and her head was surrounded by a large, silvery bubble. Between us floated a large harbor seal so big that he had to be a selkie. He had big dark eyes with eyelashes about a foot long and a sleek round head and shoulders like a troll. There was a badge on a cord around his neck. It read HARBOR POLICE.

The police-selkie saw me looking at him. "Your friend seems upset," he said.

"Yeah, well, she doesn't like people sneaking up on her. Neither do I."

"Well, I don't like strange land folk splashing around the harbor." A crumb of water-soaked bread drifted down past his nose. "And you've been littering. That's a serious offense, you know."

"It's just bread," I said. "Biodegradable and completely edible. I was trying to attract a magic fish, but you're even better. Can you direct me to the Court of the Mermaid Queen?" I remembered my manners. "Please."

"You want to see the Mermaid Queen?" The selkie laughed. "You have to be out of your mind. The Mermaid Queen eats Land Folk for breakfast. Raw. It would be far kinder to drown you. Unless you can give me a good reason not to."

"I'm on a quest," I said proudly.

"A quest, huh?" The police-selkie sounded surprised. "A kid like you? What are you after?"

I didn't think it was a good idea to say anything about the Mirror, so I settled for "I can't tell you," which was the exact truth. The selkie lifted his upper lip, displaying his long, white, sharp dog-teeth. "I would if I could, believe me," I said hastily. "The thing is, I can only tell the Mermaid Queen."

"You're after the Mirror, huh?" the selkie said wisely. "You won't get it, of course, but I understand that you have to try. I'll see if I can set up an audience for you.

That fairy changeling, is she your official magic companion?" I nodded. "I've heard that fairy changelings aren't really up to much in the way of magic. You sure you don't want me to let her drown, maybe pick up a better companion along the way?"

This time, I didn't even think about it. "I'm sure," I said. "Thanks anyway."

"Your call." The selkie pulled a wand with a circle on top of it out of his belt. "Now, if you'll just swim a little closer to her, we'll be on our way."

I finned myself up to Changeling. The selkie held the wand to his muzzle and blew a huge bubble around us. Changeling immediately curled up on the bottom of the bubble with her sea-soaked jacket pulled up around her ears. I plastered myself against a transparent side and watched New York Harbor drift slowly by us.

I knew a lot about Fresh Water Folk, but all I'd learned about Sea Folk were their names and descriptions and a couple of stories the moral of which was "Don't go near the water." But heroes on quests never get drowned.

At first, mostly what I saw was a brownish-yellow murk dotted with a lot of Outside garbage I recognized from the Park: banana peels and paper coffee cups, disintegrating newspapers and plastic bags. Then something large and yellow flashed by the bubble. "Ooh," I said, and "Wow," as a school of mermaids in shiny yellow vests swooped and circled around us, scooping up the garbage in their nets. I noticed that their hair was cut short and none of them was wearing pearls. Or singing. So much for Changeling's mermaid lore.

When the mermaids had swirled away from us in a neat, yellow wave, I looked eagerly around for something else—a whale, maybe, or a sea monster. A large, misty shadow below us seemed promising until we got closer and I saw it was a wooden ship, half buried in mud and covered in rust and barnacles. The police-selkie pushed our bubble down inside and wedged us under a piece of deck.

"This here's the brig," he said. "It's really a brigantine, but the Queen likes her little joke. Don't bounce around too much. These bubbles aren't entirely splinter proof."

And then he swam away.

CHAPTER
14

CHEATING'S ONLY AGAINST THE RULES WHEN YOU GET CAUGHT.

Neef's Rules for Changelings

It was a long wait. Tucked under the brigantine's deck at the bottom of New York Harbor, I couldn't tell where the sun was. Changeling went to sleep. I didn't. Whenever I tried to think of a plan to get the Magical Magnifying Mirror, I'd get distracted by how cold and wet I was and wonder why I'd ever wanted to go on an adventure in the first place and whether exile Outside would be more or less horrible than being eaten by the Wild Hunt.

When I was very little and wouldn't do what Astris told me, she would threaten to send me Outside if I didn't behave. It worked every time. If the stories are right, Outside is a dangerous place. Ravens don't feed you, animals don't talk, and mortals may hate you if you're wearing the wrong clothes. The worst thing is that there isn't any magic except what you bring with you. I might be ready for an adventure outside Central Park, but I couldn't imagine I'd ever be ready for an adventure Outside.

I missed Astris. I missed the Pooka. I missed Bastet and the Old Market Woman and the Water Rat. I even missed the amorini. And I sure could use a moss woman right about now.

Eventually Changeling woke up, and when she did, she started to whine. She was wet. She was cold. She did not like this place. She wanted to go home.

"Could you just shut up about home?" I said finally. "I want to go home, too, but you don't hear me whining about it."

"I do not understand," Changeling said. "Your home is dangerous and frightening. Things chase you. And you live with a rat. Why do you want to go back?"

I wasn't about to discuss Astris and the Pooka with someone who said "rat" in that disgusted tone of voice. "What's so great about your home?" I asked.

"It's comfortable and safe," she said. "My room is arranged exactly as I like it, and I know where everything is. I have a collection of pressed flowers. I am a huge fan of flowers. They are colorful and symmetrical. I am going to embroider flowers onto all my clothes."

That sounded like something a supernatural would do, all right. "Did you make your jacket?" I asked.

"No. Mom purchased it at Levi's. But I embroidered it."

"It's beautiful," I said honestly.

"Thank you. The flowers are all botanically correct."

I wasn't really interested in the flowers. "Tell me about your room."

Her room was robin's-egg blue, with flowered curtains and a desk and a computer and a bookcase and framed botanical sketches on the walls. It was very weird to think that it was my room, too, in a way, or the room I might have had if I hadn't been brought to New York Between.

"The walls are blue?" I asked suddenly. "What happened to the fairy-tale mural?"

"That is a very odd question," Changeling said. "There used to be a mural on my wall when I was very small. I did not like it. The fairies were not accurately drawn."

I knew that. The mural fairies had been pink and cute and fluffy—not like real fairies at all. But I'd loved them anyway. "Are there stars on the ceiling?" I asked.

"We moved from that apartment when I was six, and I think most of the stars had fallen off by then." A thoughtful pause. "How do you know about the stars and the mural?"

The truth was, I didn't know. My questions had just kind of flown out of my mouth. "Magic," I said shortly. "Tell me about Michiko."

"Michiko is our au pair. That means she looks after me in return for a place to live while she pursues her studies at New York University. She is a big fan of anime. Anime is—"

I interrupted before she got started on another speech.

"I'd rather hear about your, um, mom. What does she look like?"

"She is of medium height and rather small-boned. Her eyes are hazel and her hair is dark brown and very curly, just like mine. She says we should be grateful—women pay good money to get their hair to look like ours. However, I think it is not very reasonable to want tight curls. They are hard to comb."

"You can say that again."

She began obediently, "I think it is not very—"

"Reasonable to want tight curls. Got it." I was feeling weirder and weirder. "What about your father?"

"Dad is getting bald," she said. "But he is very distinguished-looking nonetheless. He is also extremely intelligent. Mom says he can make a computer roll over and purr, but I think she must be teasing. If a computer rolls over, it breaks. Dad would never do that."

She went on for a while about Mom and Dad and Michiko and someone called Strumble, who, I gathered, was a (non-talking) dog. "I miss them," she said at last. "I am worried that they must be anxious about me."

I moved restlessly, making our bubble bounce. "We have to finish the quest first. Maybe we'd better make a plan."

A long silence followed while I pulled myself together and tried to remember my questing lessons. Quests, I recalled, are traditionally achieved by force, by magic, or by trickery. I wasn't a fighter and I didn't have any magic, which left me with—"the Riddle Game!" I exclaimed.

"I do not understand."

I couldn't believe my ears. "Are you dumb or something? The Riddle Game is the oldest game there is. If I ask the Mermaid Queen a riddle she can't answer, she has to give me a boon. The catch is, after playing it for so long, the Folk know the answers to every riddle there is. Which means I'll have to make up a new one. Unless you've got a better idea?"

"I am not dumb," Changeling said stonily. "A riddle is a question whose answer derives from a pun or a metaphor. I think riddles are dumb."

"Then it's a good thing I'm the one who's making one up," I said. "Now shut up and let me think."

I pulled a springy curl into my mouth and sucked. Astris hated when I sucked my hair, and I hadn't done it in a long time. But it helped me think and Astris wasn't there. The curl tasted salty.

"Questions," I muttered. "Puns and metaphors. Come on, Neef. How hard can it be to make up a riddle?"

The answer to that, after I'd chewed through about half an inch of hair, was really, really, really hard. It took me a while just to work out that you had to think of an answer before you could figure out the clue. And then you had to turn it into a poem, if possible.

The best riddles have one-word answers. For obvious reasons, I kept thinking of things like "dark" and "mud" and "boat" and "fish," which the Mermaid Queen would have to be a total lamebrain not to guess. What I needed was something totally land-based.

In the end, the riddle came to me in a flash: question, answer, and all. I mulled it over for a while, changed it around so it would sound poetic, and then I said, "I got the riddle, Changeling. You want to hear it?"

"Riddles are dumb," Changeling said. "Besides, someone is coming."

"How do you know?"

"The water sounds different."

I strained my ears until they ached, but all I heard was a slow, regular swishing and some deep-voiced throbs that I thought had been there all along. A faint light began to filter through the rotting deck like daylight through leaves, heralding a school of tiny, glowing fish. They were followed by six mermaids who were even tougher looking than the Harbor garbage collectors. Their hair was short and stiff and prickly like spiny coral, and their fins were pierced and threaded with shiny brown tape. They wore tight black vests held together with big silver pins, and tridents tattooed on their right arms.

Without a word, they fitted a net around our bubble and maneuvered us out of the wreck like a chunk of extra-large garbage. Then they towed us across the Harbor with the light-fish swimming ahead of us to show the way. I bounced from side to side trying to see everything at once, while Changeling sat rigidly with her legs crossed and her eyes closed, Folkishly determined to see nothing at all.

Like Central Park, New York Harbor was much busier at night. Mermen with green skin and spiny heads flirted with our merguards, who ignored them. Ugly, knobby, magical fish darted up and gaped at us, then peeled off on their own business. I saw a troop of police-selkies skimming along the silty bottom and waved at them in case one of them was our friend. None of them waved back.

After a while, I saw something huge drifting ahead. At first I thought it might be another wreck, but as we got closer, the shape got clearer. I made out a long bag and a cluster of tentacles that seemed to beckon us forward. We headed straight for it, and soon I was looking straight into the kraken's cold blue eye. Its wicked curved beak opened a little, almost as if it was laughing at me, then it bunched its huge tentacles and shot away in a cloud of black ink.

The bubble bounced and spun, tossing Changeling and me around like pebbles in a bowl. Gradually, the water cleared.

We were heading straight toward a high wall. It was all rocky and gooey and stuck with rusty iron bars and garbage—not at all the kind of place I'd expect a powerful Genius to live.

The merguards steered our bubble into a dark slit that looked way too skinny for it. There was a terrifying moment of blackness, with the walls squeezing us like a pair of hands. Crushed up against me, Changeling screeched. I didn't blame her.

We popped out of the slit into a shifting mass of huge, round eyes and huge, gulping mouths and huge, sharp teeth. I didn't see a lot of arms, but I saw plenty of claws, and they were all pointed toward our bubble. It was like the Wild Hunt at the Solstice Dance, only wetter.

I untangled myself from Changeling and tried to tune out her panicked screeching. I couldn't pay attention to her now; I had a Riddle Game to play and a Magical Magnifying Mirror to win. I cocked my chin in what I hoped was a heroic pose and repeated my riddle under my breath. I was afraid it sounded pretty lame, but it was the best I could do. Anyway, it was way too late to think of a new one.

The Sea Folk scattered. The merguards towed us down the middle of a long hall between rows of tall, lumpy pillars. They were stuck with bright, shiny things—I think I saw Coke cans and something that looked like a bicycle fender, as well as a big silver tray and jewels. A lot of jewels.

The jewel motif was continued on Mermaid Queen's throne. It was an open shell totally encrusted with jewels that glittered and sparked in the light-fish glow like sun on rippled water. The bottom was lined with something pink and soft that cradled the Mermaid Queen like a shiny black pearl.

I guess I'd expected the Genius of New York Harbor to be kind of like the Green Lady, only with a fish's tail instead of high-heeled boots: someone beautiful and scary and proud.

The Mermaid Queen was just scary.

Under her black vest, her skin was solid tattoos from forehead to tail-tip. I made out a fish on each cheek, a black anchor on one arm, and a whalelike object that took up one entire side of her tail. Her fins were pierced with studs and rings; her hair stood out around her head like a spiky, orange crown. Around her middle, where maid turned into mer, she wore a golden chain with a disk hanging from it like a miniature moon.

So far, my quest was a complete success: I'd found the Queen and I'd found her Magical Magnifying Mirror. Now, all I had to do was get it away from her. My mouth was dry and my brain even dryer. I wished as hard as I could that the Pooka would appear and help me out. Needless to say, nothing happened.

The Mermaid Queen blinked her round, black eyes and waved her tail fin lazily. "Word is, you're on a quest," she said. "You want to tell me about it?"

I bowed, which isn't all that easy to do when you're standing in a bubble. *Say something, Neef*, I told myself. *Anything*.

"Greetings, great Queen of New York Harbor," I croaked. "Um. Nice tattoos."

"I know," the Mermaid Queen said. "Wanna see my submarine dance?"

She floated up from her throne and sent a long ripple through the thing I'd thought was a whale. "Cool," I said weakly.

"It's a nuclear sub," the Mermaid Queen said, settling back down. "I know all about submarines, you know. I know everything. I know how the currents run and the shallows shift. I know when a ship is heading into New York Harbor and what her tonnage is and what her captain eats for breakfast."

She gave me a fishy look and I pulled myself together. "You do? Wow. That's way more than the Green Lady of Central Park knows."

The Mermaid Queen twirled the Mirror on its chain. "You better believe it, sister. If it's happening or if it's happened or if it's been written down anywhere, I can see it. All I have to do is ask, and my Mirror shows it to me. So. What's the story with this quest?" She frowned at me, pleating the trident tattooed on her forehead. "You better not be after my Mirror. Because that would be *so* boring. Everyone's always after my Mirror."

There's this thing my brain does sometimes when I'm really panicked. I'm sure it's totally stalled, then I open my mouth and discover that it's been working behind my back. "I'm on a quest for a riddle nobody can answer," I heard myself say. "I think I've got one, but I can't tell unless I try it out. Since you know everything, I thought I'd ask you."

The Mermaid Queen grinned, puffing up the fish tattooed on her cheeks. "I don't work for free, you know. What's it worth to you?"

I had no idea, but kept talking anyway. "My spidersilk dress."

She wrinkled the trident on her forehead again. "Your dress? Why would I want a spidersilk dress? It's so not me, you know? Think again."

I shrugged. "You don't want my dress, it's no skin off my teeth. It's not like I *want* to get rid of it."

She flicked her tail fin. "A magic dress, huh? What does it do?"

"Why should I tell you? You don't want it."

"Maybe I changed my mind."

"Actually," I said, "I've changed mine. A challenge isn't any fun if only one person's risking something. Forget the whole thing. I'll find someone else to ask."

She floated upright. "So it's a challenge now? I knew it. Fine. Let's rumble."

When you're on a wild ride, the Pooka always said, you just have to keep going and trust your luck. I took a deep breath. "Challenger calls the wager. That's the rule. I put up my dress. What do you put up?"

"My Mirror," said the Mermaid Queen. "That's what you're fishing for, isn't it? It's not like I'm actually risking anything. It can answer every riddle that's ever been asked. It remembers everything it's ever heard or seen. And you're, what? Some dry-behind-the-ears mortal changeling? I can't lose. Bring it on."

My heart was pounding so hard it was making the front of my dress quiver. What if my riddle wasn't new? What if the Mirror figured it out anyway?

The Queen waved the Mirror at me. "Whatcha waiting for? Lay it on me."

I took a deep breath of magic-smelling air. "*Needle feet, feather pelt, candle eyes, engine belly. Who am I?*"

The Mermaid Queen scrunched her face first to one side and then to the other, doing hideous things to the fish on her cheeks. "I don't remember hearing that one before," she said, surprised. "Run it by me again."

I repeated it. She lifted the Mirror and whispered at it, then peered into it intently. I held my breath while she frowned, whispered some more, tapped on the frame, looked again, lowered the Mirror to her scaly lap.

"You gotta give me three guesses," she said.

I wanted to say no. Boy, did I want to say no. But something told me it would be a mistake. "Sure," I said. "Take your time."

"Is it a tugboat with an icebreaker on front?"

I was so relieved, I had to bite the inside of my cheek to keep from laughing. "No," I said. "It's not a tugboat."

She looked down at the Mirror. "A subway?"

I didn't know what a subway was, but I did know it wasn't the answer to the riddle. "Nope."

More whispering and tapping. I bounced between terrified and hopeful so many times that I didn't even know how I felt anymore, except ready for this to be over. "Give up?" I asked.

"No," she snapped. "I don't. Did you make this up?"

"Yes."

"That's cheating," the Mermaid Queen said hopefully.

"No, it's not. Do you give up?"

"No!" She waved her tail fin so hard the bubble scudded backwards. I lost my balance and fell. Changeling had quieted down, but when I sat on her, she started screeching again. I heard the merguards snickering as I got to my feet.

"Okay," the Mermaid Queen said. "I got it."

My heart jumped into my mouth.

"You think you're real smart, don't you?" she sneered. "Well, you can just take off that dress and get ready to swim to shore. The answer to your riddle is the clock in Grand Central Station, the one with the eagle on it."

I swallowed my heart again. "No," I said. "It isn't."

"Oh, no? Then what is it?"

"I don't have to tell you."

Her fishy eyes got narrow and her lips lifted just enough to show the sharp tips of her teeth. "Shark poop. How do I know your riddle even has an answer, huh? If it doesn't, you're a cheat and a liar and I'm allowed to drown you." She looked wistful. "I haven't drowned any-body in ages, not up close and personal."

She unpinned the top safety pin holding her vest to-gether and tested the point on her fingertip, which bled a cloudy halo of dark blood.

"You wish," I said. "Ready? The answer to the riddle is 'a cat.'"

"A cat?" The Mermaid Queen darted upright. "You're making that up. Cats aren't what you said. I've seen cats. They're soggy and limp."

"Only if they're drowned," I said. "Live cats are soft and furry. And they purr. Ask your Mirror, if you don't believe me."

Not surprisingly, the Mermaid Queen was a sore loser.

She argued about cats, the form of the riddle, and the terms of the bargain. After a while, I was tempted to give up and call it a draw just so she would shut up. In the end, only the fact that I was sure she'd drown us if I did kept me arguing. She even pitched a Genius-sized fairy fit that bounced the bubble all around the hall, making Changeling scream and my stomach flip over like a pan-cake.

Finally, however, the Mermaid Queen gave in. "You win," she snapped. "Take it. Stupid Mirror. What good is it, anyway, if it can't even figure out the answer to a stupid riddle?" She unwound the chain from her waist, piled it in her hand with the Mirror on top, and handed it to the biggest and spikiest of the merguards. "Listen carefully, Flotsam, and do *exactly* what I tell you. Take these changelings to the pier, give them the Mirror, and let them go."

"You got it, Harbor Lady," the merguard said.

The trip back to land was a lot faster than the trip out. I wanted to replay the Riddle Game with Changeling so she could tell me how great I'd been, but she was way past hearing me. I wished again that the Pooka had been there. I was sure he'd be proud of my bargaining skills. I was. The nervous, jittery feeling in my stomach was just because the merguards were swimming so fast that the bubble was bouncing a lot.

We drifted to a stop. Flotsam grinned at me with all her sharp teeth. Then she undid one of the pins in her vest and shoved it through the bubble's side. As the cold water rushed in on us, I felt something hard being shoved into my hand.

"Here's your prize, sucker," she said. "Have a nice swim."

CHAPTER
15

THERE'S ALWAYS A CATCH TO A MAGIC TALISMAN.
Neef's Rules for Changelings

"Let them go," the Queen had said. Very funny.

Gasping and coughing, I broke the surface and tried to get Changeling's head above water. She was limp and heavy, not even fighting me. The pier looked a long way away. Luckily, a couple of burly selkies who were hanging out on the pier saw us thrashing around. They dove in, hauled us out, and thumped on Changeling until she coughed up all the Harbor water she'd swallowed. Then they yelled at us for swimming without proper supervision. I promised we wouldn't do it again. They let us off with a warning and left us shivering in a widening pool of cold salt water.

I looked around. In front of Castle Clinton, I saw a crowd of misty men and women surrounded by boxes and suitcases. Some of the women carried babies tied to their backs in shawls. They were all waiting for something, and I could tell they'd been waiting for a long, long time. They didn't even notice us.

The sky paled and so did the ghosts, until they faded out completely.

Changeling was shivering and clutching her soggy flower-garden jacket around her as if she thought it would make her warmer. "I am very cold," she said through chattering teeth.

I sighed. "You'll feel better if you eat something. Are you tired of bread and cheese yet? I could ask Satchel for a chicken leg or something."

"B-bread and cheese will be fine."

I looked for someplace away from the water where we could eat and dry out in peace and finally found a kind of den between the back wall of Castle Clinton and a couple of Dumpsters. The space was already occupied by a dirty mortal in a ragged coat and boots tied on with cloth. But he was asleep, so he didn't count.

Changeling eyed him nervously. "That is a street person," she said. "He probably drinks too much or takes drugs. It is not safe to be around him."

"He's asleep," I said. "And when he wakes up, he'll go right back Outside, so he won't bother us."

"I do not understand," Changeling said. "He is already outside."

I wondered if the Pooka or Astris ever got tired of explaining obvious stuff to me. "I meant New York Outside, where you live. Usually, mortals don't come to our New York unless they're asleep. Here's your cheese."

I could tell she wasn't convinced—she kept glancing at him. But she shut up and ate. I took a bite myself, then fished the Magical Mirror out of my shirt where I'd stuffed it while the selkies were thumping on Changeling.

The Mirror certainly wasn't very magical to look at: two palm-sized circles of silvered glass set back-to-back in a plain metal frame. The first side showed me nothing but a big pinkish blur. I moved the Mirror closer, and my eye swam into focus. It practically filled the Mirror, greenish flecks in a brown iris, pink veins doodled through the surrounding white, eyelashes coarse as a cat's whiskers.

I put the Mirror to my mouth as the Mermaid Queen had done and whispered, "How do I get a ticket for *Peter Pan*?"

The Mirror's answer was a view of my lips, magnified to ogreish hugeness. The other side was just as useless.

"I wish we'd asked the Mermaid Queen how to make this thing work," I said. "It's probably something icky, like polishing it with demon's earwax."

Changeling reached for it. "I would like to see that, please."

I stared at her hand.

It was clean from our seawater bath and pale with cold. Three cloud-shaped birthmarks along her pinky finger showed up clear and red. I snuck a look at my own right hand. There they were: the exact same marks.

"I want to see it," Changeling repeated, and made a grab for the Mirror.

She had my birthmarks. She had my hair. She had my face and my eyes. But she didn't know any of the things I knew or care about any of the things I cared about. She hated rats. Well, I hated her.

I thrust the Mirror at her. "Here," I said roughly. "Knock yourself out. Just remember that if you break it, you'll never go home."

Changeling held the Mirror to her eye, then tapped searchingly along the edge of the frame. She held the Mirror to her ear. She started to hum—happily, this time. I turned my back and settled down to some serious thinking.

The next item on my quest list was the ticket to *Peter Pan*, which seemed harmless enough. After nearly getting drowned, I wasn't up for tackling the Dragon of Wall Street.

The most obvious thing to do, of course, was to trade something for the ticket. Too bad all I had was one soggy, useless fairy changeling and a magic Satchel. The Mermaid Queen's Mirror, of course, was out.

That left me with basically three choices: another contest, working for the ticket, or stealing it like Jack stole the giant's magic radio in "Jack and the Extension Ladder." It felt like pressing my luck to try the Riddle Game again, which was the only nonmagical contest I knew.

And it didn't feel right to work for any Genius other than my own Green Lady.

Which left stealing.

"Hey, Changeling," I said. "You've been living with wild mortals. You got any ideas how we can steal a ticket to *Peter Pan*?"

Changeling looked up from the Mirror. "It's against the law to steal. If you steal, you are a thief. Thieves go to jail."

It was "Riddles are dumb" all over again. I gritted my teeth. "Things are different here, okay? People steal things all the time. If I get caught, I just have to give whoever I steal it from something of equal value, and everybody's happy."

"Stealing is *against the law*."

"If I can't steal the ticket, how am I supposed to get it?"

Ignoring my question, Changeling bent over the Mirror again. I put a salty curl in my mouth and chewed hard while I thought. But the only idea I could come up with was to sell Changeling to a demon for gold, which, however tempting, was impossible because I'd promised to protect her.

The day got warmer. The spidersilk dress was dry, but my hair was damp and sticky, and my skin itched.

I poked Changeling. "Come on, Changeling. Time to get moving. You can carry the Mirror if you want, but you have to keep it hidden."

Changeling slipped the golden chain around her neck

and tucked the Mirror down the front of her blouse. "You're not going to steal anything, are you?"

"No, Changeling. I'm not going to steal anything," I said.

As we slipped out from behind the Dumpster, I tripped over the street person, who groaned, opened his eyes, and immediately disappeared.

"See?" I said to Changeling, who was staring round-eyed at the empty space where he had been. "I told you he wouldn't bother us."

After our adventures in New York Harbor, the Between-ways didn't seem like such a big deal. Changeling grabbed my skirt, then closed her eyes and muttered, *"Broadway-BroadwayBroadway,"* while I kept an eye out for our stop. Simple.

Broadway is famous for its nightlife, which is the only kind of life anyone can have in a place where the sun never rises. The Pooka had gone to Broadway to see *Finian's Rainbow* once and come back full of stories. He'd hated the play, but he loved the crowds and the lights and the Broadway Folk, who aren't like any other supernaturals in the City. I knew about out-of-work vampires playing scenes on street corners, hoping a manager or director would see them and cast them in a play. I knew about gaffers and hoofers and best boys and the long lines of Folk from all over the City waiting to buy tickets for popular plays. I was ready.

Before long, I saw a huge, flashing BROADWAY! in red and white lights surrounded with blinking gold stars. Towing Changeling, I dashed off the Betweenway, across the crowded platform, and through a door outlined in glowing zigzags.

Outside of the Solstice Dance, I'd never seen so many Folk in one place in my life. The street was a solid mass of them, chattering and laughing: fox maidens arm in arm with kobolds, demons squiring succubae, sidhe with peris or possibly even mortals. In the blinking lights, it was hard to tell. Everybody seemed to know where they were going; everybody looked cheerful.

And then there were the lights. They blazed from windows and across building fronts, blinking, swirling, doing tricks. Across from the Betweenways station, I saw a glowing green bottle drink itself over and over next to a bright pink cat switching its glittering tail in front of its grin. Down the street, a bright blue bird flapped its wings above a sign made out of twinkling lights:

Limited Engagement

THE BLUEBIRD

Starring

Jimmy Durante

and

The Infant Phenomenon as

THE BLUEBIRD

A tap on my arm woke me from my trance. I looked down to see a skinny supernatural in a lime-and-purple-checked jacket. "You ladies look like you might be in the market for some entertainment," he said.

He was bald and blue-faced, and his lips didn't quite cover his very sharp teeth. He looked like a kind of ghoul—mostly interested in dead bodies, not very aggressive. Still, I was cautious. "Depends on the entertainment."

The ghoul opened his jacket, displaying rows of colored discs stuck into the lining. "What is your pleasure, ladies? A pair on the aisle to *Wicked*? Balcony center for *Babes in Toyland*?"

This was just too good to be true. "Got anything for *Peter Pan*?" I asked.

Yellow teeth flashed in a ghoulish grin. "Today is your lucky day," he said. "It is not every scalper who can produce"—he selected two of the discs—"a pair to *Peter Pan* out of thin air."

I eyed the tickets greedily. "How much?" I asked. "I only need one. The thing is, I don't have any gold."

"Gold?" The scalper waved one blue claw airily. "What would I want with gold? All I am asking is a hand—your choice. Cheap at twice the price."

"Are you out of your mind?"

He looked pleased. "Yeah, I know. I'm too soft-hearted. All the other scalpers are asking an arm and a leg."

I started to edge away. "Thanks anyway," I said. "I think I'll try at the theatre. Can you tell me where it is?"

But the scalper had already turned his back on me and was talking to a pair of elves.

Fine. We'd just have to do this the hard way.

I looked around for Changeling. She wasn't beside me; she wasn't by the Betweenway entrance; she wasn't anywhere.

OdearOdearOdear, as the moss woman would say.

I walked down the street, trusting to luck and a hunch that she'd be interested in the moving lights. Sure enough, I found her staring up at the self-drinking green bottle with her mouth open.

"Why can't you stay put?" I snapped at her. "I've got better things to do than go looking for you."

No response. The bottle emptied and filled again, reflected in her unblinking eyes. Angrily I grabbed her jacket and shook her. She took a swing at me. I danced out of reach and crashed into a passerby.

I staggered. The passerby caught my shoulder and inquired, in a voice like a tree full of birds, why I couldn't watch where I was going.

Too embarrassed to move, I muttered an apology to a pair of flesh-colored tights and sparkly golden shoes. The hand on my shoulder moved to my chin and forced me to raise my head. I looked up into a pair of very blue eyes, heavily shadowed and mascaraed, with a mop of shiny blonde curls above them. Above the curls was a top hat, which was gold and shiny, like the shoes. The girl wearing all this splendor was maybe twice as tall as me, and a lot thinner.

So was the girl next to her, who had her arm around the first one's waist, and the girl next to her, who had *her* arm around the second, and so on down a line of six blondes, all dressed in gold bathing suits and top hats and sparkly gold high-heeled shoes.

"And where *are* you going?" the golden girls caroled.

"I was looking for the theatre where *Peter Pan* is playing," I said. "Do you know where it is?"

Six pairs of blue eyes exchanged glances. Six red mouths opened. Six sweet, high voices spoke in perfect unison. "They're not auditioning. They're looking for boys, not girls. And they wouldn't take *you* anyway. You're too fat and clumsy."

Folk say this kind of thing all the time. They don't mean to hurt your feelings—they're just telling you the truth as they see it. I was used to it, but Changeling wasn't. "That was a very mean thing to say," she complained. "Furthermore, it is untrue. I am not fat. I am well within the normal weight for a preadolescent girl of my height and body type."

The girls took two steps back, bowed, and kicked up their right legs, missing my nose by about an inch. "Oh!" they chimed. "You're not Theatre Folk!"

"No," I said. "We're changelings."

"You're not a fledgling chorus line?"

This was a new one on me. The Pooka had told me about hoofers, who dance in musicals, but he'd never mentioned a chorus line. "What's that?"

The girls executed a complicated series of dance steps, ending in another high kick, this one staggered, like a breaking wave. Passing Folk broke into applause. I did, too, but Changeling stuffed her hands in her pockets and scowled.

"Thank you," said the girls, and bowed double. Magically, their top hats didn't fall off. "I'm a chorus line. *The* Chorus Line. The *original* Chorus Line. Every other chorus line is just a cheap knockoff."

"I'll remember that," I said. "Um. Do you know where *Peter Pan* is playing?"

The Chorus Line's smile switched off. "It's not."

"Isn't it the hottest show on Broadway?"

The Chorus Line wrinkled her six foreheads. "Do yourself a favor, chickens. Go home. Forget the bright lights. Forget *Peter Pan*. Get a real job, marry a nice man, make your mother happy."

This made no sense at all. "If you don't want to tell me," I said, "you should just say so, and I'll ask somebody else."

"Don't do that." The Chorus Line gathered around us, her outside parts linking arms, so she surrounded us completely. Changeling closed her eyes nervously. "Listen," the Chorus Line said. "I'm not supposed to talk about this, but I can tell *you*. Look around. What do you see?"

I peered out between two of the Chorus Line. Noise, lights, crowds: check. But what had happened to the glittering pink cat? And the theatre where *The Bluebird* was playing?

The Chorus Line followed my gaze. "The Casino Theatre," she said. "It's gone dark. So has the Republic, the Empire, and Belasco's. And the Follies is flickering. Broadway's dying, chickens, and nobody knows how to stop it."

I wondered whether the fact that *Peter Pan* had closed would get me off the hook with the Lady. Somehow I didn't think so. "That's terrible!" I said.

"You can say that again." The blended voice was sad.

"What's wrong?"

The Chorus Line lowered her voices to a gossipy buzz. "It's all the Producer's fault. Some fast talker conned him into putting Broadway on a computer. Everything—the plays, the music, the theatres, the lights. It worked really well for a while, but now it's gone buggy, and nobody knows how to fix it."

At the word "computer," Changeling gave a little twitch. Hadn't she said something about fixing her dad's computer? And I'd read two complete issues of *Macworld*.

"We know about computers," I said.

The Chorus Line rippled with surprise. "You do?"

"We're experts," I exaggerated. "Take me to the Producer."

"The Producer's the Genius of Broadway, you know," the Chorus Line said doubtfully. "It's not easy to get in to see him. Do you really think you can get rid of those bugs?"

I didn't have a clue, but I did think that once we got into the Producer's office, anything could happen. If worst came to worst, I was sure we could work out some kind of a deal, maybe go on a quest for a computer wizard or something. I didn't know much about Tech Folk, but I hadn't known much about mermaids, either.

Or maybe we'd actually get rid of the Producer's bugs. It was worth a try, anyway.

"No problem," I said. "Lead us to it."

CHAPTER
16

IF YOU TALK BIG, YOU SHOULD BE ABLE
TO DELIVER THE GOODS.

Neef's Rules for Changelings

The Chorus Line forged through the Broadway crowds like a troop of pixies through a meadow, prancing down the sidewalk and kicking out with her twelve high-heeled golden shoes. Changeling and I scuttled breathlessly behind her, so close that we bumped into her when she stopped.

"Oopsy-daisy," she said. "Well, this is it: the Producer's Office. Ain't it the limit? Well, chickens—see you in the funny papers." Before I could thank her, she wheeled neatly and high-stepped away.

I looked up. The Producer's Office looked like a palace a djinn might build for a giant with a taste for gold leaf and theatre. The Office's walls soared up high and spread out wide, and every inch of them was decorated with golden gargoyles and feather pens and masks of comedy and tragedy and huge mosaics showing scenes from famous plays like *A Midsummer Night's Dream* and *Peter Pan*.

As I stood gawking at Peter Pan fighting Captain Hook, someone bumped into me, growling something about tourists and hicks. I pulled myself together and headed for the door.

There were three sets of double doors, each big enough to admit a medium-sized dragon. The outer two were locked and chained. The central one was guarded by a bigger-than-life-sized statue of a golden griffin. A little golden bell dangled from its beak.

I reached up to ring it, and the griffin flickered violently. Startled, I jumped back and waited until I was pretty sure nothing worse was going to happen, then tried again. This time, my hand went through the bell like it wasn't there.

Third time, I told myself, *is a charm.*

On my next try, the bell buzzed loudly. I jumped, and the griffin blinked.

"You two dolls got an appointment?" Its beak didn't move when it spoke and it had a bad case of static, so its question sounded more like, "You *crackle* dolls *crackle* appointment?" But I got the drift.

"I'm sure the Producer will see me without one," I said firmly.

"You are sure he will see you, huh?" The griffin's voice was a little stronger. "Me, I am not so sure. The Producer does not talk to little dolls as a general rule, unless they are represented by an agent. You dolls got an agent?"

"Do we look like we got an agent?" I asked.

The griffin coughed, or maybe it was laughing. "You have moxie, little doll. I will give you that. But it takes more than moxie to see"—the griffin winked out completely for a second—"without an appointment."

"That griffin is a hologram," Changeling said.

The griffin blinked and focused on her. So did I. "What does a little doll like you know about holograms?" it asked.

"A hologram," Changeling said, "is a three-dimensional illustration, created with an optical process using lasers. I have never heard of a free-standing one, but I believe that they are theoretically possible. This one is almost certainly malfunctioning."

I didn't understand what she was saying, but apparently the griffin did. "That little doll is not as dumb as she looks," it crackled. "Come on in."

The big doors jerked open, sticking unevenly halfway. Changeling froze, so I grabbed her jacket and hauled her in after me.

The Producer's lobby was as grand as the outside of the building, only more so. Acres of plush red carpet! Miles of gilded carving! Hundreds of chandeliers like crystal waterfalls! Mirrors! Paintings! Statues galore! No doors I could see, but there was a long golden staircase that curved gracefully up to a golden balcony. As we crossed the hall toward it, I caught sight of two wild-haired bogles sneaking across the luxurious carpet. One of them looked into my eyes with terrified astonishment. It was not a pleasant moment when I realized that the bogles were Changeling and me.

The Pooka always said that attitude counts more with Folk than appearance. I threw back my shoulders and marched up those golden stairs like I owned them. At the top, a second griffin flickered and fizzed as if it couldn't make up its mind whether it was really there or not.

"The elevator is to your *crackle*," the griffin said. "Shake a leg, dolls. The Producer *crackle crackle*."

Luckily, there was only one elevator in sight and only one button on the panel inside. I pushed the button and the door hissed closed, shutting Changeling and me into a mirrored cube. Faced once again with my boglelike reflection, I brushed at my skirt and picked some dried seaweed out of my hair. It didn't help much.

The elevator rose slowly, groaning and bouncing like a spider on a thread. I began to worry that the Producer's buggy computer was about to drop it or dematerialize it or make it go sideways. My reflection turned a delicate green. Changeling's reflection didn't change at all.

There was a soft *ding* and the elevator quivered to a stop. The doors whooshed open and I stumbled grate-fully out into a long hall. At the far end, a third griffin hologram lay across the threshold of a gilded door. The griffin looked about like I felt: You could see the door's golden curlicues clear though it.

It got to its feet, flickering madly. "The Producer *crackle*," it informed us. "If he finds out that you little *crackle* are *crackle* with some cockamamie *crackle*, he is going to be very *crackle crackle*."

This did not sound promising, but I wasn't going to turn back now. I glanced at Changeling, who was scowling at the griffin as if she found it offensive. "Let's get this show on the road," I said, holding on to my attitude as hard as I could.

"Your funeral," the griffin said clearly, and flickered out as the door swung wide.

Given the Producer's taste for gold and scarlet, I was expecting his private office to be really special. It was special, all right: dingy gray paint, a speckledy linoleum floor, a beat-up wooden desk, a huge dented gray metal cabinet with double doors, a ratty office chair, a few torn posters tacked to the walls, a cracked leather sofa. The only really colorful things in the room were a toy theatre with red velvet curtains and the Producer himself.

Except for his clothes, the Producer looked a lot like the troll who lived under Glen Span Arch. He was about twice as tall as me and more than twice as wide, with a head like a fireplug and a mouth like a baby's and little blue marble eyes. The Glen Span troll, however, wouldn't have been caught dead in a mustard-colored suit with red checks and a brown fedora pushed to the back of his head.

The Producer leaned back in the ratty chair and put his two-toned shoes on the beat-up desk. "A little bird tells me you dolls want to talk," he said. "So talk."

I took a deep breath, crossed my fingers behind my back for luck, and said that I'd heard that the Broadway computer was full of bugs. Since my companion and I knew something about computers, we thought we'd drop by and see if we could help him out.

The Producer of Broadway laughed, showing flat yellow teeth. "Help me out, huh? What kind of a chump do you take me for? Everybody knows dolls are ignorant on the subject of computers. You are lucky I am a Genius with a sense of humor, or I would bop you in the beezer."

"Then it's a good thing I'm not a doll, isn't it?" I said.

"You are not a doll?" He squinted his blue marbles at me. "Then what are you? Chopped liver?"

"A mortal changeling."

The Producer laughed. It was not a happy sound. "Are you thinking that is some kind of a recommendation? I am somewhat sore on the subject of mortals at this time. The citizen that sells me this turkey is part mortal himself. He tells the tale that this computer is a mortal-fairy hybrid, only one of its kind, completely resistant to gremlins and theatre critics. He does not mention bugs." The Producer ground his trollish teeth. "When I find this citizen, I will bite his head off, and then I will close him down so fast he will not know what hit him. That will teach him to sell the Producer of Broadway a turkey, at that."

I didn't remember anything in *Macworld* about turkeys. I swallowed. "That's very interesting," I said weakly.

The Producer snorted. "That is what they all say. For weeks, there is a parade of nerds and geeks and hackers through my office and every one of them says my problem is 'interesting.' I am thinking that 'interesting' is Tech Folk talk for 'kaput.' I even find this guy who says he is a computer wizard straight from Cyberspace. He is a very strange citizen indeed, just a head and a box and a couple of long, wiggly arms. And what does he do?" The Producer took a bright yellow handkerchief out of his breast pocket and swiped his face with it. "He makes it worse."

The only way to kill a troll was to trick him into staying outside until the sun came up, when he'd turn to stone—not really useful in a place where it was always night. And I wasn't sure sunlight would work on a Genius, however troll-like, even if I wanted to kill him. Which I didn't.

"Well, well," the Producer said. "Your stand-in has found my computer."

I spun around to see Changeling poking at the golden curlicues on the toy theatre. To my astonishment, the scarlet curtains parted to reveal a dark screen labeled "Fire Curtain." I glanced at the Producer to see how he

felt about Changeling touching something without asking first.

Surprisingly, the Producer was grinning happily.
"That is one smart little doll. The other guys all look in
the cabinet." He swiveled his chair to the gray metal cabinet behind his desk and yanked open its doors. A bearded
head sporting a pointy hat stared back at me with an expression of horrified astonishment: the computer wizard,
I guessed. Ranged on the shelves around it were smaller
heads, most of them wearing heavy black glasses repaired
with duct tape and paper clips.

"Get it?" the Producer asked.

I swallowed. "Got it."

"Good. I will leave you dolls alone. I cannot stand to
watch computer magic. It makes me nervous."

When the door had closed behind him, I turned to
Changeling. "It's no use. This is just too dangerous. When
the coast is clear, we'll go look for some stairs and get out
of here. I'll think of some other way to get the ticket."

"Why?" Changeling asked.

If I'd known what a beezer was, I would have bopped
hers myself. "Why? Because I don't want our heads to
end up in the Producer's collection, that's why."

"You said you knew how to fix the computer."

"I was wrong."

I tiptoed to the office door and cracked it open. The
griffin was still lying across it, looking so faded and flick-

ery that I doubted it would be able to stop us. However, the Producer was slouched in a golden chair with his feet on a stool and his hat pulled down over his forehead. His marble-blue eyes met mine.

"I hope you dolls are not thinking of taking it on the lam," he rumbled. "Because if you are, I will have to bite your heads off."

"Of course not," I said quickly.

"Good. Now get back in there."

I shut the door softly.

Changeling had pulled the Mermaid's Mirror out of her shirt, and was humming in an absorbed kind of way. "Hey, Changeling," I said, and nudged her gently with my toe, but she didn't even notice.

I wheeled the Producer's chair over to the toy theatre and sat down.

Macworld was all about computers with screens and keyboards; the Producer's computer was a toy theatre. Still, a computer's a computer, right? I looked for a button labeled ON, but wasn't surprised not to find one.

Gingerly, I poked at a golden curlicue. Nothing happened. I poked at another. A panel below the theatre opened and a flat board studded with rows of buttons popped out.

Eureka! I pulled a curl into my mouth and studied the board. The buttons were marked with tiny faces: a smiling one; a frowning one; two winking, smiling ones (right eye and left eye); two winking, frowning ones (ditto); four with their mouths turned up on one side and one eyebrow raised; and so on and on in tiny, bewildering variation.

I didn't like the look of the frowny face. The smiley face, however, seemed inviting. I moved my finger toward it.

Changeling leaned over my shoulder, so close that her hair tickled my cheek. "What are you doing?" she asked.

I spat out the curl. "Fixing the computer. Go away, Changeling. You're making me nervous."

She didn't move. "Do you know what kind of computer this is? What operating system is it running? Do you have the manual?"

"What's a manual?"

"It is dangerous to work on a computer without reading the manual."

"It's dangerous *not* to work on it. Did you see those heads in the cabinet? Now leave me alone. I have to concentrate."

Changeling pulled back, but she didn't go away. Irritated, I pushed the smiley-face button and held my breath. The fire curtain rolled up slowly. Behind it was a stage, bare of everything but a hideous browny-yellowy thing as big as my fist.

I looked at the bug; the bug looked back. It had a face like a gargoyle and far too many legs, and its curved mouth parts were busily munching something bright and twitching. I shuddered and turned my attention back to the buttons. There was one with a wavy mouth that looked kind of friendly. I pressed it hopefully.

The bug swallowed the bright thing, stretched its mandibles in a bored kind of way, and scuttled to the front of the stage. I yeeped, and the door opened.

"You got a problem in here?" the Producer asked.

I turned and grinned crazily at him. "No, no. Everything's fine. Just fine."

"Good," the Producer said darkly, and closed the door.

I turned back to the stage. The fist-sized bug had been replaced by a whole troop of smaller bugs. I hit a couple of buttons, more or less at random. The first one made the bugs arrange themselves into rows; the second made them march back and forth across the stage. Desperately, I reached for the frowny face.

Changeling slapped my hand. Hard.

"Ow! What did you do that for?"

"You are not approaching the task rationally. You obviously do not know anything about computers at all. You do not even know where to begin."

I got up, sending the chair rattling across the floor. "Okay, fine. Let's approach it rationally. It's a toy theatre that runs Broadway. Where do *you* think we should begin?"

Changeling held up the Mermaid's Mirror. The silvery surface was filled edge to edge with a complicated diagram.

"I think we should begin by consulting the manual," she said.

I gaped at it, then wheeled the chair back to the theatre for her to sit in.

Changeling studied the diagram, then punched a winking face and a worried one. The bugs formed a series of concentric spinning circles like an archery target. It gave me an instant headache, but Changeling started to hum happily. She consulted with the Mirror for a while, stared at the buttons, then pressed a surprised face. The bugs changed from yellowy-brown to violent green. She went back to the Mirror.

I was chewing on my hair again out of sheer nervousness. It tasted terrible. I spat it out. Changeling looked up impatiently. "Go away. You are bothering me."

The Producer's office walls were plastered with posters for plays—*A Midsummer Night's Dream* and *Wicked* and *Peter Pan*—and framed drawings of actors signed with little hearts and *x*'s and inscriptions like "With Love and Nibbles" and "Forever Yours" and "For the Big Enchilada." Judging from the toothy smiles, most of them were vampires.

When I was bored with the pictures, I turned to the desk. It was piled with scripts and letters from theatre managers complaining about the electrical service and striking gaffers and slow deliveries of nectar to the concession stands. When I'd paged through the scripts, I was out of things to look at—except for the cabinet full of Tech heads, which I'd already seen as much of as I wanted to.

Beyond the desk, there was a window covered with wooden slats. I found a string hanging down one side and fiddled with it until I got the slats to raise and then I looked out.

Except when I was dangling from Carlyle's claws, I'd never been this high up. Broadway sparkled below me like a giant's necklace—ruby and diamond, emerald and sapphire. From this distance, it looked oddly peaceful. I leaned my forehead against the window and imagined what it might be like to live among Theatre Folk, meeting supernaturals from all over the City, maybe even other mortal changelings. It might be fun. It would certainly be different. I hadn't seen any trees, for instance, and the lights of Broadway drowned out the stars. The sun, of course, didn't shine at all.

Broadway was a nice place to visit, I decided. But I wouldn't want to live there.

Three different sets of lights flickered and dimmed, one after another, leaving large black gaps in the twinkling chain. I shivered and turned to see how Changeling was doing.

Over at the theatre, things looked hopeful: The swarm of bugs on the stage was a lot smaller than it had been. As I leaned over Changeling's shoulder, though, there was a sudden population explosion. Thousands of huge, gnarly bugs swarmed everywhere, their mouth parts gaping hungrily. They climbed the scarlet curtains, threatening to spill out over the control board and overrun the office.

I screamed.

Changeling pushed three buttons at once.

The bugs disappeared.

A tiny flashing light darted onto the empty stage, tinkled in an annoyed way, and exited into the wings just as the office door burst open and the Producer barreled in, looking ready to bite off the first head he saw.

"The bugs are gone!" I yelled. "Everything's okay now!" But the Producer had already shoved Changeling aside, chair and all, and was staring at the little theatre with horror.

"This stage is empty!" he growled. "Where are the programs? Where is my data? Where is Broadway?" He glared from me to Changeling, who had rolled all the way to the window. "You chiselers. Biting off your heads is too good for you. I will cook you in a pie. I will have your guts for garters."

I gaped at him helplessly, too scared to think. Changeling rubbed her face and yawned. "There is no reason to raise your voice," she said placidly. "Your computer is rebooting."

The Producer eyed her suspiciously. "Rebooting?"

"Yes. I have debugged it and defragged it and installed an antivirus program. The Hard Drive says to tell you that you are one lucky customer and next time remember to back up your data. Only chumps forget to back up their data. What is a chump?"

The Producer looked like he'd been bopped in the beezer. "Say again?"

Changeling repeated what she'd just said, only with a lot more words. To me, it sounded like a foreign language based on English. I don't know what it sounded like to the Producer. He looked so confused that if it hadn't been for the gray cabinet, I might almost have felt sorry for him.

When Changeling finally stopped talking, the Producer shook his head very slowly and said, "I never heard a doll use so many jawbreakers, at that. Give it to me straight: Is my computer busted or not?"

Seeing that Changeling was about to go through it all again, I said, "No, it's not busted. It's as good as new. Better."

"That is swell." The Producer cracked his knuckles like fireworks. "If it is true. I know what you mortals are like. You make things up like crazy. I will test the computer as follows, and if it works, you will get a reward. If it does not work, I will not only bite your heads off, but grind your bones to make my bread. You got that?"

I nodded.

The Producer sat down in front of the toy theatre. Suddenly I was horribly sure that the computer wasn't going to work. He must have felt the same way, because he touched a puzzled-looking face as if it might bite him. We both held our breaths.

A dwarflike supernatural trudged onto the stage. "What?"

The Producer let out a whoosh of breath and ordered up a pair of tickets for *Wicked*, pronto.

The Tech dwarf trudged off again.

"See," the Producer said to me, "the Tech Folk charge many potatoes for computer fixing, but I am thinking, what use are potatoes to a couple of little dolls, except to buy tickets to a show? I propose to you that we cut out the middleman and I reward you with a pair of house seats for *Wicked*, one for you and one for your stand-in. I understand that little dolls love *Wicked* more than somewhat."

When a Genius offers you a reward, you're not supposed to tell him you'd rather have something else. But the thought of having to do a trade with Sammy the Scalper inspired me. I told the Producer how kind he was, and how seeing *Wicked* was truly what every little doll dreamed about, only this fairy I knew was friends with the original Tinkerbell in *Peter Pan*, and she said it was the best show on Broadway, and I wanted to see it so much, and couldn't he please, please consider making it a ticket to *Peter Pan* instead?

Finally the Producer laughed and said he'd come

across with a deuce to the Pan play, and I was a queer duck, at that. But I had plenty of moxie, and he liked that in a little doll.

While he punched a couple more faces and talked to the Tech dwarf some more, I went to the window. The bright necklace of Broadway sparkled below me, un-broken and unshadowed. I wanted to show Changeling what she'd done, but She was gazing at the computer like someone saying good-bye to a friend.

At last the Tech dwarf came on from the wings trun-dling two shimmering discs, which it rolled out over the footlights. The Producer caught them neatly, slid them into an envelope, and handed it to me. "Here you go, little dolls," the Producer said. "Orchestra center, with the original Tinkerbell, just like you want. If they give you any lip, tell them the Producer sends you."

CHAPTER
17

A VAMPIRE'S BARK IS WORSE THAN ITS BITE.

Neef's Rules for Changelings

Debugging the Producer's computer had done more than just turn Broadway's lights back on. The elevator zipped us smoothly to the lobby, and all three griffins were sharp and bright and solid. Outside, the sidewalk swarmed with agents waving portraits and scripts and yelling that they had to see the Producer, right away. The door griffin was yelling back at them that nobody saw the Producer without an appointment. Everyone was happy, except Changeling, who started gulping air in a panicky, fairy-fittish kind of way.

Grabbing her jacket, I kicked and shoved my way through the mob of agents and looked around. Every place that wasn't a theatre was a shop or a food stand, lit up like a fairy hill and swarming with Folk chattering and shrieking with laughter. I caught sight of a promising gap between the Belasco Theatre and a store selling shadows autographed by Peter Pan.

It turned out to be a narrow alley, paved with cobblestones. At the far end, I saw a faint, yellowish glow and scurried toward it.

The alley ended in a quiet courtyard. A lamp shed its gentle golden light over a stone fountain with a statue in it. When Changeling sat down on the basin's edge, I noticed that the statue was a large, howling wolf. Beyond it was an arched door with THE BRAM STOKER written over it in spiky scarlet letters.

Wolf plus Bram Stoker equals vampires.

Although vampires sometimes hunted mortals in the Park on moonlit nights, I'd never actually seen one. Of course I'd been taught basic anti-vampire lore: Carry garlic if you're out at night; don't talk to anybody in a black cloak; and if you get caught, don't look them in the eyes. The best strategy, of course, was not to meet one in the first place.

I grabbed Changeling and spun around, intending to head back to the street. But Changeling wasn't going to go back to Broadway without putting up a fight. My panicked attempt to persuade her was interrupted by a long, piercing creak, like a massive ironbound door opening very slowly. I looked up and saw two shadowy figures glide into the courtyard.

"Look, Honey," one of them said. "Somebody ordered takeout."

I wanted to close my eyes, but it was already too late. I could see and hear, but I couldn't move even an eyelash. Changeling had stopped kicking me, so I knew they'd gotten her, too.

The vampires strolled toward us. The one who had spoken was a man dressed in a black silk cloak and fancy suit. His companion was a little girl with golden ringlets wearing pink ruffles and shoes that rang brightly on the cobbles with every step. *Oh, great,* I thought. *I'm going to be eaten by Shirley Temple.*

"Well, well, well," the man said. "What have we here? Mortal, do you think? I hope so. I could use a bite before the audition."

He came right up to me, sniffed at my neck, and pulled back in a hurry. "Phew! This one stinks of fairy."

"This one, too. Oh!" The girl vampire clapped her little white hands. "Do you think they're changelings, Raoul? What fun!"

The man rolled his eyes. They were a rich, dark burgundy and very large, so it was not a pretty sight. "Cut it out, Honey," he said. "Can't you act your age?"

"Which one?" Honey asked sweetly.

The man lifted his upper lip at her. "Oh, please, don't start. I'm much too hungry to deal with one of your snits." He sniffed my neck again, a questioning kind of snuffle. It tickled.

"*Mostly* mortal," he said. "Maybe just a little sip. . . ."

"Aren't you allergic to changelings? Don't they give

you big, fat hives? Won't the itching distract you at the audition?"

The warm pressure lifted from my neck. Raoul rubbed the back of his hand against his lips. "You're impossible!"

Honey flashed a pair of pearly little kitten fangs at him.

"We haven't got time for this," Raoul said. "Every out-of-work vampire in the City's going to be at that audition. I can't afford to be late. And I've got to stop at the Blood Bank. Are you coming or not?"

Honey tip-tapped around behind us. I felt the slither of spidersilk against my legs as she plucked at my skirt. "No," she said around my shoulder. "I hate auditions. It's all your fault anyway. You're the one who bit me when I was eight. If you'd waited a few years, I wouldn't be stuck playing cute little girls until the end of eternity."

Raoul ground his teeth. "Cute little monsters is more like it. You need the work, Honey. All those pots of A-negative don't come cheap, you know. Besides, this is a great part. Little Miss Marker. You were born for it."

A sharp clack must have been Honey stamping her foot on the cobbles. "No. I *won't* go to the stupid audition. I want to play with the changelings!"

"So play," Raoul sneered. "I hope they give you blisters." He twirled his cloak around him with a practiced sweep of his arm and stalked out of the alley.

"He's been like that since Mr. Lugosi flew out from

Hollywood and took over the lead in *Dracula*," Honey said, sounding suddenly less whiny. She came around in front of me. "Tell me, darlings, are you stupid or merely ignorant? Don't you know it's *fatal* to wander down dark alleys? *We* can't eat you, but there are plenty of Folk who'd adore the chance of a fresh changeling or two. Don't you have a word to say for yourself?"

I glared at her. Hard. She giggled. "Oh. Sorry." She waved an airy hand. "As you were."

I flopped down like a puppet whose strings have been cut. Changeling collapsed on top of me and wiggled away hastily. I rubbed my neck where I could still feel the tickle of Raoul's breath.

"Thanks," I said.

"You're welcome," Honey said. "Now, answer my question. What's a pair of changelings doing wandering around the back alleys of Broadway without so much as a Cap of Invisibility? Didn't your fairy godparents teach you *anything*?"

"They taught me lots," I said indignantly. "I can say 'I am under the protection of the Genius of Central Park' in about a million languages. And I know lots of Folk lore. You want to know how to make a leshii leave you alone?"

Honey squealed delightedly. "Ooh, you're a *country* girl! What brings you so far from the fields you know?"

I stood up, a little shaky around the knees. "I'm on a quest."

"A quest?" She started to clap her hands, caught herself, and clasped them behind her back. "How exciting. I adore quests. Do tell me all about it."

"Okay, I'll tell you." I glanced at Changeling, who was sitting on the cobblestones with her arms around her knees and her head down, humming frantically. "Can we go somewhere else?"

"What am I thinking?" Honey exclaimed. "You're exhausted, poor dears. Come have some hot chocolate, and I'll see if we can fix you up with a coffin to sleep in."

"Oh, we can't spend the night," I said hastily. "Thanks anyway."

"You've got nothing the fear, darling. Vampires really are allergic to fairies." Honey held up her hand. The tips of her fingers were blistered and red. "Your skirt is pure fairy magic. Satisfied?"

"Hot chocolate sounds good," I said.

According to its brochure, the Bram Stoker was "a full-service residential hotel for the discriminating urban vampire." Its lobby was decorated entirely in black and white, with curly tufted sofas and black marble urns full of red roses tucked into every corner.

Honey led us to one of the sofas and waved. A very tall vampire in a black suit detached himself from the shadows, glided up to us, and bowed.

"Nosferatu darling," Honey said. "Be an angel and

bring us two hot chocolates and a pot of A-negative. And tell Management my friends will be needing somewhere to sleep."

Nosferatu's nose quivered; he swept his arm protectively across his face. "Changelings!" he hissed.

I didn't think much of him either. He was as bald as Sammy the Scalper, with fangs as long as my finger and eyes like scarlet eggs in wrinkly nests.

"Management will not be pleased," he said.

"Ask anyway," said Honey, and waved him away. "Now, darling," she said. "Tell me *everything*!"

I thought I didn't feel like talking, but telling my story to Honey wasn't like telling it to anybody else. Most Folk just sit there while you're telling them a story, looking out over your shoulder or cleaning their claws or cobbling shoes or whatever. You never really know whether they're listening unless you change something or leave something out, and then they correct you.

Honey listened with her whole body, red-violet eyes wide, oohing and aahing and giggling and shivering in all the right places. She didn't care if I stuck to the traditional rules of storytelling—in fact, she asked questions that made it impossible. Before long, I'd forgotten she was a bloodsucking ex-mortal and was telling her my adventures without even thinking about which fairy-tale pattern they fit into.

I was just describing the Mermaid Queen's tattoos,

with special attention to the nuclear submarine, when Nosferatu glided up with a silver tray filled with pots and cups. "Two chocolates and one A-negative, Miss Honey. Management says that you may accommodate the changelings in your suite. But do try and keep them from running about the halls. Some of our older guests are particularly sensitive."

Honey lifted her upper lip just enough to display the tips of her fangs. "How *sweet* of Management to care."

Nosferatu sniffed. "There will be an extra cleaning charge, of course—to decontaminate whatever they may touch."

"I just *adore* the Bram Stoker," Honey said sarcastically, sounding a lot like Eloise. "Go on, darling," she said when Nosferatu had hissed himself away. "What happened next?"

I took a sweet, burning gulp of hot chocolate and picked up the story at the Riddle Game. Honey insisted on trying to guess the riddle and couldn't, although her second guess—a magic rat—came close. I was feeling better than I had since seeing the Producer's cabinet of Tech heads. Changeling had finished her chocolate and was fast asleep in the corner of the sofa with her mouth open, looking about as heroic as a ham sandwich.

This is my *quest*, I thought. I'm *the hero around here.* And before I knew it, I was telling Honey that I had fixed the Producer of Broadway's computer all by myself.

Honey's eyes sparkled at me. "Well, aren't you the bee's knees! Last time I was in Central Park, it was all too Olde Worlde for words. I wouldn't have guessed anyone there would even have heard of computers, let alone learned how to fix them. Well, you live and learn, don't you?"

I quickly took another sip of chocolate and tried to think of a response that wouldn't sound lame. The silence was getting really uncomfortable when Honey asked, "Do you remember much about your life before you were changed?"

"Not really," I said cautiously. "I don't think about it."

"Perhaps they took you when you were very young. I was eight when I crossed over." She smiled sadly. "I remember lots about being mortal. I was the original Gwendolyn in *The Poor Little Rich Girl*. *The New York Times* called my performance 'heartbreaking.'"

She'd listened to my story; it was my turn to listen to hers. I made an encouraging noise.

"The stage was wonderful," she went on. "Still, what I remember best is things like Mama taking me to Central Park and feeding the pigeons on Sunday afternoons. Sometimes we'd walk down to the lake and Papa would rent a rowboat and I'd trail my hand in the water and Mama would scold me because the water was dirty." She played with a pink frill on her skirt. "Sometimes I splashed her. I wasn't a very nice child, I'm afraid."

I stifled a yawn. "My mom wouldn't let me feed the

pigeons," I said. "She called them flying rats."

"Your mom?" Honey asked, startled. "Don't you mean your fairy godmother?"

I shook my head. It felt swollen and strange, almost as if it belonged to someone else. "No. My fairy godmother is a white rat. She likes pigeons. Mom hated rats and snakes and pigeons and cockroaches. Dad said we ought to get a cat, but she wasn't big on cats." I looked at Honey. "I feel really weird. Did you put some kind of spell on me?"

Honey laughed. "Just conversation, darling. It's a kind of human magic. What else do you remember?"

I told her about my room with the fairy-tale mural and the stars, which somehow reminded me of the wooden sailboat Daddy built for us to sail on the Boat Pond. "It had a lavender ribbon flying from its masthead," I said, and then, "Changeling fixed the Producer's computer."

"I know," Honey said.

She was sitting with her ankles crossed, her shiny black Mary Janes dangling above the black plush carpet, her blistered hands folded in her frilly pink lap. Her expression, even without whiskers, reminded me of Astris when I'd been acting particularly mortal.

"I wish I hadn't lied," I said shyly.

"Apology accepted," she said. "It's natural for mortals to beef up their parts a little, but keep this in mind: If you start lying about things, after a while you're in danger of forgetting what's real and what isn't."

"Isn't everything real here?"

She looked serious. "No," she said. "But it could be. That's why Folk don't lie. And they have a very short way with mortals who do. Take it from one who knows: Being a has-been mortal in New York Between is no day at the races."

"I like the Folk." I sighed. "When I was smaller, I used to wish and wish I was a fairy, until my fairy godmother made me lay off."

Honey gave my hand a snowflake-cold touch. "I'll let you into a little secret, darling. You are—a tiny part of you, anyway."

I snatched my hand away. "That's not funny."

Honey leaned forward earnestly. "Scout's honor, darling. Think about it. You eat supernatural food, you breathe supernatural air, you live and play exclusively with supernaturals. You shouldn't be surprised if some supernaturalness rubs off on you. You look maybe ten, eleven years old, but you're probably older." She studied me, her curly blonde head cocked. "Do you even know what I'm talking about?"

"No," I said shortly, feeling stupid.

"It's not your fault, darling—Park Folk are notoriously ignorant about all things mortal. Pay attention now. I'm going to give you your first lesson in human time. Outside mortals count time in years—that's roughly from Winter Solstice to Winter Solstice. Every year, they grow older. Are you following me so far?"

I thought this over. "Does getting older have anything

to do with getting bigger? I know I've been growing a lot lately." I looked down my body in alarm. "How big am I going to get? Ogre size? Giant size?"

Honey laughed. "Calm down, darling. You're already nearly as big as you're going to get. So is Changeling. Because she started as a fairy, she grows more slowly than a mortal. As she spends more time in the mortal world, she'll start aging faster. Understand?"

"Not really," I muttered. My eyes drifted shut. It was nice and quiet there in the dark, and I would have been happy to stay there and just go to sleep if Honey's pixyish giggle hadn't jerked me awake. I picked up my chocolate cup to see if there was any left. There was, but it was cold and sludgy, kind of like my brain.

"Time for all good changelings to be in bed," Honey said. She got up and slung Changeling over her shoulder, careful not to touch anything but her clothes. Vampires, I remembered, are a lot stronger than they look.

"Come along, darling. Next stop, beddy-bye."

CHAPTER
18

FOLK OF A FEATHER FLOCK TOGETHER.

Neef's Rules for Changelings

When I woke up, I was so warm and comfortable I thought at first I was back in my own bed in Belvedere Castle. Then I realized it was much too quiet, and the air smelled stuffy and kind of flowery.

I opened my eyes. Reflected candlelight danced in the shiny side of a big black box about an inch from my nose. I wallowed upright in a huge pile of velvet-covered cushions and stretched.

Honey peered down at me over the edge of the box. "You slept like the dead," she said. "The maid's been trying to get in and fumigate for hours."

Her voice brought it all back: Sammy the Scalper, the Chorus Line, the Producer and his cabinet of Tech heads, the lights of Broadway going out, Changeling turning them back on again.

"Where's Changeling?" I asked.

"Changeling's taking a bath, darling. Your Satchel is on the breakfast table, hobnobbing with my magic coffee-grinder. The Bram Stoker doesn't do solid food, I'm afraid."

Honey's room was decorated entirely in red, black, and pale yellow. So was Honey. She'd lost the Shirley Temple look for black tights and a loose red silk shirt, and had scraped her blonde ringlets back into a curly ponytail.

A door opened and Changeling walked into the room.

I wasn't sure, this morning, exactly how I felt about Changeling. On the one hand, she was so totally not from around here. She didn't know Folk lore; she didn't know the rules. I wasn't even sure she really believed in fairies yet. If she *looked* just like me, she should *be* just like me, you know? Like nixies are like other nixies? But she wasn't.

On the other hand, she could see things I couldn't and knew things I didn't. Without Changeling's Tech magic, I'd be negotiating with Sammy the Scalper over which body part to trade for a ticket to *Peter Pan*. Or decorating the Producer's cabinet of heads. I owed her. Big-time. And I didn't feel good about *that* either.

Changeling marched over to me. She still wore her embroidered jacket, its flowers a little faded from their bath in New York Harbor, but she'd traded her ragged skirt and T-shirt for black jeans and a crisp white shirt.

"Honey told me that my old clothing was not appropriate for Wall Street," she told me. "I did not allow her to replace my jacket, however." She examined me with a slight frown. "Do you think that dress is appropriate for Wall Street?"

"Probably not." I bit my lip. "You look very nice, Changeling."

"Thank you."

All at once, I realized just how grubby and itchy I felt. I scrambled out of my nest and told Honey I wanted a bath.

Honey's bathroom was mostly occupied by a black marble bathtub the size of a small pond. Honey showed me how to turn on the water and where she kept the bath oil, and left me alone.

I stripped off the spidersilk dress, washed my hair and skin in the rose-scented water, and then just floated.

What I should have been doing was planning how to find the Dragon of Wall Street and how I was going to get his Scales from him once I found him. But every time I tried to focus on the subject of dragons, my mind skated off to what Honey had told me about changelings.

It made a Folkish kind of sense. Living with the Folk, I was growing Folk-y. Living with mortals, Changeling was growing mortal. But what did that *mean*, exactly? Would I grow magic as I grew Folkier? Would Changeling eventually lose hers? Was her skill with computers mortal knowledge or fairy magic? What kind of supernatural had she been originally? How had she been chosen to lead the life I would have had if the Folk hadn't switched us?

Honey tapped on the door.

"I do hope you haven't drowned," she called out. "Management would absolutely hate that."

"Out in a minute," I shouted.

What about Honey? She used to be mortal like me. Now she was a supernatural with her own set of unbreakable rules to live by. How did she deal with that? Why wasn't talking to her like talking to a moss woman or a nixie or even Astris or the Pooka? Astris liked me, but she didn't understand me. Honey understood me. But Honey drank mortal blood.

It was all very confusing.

When I was totally waterlogged, I got out and put on the black jeans and white shirt Honey had left for me—not the sneakers, though: I never wear shoes in summer. The spidersilk dress I rolled into a ball and stuffed into my pocket.

Back in the bedroom, Honey was curled up in a red leather chair with a white porcelain mug. Changeling sat at a black lacquer table eating scrambled eggs and drinking hot chocolate. I sat down to help her.

Honey wiped a trace of crimson from her upper lip, and I noticed her fingers were bandaged in white gauze.

"Does it hurt?" I asked around a mouthful of egg.

"It itches," she said. "My fault entirely. I couldn't resist touching your dress. I've never seen a real spidersilk one before." She put the mug on the floor and unfolded her legs. "This is all very cozy, darlings, but we really need to discuss this Wall Street expedition of yours. What are your plans?"

I took another bite of egg and chewed, thinking fast.

The Financial Maze belonged to the Folk who lived for gold: giants, kobolds, wyrms, some dwarves. No big European dragons—the Dragon of Wall Street had long ago eaten all the serious competition. Not for the first time, I wished that I knew more than the basic facts about the non-Park neighborhoods of New York.

I swallowed. "Well, I thought I'd get as close as I could and trust to luck."

Honey's fangs showed at the corners of her smile. "Wall Street isn't like New York Harbor, darling," she said. "It's not even like Broadway. You can't count on running into a friendly investor or a helpful broker who'll show you the ropes. There's no such creature."

"Then I'll just have to do without help. If you can tell us how to get to the Treasury, maybe I can ask for a job— you know, like that debutante whose date got stolen by the ogre's daughter? She pretended to be a housekeeper until she figured out how to break the spell the ogre had laid on him."

Honey laughed. "The only job you're likely to get at the Treasury is as an afternoon snack."

I was getting annoyed. "Then what am I supposed to

do? Because if I don't get the Dragon's Scales, I'll never get home. Changeling either."

"Calm down, darling. I'm just introducing a note of reality into your charming fantasy. Not to beat around the bush, what you need is a native guide."

"Does that mean you're coming with us?"

Honey shook her head. "Daylight, you know. *Ruinous* for my complexion. No, I'm going to send you to my friend Fleet. She's lived in the Maze all her life."

Another strange supernatural; another new adventure. It was hard to remember I'd ever wanted one. I poured some more hot chocolate. "What kind of supernatural is Fleet?" I asked resignedly. "How does she like to be asked for things? What will I have to give her in return?"

"Oh, Fleet's not a supernatural," Honey said. "She's a mortal changeling. Like you."

I stared at Honey, who gave a Shirley Temple–esque giggle. "I surprised you, didn't I? It's true, though. There's a whole street of changelings in the Maze. Maiden Lane. But first you have to get there." She turned to Changeling. "You're good at remembering things, aren't you?"

While Honey and I talked, Changeling had piled the dirty plates on one corner of the table with the forks laid neatly across them, and was arranging some little enamel boxes she'd found in a flowerlike pattern. "I have an eidetic memory," she said without looking up from her work. "What do you want me to remember?"

"A series of directions," Honey said. "Street names,

left turns, right turns, things like that. You have to get it exactly right. A mistake could be fatal."

"I will not make a mistake," Changeling said.

I tried to pay attention while Honey taught Changeling the way to Maiden Lane, I really did. But there aren't any streets in the Park. Names and turns slid in one ear and out the other like water through a pipe. Instead, I watched Changeling arrange boxes. Her hair had dried into a crinkly halo. I touched my own curls and wondered how alike we actually looked. I thought my eyes might be a little greener and my face a little rounder, but I wasn't sure. I wished that Honey's room had a mirror.

Changeling glanced up and caught me staring at her. I laughed nervously, and Changeling turned back to her boxes. "What comes after Worth Street?" she asked Honey, and then it was all "turn left" here and "take the third right" there until Honey was satisfied that Changeling had the directions memorized. Then it was time to go.

I picked up Satchel and slung it across my chest. "I hope Management won't charge you too much for all those contaminated cushions," I said, looking at the black-and-red nest beside the coffin.

Honey smiled a rather nasty smile. "Management can go file its fangs," she said. "Come on, darlings. You don't want to be caught in the Financial Maze after dark."

The hall seemed to be empty of sensitive vampires. We followed Honey through a maze of long corridors lined with shiny wooden doors with brass plaques on them:

"Lillie Langtry," "Lynn Fontanne," "George M. Cohan." Finally, we came to a hall so encrusted with painted red dragons and gold curlicues and Chinese characters for luck and joy that at first I didn't even see that there was a door at the end.

"This opens on Canal, at the heart of Chinatown," Honey said. "The Financial Maze is the next district south. Do watch where you're going, darlings. Canal is delightful, but the Financial Maze is something of a Forest Perilous." She sighed. "I wish I could come with you. I so want to know how it all comes out."

I wanted to tell Honey how much I liked her and how grateful I was for the cushions and the bath and the clothes. But I wasn't sure that vampires like to be thanked, so I said, "Would you like me to come back and tell you about it?"

"You darling!" She threw her arms around my waist in a big hug. Even through my clothes, I could feel how cold she was. "Break a leg. And don't worry about a thing, darling. You and Changeling are a great double act. The Dragon won't know what hit him."

The dragon door led to a room about the size of the Producer's elevator, with a second door in the facing wall. When Honey closed the door on her side, we were in total darkness. Then I heard a click, and Changeling swung the second door open onto bright sunlight and the chatter of many voices.

CHAPTER
19

IF SOMETHING SEEMS TOO GOOD TO BE TRUE,
IT'S PROBABLY TRYING TO KILL YOU.

Neef's Rules for Changelings

We stood outside the Bram Stoker's back door, breathing in the sharp perfume of unfamiliar spices. The street was an immersion course in Chinese Folk lore. In the space of a few breaths, I saw a troop of monkey spirits with long tails waving from the back of their camouflage shorts, three doll-like hu-hsien in miniskirts and high-heeled boots, five blue demons, a pair of fu dogs (one red, one green), and countless tiny flying dragons like bright silk scarves. Red-and-gold signs advertised shops and services: CELESTIAL CLOTH BY CHIH NÜ, THE CHIN CHIA GRAMMAR SCHOOL FOR YOUNG SUPERNATURALS, and LI ORGANIZING SERVICES.

The crowd thinned out, and I caught sight of a wide slate-gray canal dotted with red-sailed boats and gilded barges. The sky was blue, scarlet flags were flying, and everybody seemed to be shouting cheerfully. I turned to Changeling to see how she was handling the noise.

Changeling was handling it just fine. Changeling on a mission was a different creature from Changeling tagging along on somebody else's adventure.

"What are you waiting for?" she asked. "We have to go this way." And she barged through a knee-high flock of shinseën, who wagged their white beards and scolded her in high, old-man voices. I followed, apologizing.

I wasn't in a hurry to leave Chinatown. Countless stalls spilled their piles of cabbages and magic fish and amulets and embroidered slippers and bolts of violently colored silk into the street. A tray of tiny, jewel-bright frogs caught my eye. I bent over them, enchanted; a jade green one winked a ruby eye at me. Changeling jigged impatiently. "We have to *go*," she announced.

"Just a sec. I want to see this frog," I said, but she kept bugging me until I gave in. We walked along the canal to a red-and-gold bridge, which we crossed at a trot. Changeling paused to check a sign, then turned down a side street.

The side street was, if anything, noisier and more jam-packed than Canal, but Changeling wasn't fazed. She wove through the Chinese Folk like a needle, trailing me, threadlike, behind her. The street branched and branched again. To my relief, the crowds thinned, then vanished completely. Changeling didn't even seem to notice, but marched purposefully on, turning right and left, seemingly at random, but heading always southward, deeper into the Financial Maze.

I wasn't liking the Financial Maze much. To me, it

felt like an anti-Park: dusty, silent, empty, hard. Its gray buildings loomed over us like sheer, many-windowed cliffs. I was almost happy to see a will-o'-the-wisp flickering mistily at the mouth of an alley. In a world of silence and stone, it was at least familiar.

Of course, if you look at a will-o'-the-wisp, it thinks you're going to follow it. Next thing I knew, this one had darted out of the alley and started dancing around our heads. Changeling batted at it irritably. This just attracted more will-o'-the-wisps, and soon we were at the center of a misty-bright dandelion.

"Ignore them, Changeling," I begged. "They're just trying to get you to follow them. They can't hurt us as long as we know where we're going."

Changeling swung her fist at one particularly persistent wisp. "I do know where I am going," Changeling said angrily. "This is Worth. We turn right on Lafayette, cross the park, and then go left on Pearl."

The will-o'-the-wisps fled, squeaking mournfully. Changeling looked after them, puzzled.

"I knew you weren't lost," I said. "Now they know it, too. Let's go."

We tramped down Worth Street, Changeling on the lookout for Lafayette, me on the lookout for possible dangers. Where were the giants and wyrms and goblins Astris had told me about? Were they watching us from the blank windows? Finding a heavy stone to drop on our heads? Why was everything so quiet?

When we turned onto Pearl Street, I thought it was empty, too. Then a shower of golden light dazzled my eyes and a voice soothed my ears like falling water.

"Children, children, whither wander you?"

The voice belonged to a huge golden bird perched on a lamppost. Its song was to ordinary birdsong as the sun is to a candle flame.

"Are you lost?" it caroled. "I can bring you safely home. Do you want gold? I can give you endless treasure. Friends? I can make you beautiful and charming. Fame? I can put your names in every mouth in New York. Only follow me."

Changeling drifted nearer. As I hesitated, the bird promised me my heart's desire. It would lead me to Central Park, fix things with the Lady, get me an invitation to a changeling party and answers to all my questions. All I had to do was follow it.

I wanted to go wherever it led me. I really did. But a dry voice in my head that sounded a lot like the Curator kept telling me that quests don't have shortcuts.

"Don't listen, Changeling," I gasped. "I think it's like the will-o'-the-wisps. Say the streets again, and maybe it will go away."

I might as well have saved my breath. The bird took to the air in a scatter of light like the last rays of sunset, and Changeling took off after it—or she would have if I hadn't attached myself to her. She whipped around, trying to make me let go without tearing her beloved jacket.

I hung on like a burr, and the bird fluttered around our heads, showering us with impossible promises.

Out of nowhere, a whistle blew, incredibly loud and incredibly harsh.

Three things happened at once. I let go of the jacket and covered my ears, the bird disappeared like a soap bubble bursting, and Changeling let out the saddest, loudest, most desperate wail I've ever heard.

I knew how she felt, but I couldn't help thinking that this was not a good time to call attention to ourselves. "We're on Pearl, Changeling," I said as calmly as I could. "Do you remember what comes after Pearl?"

She stood in the middle of the street, repeating the directions to herself, and a giant walked into us.

It was only a little giant, as giants go—just big enough to see into a second-story window, not big enough to squash us flat. He knocked us over, then stood still, turning his head this way and that. Changeling, not surprisingly, went totally to pieces. She screamed and flailed and screamed some more. The giant tilted his face toward her, and I saw his eyes flash bright and golden, like polished coins.

A shiver went through me, more horror than fright. Clutching Changeling by the collar, I hauled her upright and pushed her flat against the wall. "Shut up," I hissed. "I know you're freaked, but you have to be quiet. I think that giant's blind, but he's not deaf."

She tried. She really tried. She managed to turn down

her screaming to a strangled moaning, which the giant would have heard just fine if the street had stayed quiet and empty. But it didn't. All at once, kobolds, demons, wyrms, giants, and goblins started pouring out of the buildings and into the narrow street, filling it with the confused thunder of heavy feet.

Our giant shook his head and shambled away.

"We've got to get out of here, Changeling," I muttered. "What's the next street?"

She shook her head, eyes squeezed shut.

"Let's see. It was north to Lafayette, left on Lafayette, left on Pearl. Or was it south to Lafayette?"

"You have it all wrong," Changeling said irritably. "We turn *right* on Lafayette, cross the park, turn left on Pearl, follow Pearl down past Fulton, John, and Platt to Maiden Lane, then left."

I grinned. "You're right. Let's get going."

I soon realized that all the Wall Street Folk were as gold-blind as the giant, but it didn't make me feel any better. We sidled down the side of the street, hugging the wall and hoping nobody bumped into us. By the time we finally made it to Maiden Lane, I'd been frightened so long I was feeling sick. I don't know how Changeling was feeling.

Just as there were no pearls on Pearl Street, there were no maidens on Maiden Lane: only a couple of scurrying kobolds and two rows of grim stone towers that reminded me of the building where the witch had stuck the Hippie Chick. I wondered if we were going to have to climb up Fleet's hair to get to her apartment. I hoped not. I don't mind heights so much, but I hate climbing ropes.

I don't know how Changeling knew which building was the right one—maybe there were signs that only fairy eyes could see. In any case, she marched up to a wall that looked like every other wall and poked it firmly with her finger. After a moment, the wall asked who we were and what we wanted.

For some reason, this was too much for Changeling, who retreated into her jacket. "We're changelings," I told the wall, speaking loudly and clearly. "We're looking for you, I think. Is your name Fleet? If it is, please let us in. Honey sent us."

There was a pause and then the voice said, "How do I know you're not a broker?"

"A what?"

"Never mind. Honey sent you, straight up?"

"Cross my heart and hope to die."

"That's easy for you to say. Brokers don't have hearts."

I looked up and down Maiden Lane. The light was fading and the wind was picking up. A fat wyrm waddled past on stumpy legs. "You have to help us," I said. "We're on a quest. And we're changelings, just like you. Please?" This last came out sounding a lot more panicked than I would have liked.

"Okay, okay." The voice was resigned. "Hold on and I'll buzz you in."

Later, Fleet and I got to be friends, but when I first met her, I didn't like her. If Changeling looked too much like me, Fleet looked too different. She was tall and slender, with polished cinnamon skin and black hair in a thousand little braids down her back like the statue of an Egyptian princess.

Usually I don't care that I'm kind of ordinary. Folk are supposed to be incredibly beautiful, unless they're incredibly ugly. But Fleet was only a mortal, like me. Plus, she kept shooting sideways glances at Changeling, like she couldn't believe she was real. And she totally refused to take us to the Dragon of Wall Street.

"Are you nuts? The Dragon's dangerous. When he chews you up, there's not enough left to spit out. My advice? Go home and forget about it."

I could feel myself getting red and hot. "Go home? Forget about it? I wish. The whole reason I'm here at all is that I *can't* go home until I've completed my quest for the Dragon's Scales."

"The Dragon's Scales?" Fleet shrieked so loud that Changeling flinched. "You're planning to steal the Dragon's Scales? You haven't got a chance!"

I got hotter. "Why not? I've already scored the Magical Magnifying Mirror of the Mermaid Queen and a pair of tickets to *Peter Pan*. And believe me, the Producer of Broadway is plenty dangerous to deal with."

Fleet wasn't impressed. "Maybe you should quit while you're ahead. New York's a big city. There are plenty of other places to live."

I wasn't so sure. What were my choices? The Financial Maze? No way. Broadway? No green things or sunshine. Battery Park? Where would I sleep? In Castle Clinton, with the ghosts? Chinatown was very cool, but not exactly homey. I could just imagine living in the Metropolitan Museum—if the Curator let me—and there were places in New York I hadn't even seen yet: the Upper West Side, Midtown, the Village, Chelsea. But I was willing to bet that none of them had nixies or corn spirits or Astris or the Water Rat. I didn't think I could bear it if I couldn't see Astris again. And what about the Pooka, stuck in the Museum being good until I got back? What about Changeling?

"No," I said. "Central Park is home, and I'm not ready to leave it yet. Besides, I've got promises riding on this."

"You shouldn't promise what you can't deliver," Fleet said. "You don't see me promising to take you to the Dragon, do you?"

"Are you telling me you don't know how to find the Dragon?"

Fleet looked insulted. "Of course I know how to find him. Blindfolded. It's just that I know better."

We were sitting in the living room of Fleet's apartment. Although it was smaller than my bedroom, it had a lot more furniture crammed into it: a round table with four chairs, a white sofa with a little table next to it, an easy chair, and a big bookcase stuffed with books. Drawings of giants and dragons and griffins and dwarves were thumbtacked all over the walls. Every flat surface was a jumble of papers and pencils and cups with mold growing in the bottom. Fleet was hunched up in the easy chair, fiddling nervously with her braids.

"Why are you so scared?" I asked. "It's not like he'll eat you or something. Aren't you under his protection?"

"I'm under his protection, all right." Fleet's pretty mouth drooped. "Way under. You are looking at one of the Dragon's Executive Assistants-in-Training."

"What's that?"

"The Dragon's very busy. He needs someone to keep Folk from interrupting him and to make coffee and appointments and things like that. He always has at least three maidens on hand, working in shifts. When one of them retires, one of us gets promoted."

I wondered what happened to retired Executive Assistants, and decided I didn't really want to know. "And you're not looking forward to the promotion?"

Fleet laughed. "You could put it that way. It's all finance and systems and keeping everything neat and organized—in other words, totally not me. I'm an artist, really."

"You are obviously not an organized person," Changeling said from the corner. "Your books are out of order."

I hadn't even known she was listening. As soon as we

got upstairs, she had gone to sit cross-legged in front of the bookcase. Apparently, she'd counted enough books to calm herself.

"I like them that way," Fleet wailed. "See? It's hopeless. Sooner or later, I'll do something really dumb and the Dragon will eat me and that will be that." Her velvety brown eyes filled with tears. She blotted them with her sleeve before they could spill over. "I'm miserable, but I'm not miserable enough to want to be eaten."

I knew exactly what she meant. Suddenly it didn't matter so much how beautiful she was.

"I understand," I said, and when Fleet looked doubtful, "No, really, I do. The Folk don't care whether we're happy or not. They only care if we follow their stupid rules. And if we don't, whammo! We're Folk food, and we don't even know why. It's not fair."

"You said it, sister." Fleet smiled at me, beautiful as a fairy-tale princess.

Princess. Hero. I had an idea.

"Hey, Fleet," I said slowly. "How about if in exchange for you leading us to the Dragon, we rescue you from him?"

"Say what?"

"We rescue you. You know, like the old stories about knights and damsels in distress? What do you say? Is it a deal?"

"And how are you going to do that?" Fleet asked sarcastically. "You got a dragon-killing sword in that satchel of yours?"

"No," I said. "It's not that kind of quest. Besides, you can't just go around killing Geniuses."

"What have you got in mind, then?"

"I'll come up with something. I've done it before. Besides, I have the Magical Magnifying Mirror of the Mermaid Queen and Changeling knows how to work it."

Fleet gave an unhappy laugh. "Which leaves us with what? A kid with a trick makeup mirror and a fairy double against a Genius of unimaginable size and power guarded by one of the best security systems in New York Between. Even a country girl like you can do the math on that one."

"We've got this far, haven't we? What are the odds against that?"

I hadn't meant it as a real question, but Changeling answered it anyway. "There is insufficient data to calculate the odds. But it is safe to say that they would be very, very high."

Fleet shrugged. "Very funny. Okay, Folklorist from Central Park. What do you know about dragons?"

The real answer was, "Not enough." But I was getting used to working with what I had. "They've all got a vulnerable spot," I said. "If we could find out what the Dragon of Wall Street's is, it would give us something to bargain with."

"Oh, I can tell you that," Fleet said gloomily. "The Dragon of Wall Street is blind. Not that it slows him down any."

Too easy. I shook my head. "That can't be it, then. There's got to be something else, something he's hiding. I'm sure Changeling and I can figure it out, if we can see him." I put my hand on Fleet's arm. "Please, Fleet, take us to the Dragon. It'll turn out fine, you'll see."

Fleet got up and paced between the window and the back wall a couple of times, dodging cast-off shoes and piles of papers. She looked at Changeling quietly rearranging her books in alphabetical order, and she looked at me.

"Okay," she said. "It's a deal. I'll take you to see the Dragon. But you guys have *got* to get me out of here. Wall Street is no place for an artist."

CHAPTER
20

DRAGONS DON'T FOLLOW THE RULES. THEY MAKE THEM.
Neef's Rules for Changelings

Once Fleet had made up her mind about the Dragon, she relaxed enough to offer us something to eat. Her version of Satchel was called Microwave, and it gave us rice and chicken in a strange, glowing, orange-pinky sauce Fleet called "sweet and sour." When we asked for macaroni and cheese, Microwave produced a bowl of lumpy stuff that looked like yellow paste poured over bits of rubber. Changeling was ecstatic.

As we ate, we talked. Fleet was all for striking while the iron was hot. I was all for waiting until morning, in case the Dragon might be asleep or out at the theatre or something.

Fleet found this very funny. "This isn't Madison Avenue," she said. "The Dragon works 24/7. And if you're worried about negotiating the Maze in the dark, don't be. I've been doing this since I was six."

So Fleet changed into what she called "business drag," a dark gray skirt and jacket, a pale gray blouse, and black shoes with very high heels. With her braids pulled back into a tight ponytail and little gold coins in her ears, she was still beautiful, but kind of scary, like an elf. Changeling wouldn't look at her.

On our way down, the elevator stopped and a boy and a dwarf got on. They were both wearing dark suits and carried the Wall Street magic bags Fleet called briefcases. The dwarf had a gray beard that would have trailed on the floor if he hadn't braided it and looped the tail through his belt. I knew right away that the boy was another mortal Assistant-in-Training. His jacket was too short in the sleeves and he was flushed, like his tie was choking him.

I smiled at the boy. He looked a little startled, but smiled back shyly.

The dwarf scowled. "Elevator etiquette!" it barked. Both Fleet and the boy jumped guiltily and stared fixedly at the elevator door. It would have been funny except that the boy's mouth was trembling like he was trying not to cry, and the dwarf was glaring at me like I was the one upsetting everybody. It was a real relief when the elevator got to the bottom and the boy and his fairy godfather disappeared into the night.

If Maiden Lane was spooky in the daytime, it was even spookier after dark, all black and silver with inky shadows. Fleet's high heels tapped sharply against the pavement, waking echoes from the high walls. It sounded like someone was following us, but whenever I turned around to look, the street was empty. In fact, we saw almost no one between Maiden Lane and Wall Street except the occasional dwarf.

"I thought you said the Financial Maze never closed down," I said to Fleet.

"It doesn't. Everybody's inside, working. The streets are only busy twice a day, when the night Folk and the day Folk change shifts. You don't want to get caught in Rush Hour if you can help it."

Right.

Wall Street turned out to be just that: a street running next to a wall that stretched as far as I could see in each direction and disappeared into the sky above. By this time, I'd realized that some places in New York looked bigger than they really were. I mean, I know how big Manhattan Island is, and believe me, if Broadway and Central Park Central and the Treasury were actually as big as they looked, there would be no room for Chinatown and Madison Avenue and the Village and everything else. Looking at the Treasury wall, though, it was easy to believe it covered the whole island.

You can tell a lot about a Genius, I think, by how hard

it is to get to see it. The Green Lady and the Curator, for instance, like to keep an eye on what's up in their territories. They don't hide in special buildings or rooms, or try to impress you with how important and powerful they are, on the theory that you'll figure it out yourself once you start talking with them. The Mermaid Queen and the Producer, on the other hand, obviously want you all softened up and humble before you even set eyes on them. The Dragon of Wall Street takes things even further. He wants you to feel like an ant. A tired, jumpy ant.

The massive door was made of some slick grayish metal with black bands, and it was huge. Fleet pushed on a corner, and a smaller door swung open, just big enough for us to enter single file. I wondered how the giants got in.

Fleet led us across an echoing stone hall to a slightly beat-up wooden counter with a sign over it that read SECURITY DESK.

"ID, please," said the guard. A kind of dragon, I thought, taking in the eagle claws, the leathery wings, and the long, snaky body. A wyvern, maybe. As it examined the white talisman Fleet extracted from her briefcase, I thought I saw a faint sheen of gold sliding along the surface of its eyes.

The wyvern waved us through an archway into a lofty corridor. Except where we were standing, it was totally dark. Fleet picked a torch out of a convenient torch stand

and tapped off into the darkness with Changeling and me pattering after like benighted travelers following a particularly determined will-o'-the-wisp.

I'm not afraid of the dark. The dark in Central Park is wide and clean and full of the music of fairy voices. When I was little, I would play hide-and-seek with the Shakespeare fairies at night, even when there wasn't a moon. The dark in the Treasury, however, was close and stale smelling and haunted by hisses and clanks. Fleet's torch sparked gleams of gold from the gray stone walls or licked bright tapestries or paintings into brief, unnerving life. At intervals were doors barred and banded with iron. One of them opened as we passed, releasing a blast of cold air and the mushroom-pale, blunt-nosed head of a giant worm.

I froze, and it irised its round, needle-toothed mouth at us. Changeling gave a squeak—or maybe that was me—and we dashed after Fleet's torch.

Twice more Fleet pulled out her talisman to be examined, once by a (non-holographic) griffin, and once by a huge, slobbery three-headed Cerberus guarding a narrow staircase. We had to go down them single file, with Fleet leading and me bringing up the rear.

At first, I worried about meeting someone horrible climbing up or something worse slithering down behind us. Then Changeling started to hum unhappily, and I started worrying about how to deal with a fairy fit on a steep staircase. I was beginning to worry about my legs snapping off at the knees, when we finally stumbled out of the staircase into a long, dark tunnel.

"My legs hurt," Changeling said, her voice flat and dead.

"Nearly there," Fleet said. "See the light?"

I did—a flickering, reddish glow that looked a long way away. It turned out to be another torch rack, set beside yet another massive door. This door was round, made of iron, and had a big wheel in the middle that I thought would take at least three giants to turn.

Fleet parked her torch in the rack and turned to me. The light gilded her coppery cheeks and cast her eyes in shadow. "You sure you want to go through with this? It's not too late to turn back."

Oh, yes it was. "Lead on," I said.

Fleet took hold of the wheel with both hands, spun it to the right, braced herself, and pulled. To my surprise, the massive door whispered smoothly open. Light blazed through it, dazzling my dark-blinded eyes. "Go on," Fleet said in my ear. "I'm right behind you."

Changeling had her hands over her face, so I took hold of her sleeve and, squinting, stepped through the door.

I've accomplished my share of impossible tasks in New York Between, but I can't possibly describe what it was like to see the Dragon of Wall Street for the first time.

"Gigantic" doesn't come close to conveying how big he is. "Humongous" doesn't cut it. There's a legend in New York that the Dragon of Wall Street exists in many different worlds simultaneously. I had never understood how that was possible until then. He was bigger than the Statue of Liberty. He was bigger than the Metropolitan Museum. He lay against the far wall of the Treasury like a knobby mountain, miles and miles away across a floor that glittered like frozen fire.

"We're standing on the Dragon's bed," Fleet told me. "It's gold, of course, tons of it. The stuff on the bottom is very, very old. Legend has it that it's the original hoard he brought with him from the Old Country."

Right. Dragons sleep on gold. And rubies and emeralds and sapphires and diamonds. Even the walkway was made of what looked like silver plates—if the Dragon bothered with anything so ordinary. Probably they were platinum or white gold or elf silver or something even more rare and precious.

Fleet eyed me anxiously. "You're awfully quiet. You don't feel gold-sick or anything, do you?"

"I'm fine. I'm just wondering what we're standing on."

"Old scales," Fleet said. "The Dragon sheds quarterly."

I wiggled my toes. The scales were smooth under my feet, and a little warm.

Changeling hunkered down at the edge of the walkway, plucked a large emerald out of the glittering jumble, examined it, and laid it down. Then she picked up some gold coins and arranged them around the emerald.

Fleet gasped. "Sweet Industrials!" she swore. "We're in trouble now!" She clicked over to Changeling and begged her to leave the hoard alone, in a voice she was obviously trying to keep low and calm. Changeling added two more coins and a small sapphire to her pattern.

Six identical giants materialized around us. They were dressed in blue, and each one carried a club bristling with spikes.

"No playing with the gold," the first one said, his voice like wheels over a loose manhole.

"No looking at the gold," the second added.

"It's best not even to think about it," the third recommended.

The fourth held out his broad, hairy hand, palm up. "Could I see a little identification here?"

Fleet fumbled in her briefcase. "It's cool," she told Giant Four, her voice shaking a little. "I'm an Executive Assistant-in-Training." She pulled out her talisman. "I've got clearance."

While the giants were examining the talisman, I swept Changeling's design back into the hoard. She protested, and I explained that dragons really hate it when other people touch their stuff. She glared at me. "Like your dad and his computer, remember?"

"The jewels are pretty. I think the Dragon should learn to share."

"Who's going to teach him? Never mind, that wasn't

a real question. For what it's worth, Changeling, I think you're right. But you still can't touch anything."

Giant Five handed the talisman back to Fleet, and Giant Six said, "ID seems to be in order. But we gotta search the visitors."

Fleet objected, but it didn't do any good. One after another, the giants searched Satchel. They sniffed at the tickets and unfolded the spidersilk dress. They peered into the Mermaid's Mirror, but all they saw was their own ugly faces. They put everything back and then they searched Fleet's briefcase and looked in our pockets and made us open our mouths so they could peer inside. Changeling told them firmly that she did not like to be touched. There must be different sets of rules for mortals and Folk, because they let her turn her own pockets inside out.

When the giants had satisfied themselves that we weren't carrying any gold or jewels, they lined up around us and marched us along the walkway toward the Dragon.

It was a very long way. We walked and walked and walked some more. Heaps of treasure served as landmarks: so far to that pile of gilded plates and candlesticks, so far to that chest of jewelry. Highlights were a life-sized troll carved from lapis lazuli and a golden elephant with a sapphire-studded house on its back. Fleet kept up a low-voiced, nervous commentary on each treasure as we passed it, but I wasn't really paying attention.

It must have been part of the magic of the Treasury that the Dragon seemed to get smaller as we got closer. By the time we were halfway across the cavern, he looked only as big as, say, the Metropolitan Museum.

I slowed down so I could study him.

His sides were a darker gray than his shed scales, striped in pale silver, with a sheen like heavy silk. His wings draped along his razor-ridged back like folded black fans. His head was something like a horse's and something like an alligator's, with a long toothy muzzle and ruby-lined nostrils big enough for a hippopotamus to stand in. His crossed claws were a dome of immense curved swords. But nothing about him was as impressive as his eyes.

They were as big as the moon, round and pearly gray, with lines of little green numbers endlessly crawling down them. I didn't have the first idea what the numbers meant, but it gave me the creeps to look at them. Fleet had been wrong: The Dragon wasn't blind. He saw the numbers just fine. They were all he saw. Probably, they were all he was interested in seeing.

Fleet elbowed me in the ribs. "Don't stare," she hissed.

"Why? He can't see me."

"He knows anyway. He knows everything. And what he doesn't know, his Executive Assistant tells him. There she is." Fleet's voice was tight with fear. "Up there." She pointed. "DowJones. The Dragon's got a lot of maidens, but she's the one who's really into her job."

I followed Fleet's finger to a square tower built near the Dragon's muzzle. On the top of the tower was a massive bowl that looked like it was made of solid gold. Beside it, a tiny figure was pouring something into the bowl from a large silver pot. A familiar, exciting scent tickled my nose.

"Keep-awake!" I exclaimed. "That's keep-awake charm!"

Fleet gave me a look. "That's coffee, Park girl. It's what the Dragon lives on. Coffee and investors."

I wondered what an investor was. I wondered whether I could catch one and trade it to the Dragon for his magical Scales. Except that he probably didn't need me to catch investors for him. And as for finding his vulnerable spot, who was I kidding?

Fleet poked me in the side. "There are the Dragon's Scales."

The Scales of Wall Street were, to my total astonishment, mortal-sized and very plain: just a brass bar on a stick, with a brass pan hanging from each end. A thing like a pointer in the middle showed when the pans were balanced. I wondered how long it would take Changeling to figure out how it worked.

Changeling, however, wasn't interested in the Scales. As soon as she noticed the Dragon's eyes, she had started her happy hum and stopped watching where she was going. She walked into one of our giant guards and he growled threateningly. She paid no attention. I took her in tow.

When we reached the coffee tower, we stopped and the six giants fell back into a watchful semicircle. Changeling stared up into the Dragon's eyes as if enchanted.

Fleet scanned the scrolling numbers with gloomy interest. "Industrials are down again," she said. "As if I cared."

I guess the Executive Assistant had seen us coming from the tower. As Fleet was speaking, I saw a tall figure in Dragon gray clicking her way across the scales toward us.

Up close, DowJones was as beautiful as Fleet, only in a white-skinned, ice-haired, frost-maiden way. Her cold gray eyes matched the pale stripe in her skirt and jacket. She looked down her elvish nose and asked if she could help us, in a voice that said she'd really rather not.

Fleet's gaze dropped, and her hands tightened on the handle of her briefcase. "Good evening, DowJones," she said nervously. "Might it be possible to have a word with Himself? If he's not busy, I mean."

DowJones lifted a perfectly arched eyebrow. "The Dragon is always busy. May I ask what this is in reference to?"

Fleet looked like she was about to trickle away down among the scales. I started to get mad. Who did Dow-Jones think she was, anyway? The queen of the fairies?

The Green Lady would eat her for breakfast. I stepped in front of her and put my hands on my hips. "Who's asking? And why?"

DowJones raked me with a scornful glance that said I was slightly less important than a sewer rat, then frowned at Fleet over my head. "If this is some kind of joke, Fleet, I'm not amused."

Fleet made a helpless noise.

"Hello?" I said. "I'm talking here. It's not Fleet's business, it's mine. I made her bring me. I'm on a quest."

DowJones's frown came back to me. "If you're here about the Scales, you should be advised that access is restricted to authorized personnel only, under the Dragon's direct supervision." She allowed herself a slight smile. "In other words, little girl, you're out of luck."

Now I was really mad. DowJones had no right to talk to me like that. She wasn't Folk, not even of any kind. I lifted my eyebrow at her, a trick I'd learned from the Pooka. "You know," I said icily, "I'd rather not discuss this with an underling."

This was clearly not how DowJones was used to being talked to. She scowled. "You *are* after the Scales, aren't you?"

Anger fizzed in my veins like coffee. "Wouldn't you like to know?" I sneered. "Are you going to let me talk to the Dragon or not? He may have forever, but I don't. Neither do you, if it comes to that."

Behind me, Fleet gave a cheep like a baby pigeon.

"You haven't told me what this is about yet," Dow-Jones said between her teeth. "Before he talks to you, he's going to want to know what kind of quest, who sent you on it, and why. It's standard operating procedure."

She made it sound like some kind of rule. Perhaps it was. "The Genius of Central Park sent me," I said briskly. "The reason is personal."

DowJones nodded. "Provisionally, I'll accept that. I do have to wonder, though, what connection a fairy changeling has to your request."

Judging from her tone, if I was a sewer rat, Changeling was the stuff floating in the sewer.

"That fairy changeling," I said, "is my magic companion."

DowJones sneered. "It must be a very *important* quest, if it rates such a *powerful* companion. Where did you pick her up? The Lost and Found?"

It was as much the way she said it as what she said, although that was bad enough. Changeling, bewitched by the numbers scrolling down the Dragon's eyes, didn't even hear her.

"You take that back," I said hotly.

DowJones smiled. "Why? Everybody knows that all fairy changelings are only good for taking our places Outside. Their magic is negligible. They grow old. They die. They don't really belong to any world. True Folk hate them.

Mortals don't like them either, but these days, they're too softhearted to get rid of them. It looks to me as if this one's parents managed to send her back. What did they do? Throw her onto a fire? Beat her until she disappeared?"

By this time, I was so mad I actually saw red. My ears rang and my skin tingled. I wanted to hurt DowJones, and I would have, too, if a huge metallic voice hadn't claimed my attention.

"May I ask just what is going on down there, Dow-Jones?" the Dragon asked.

DowJones spun on her high heels, click-clacked to the Dragon's head, and nipped into the domed space under the Dragon's claws. Not wanting her to get the first word in, I took a deep breath, cupped my hands, and yelled, "Hey, Dragon! Want to make a deal?"

There was a pause. "A deal?" the Dragon boomed. "I like a good deal."

"This one's *really* good," I said. "Just wait until you hear it."

"I doubt that. Listen, little girl, I don't have time to go through all that fairy-tale chitchat you questers are so fond of. I'll just cut to the chase.

"You want my Scales. Just like everyone else. And I don't want to give them to you. What can you possibly offer me that would make me change my mind?"

"I'll do an impossible task," I shouted. "Whatever you want. If I succeed, you give me the Scales. If I fail, I go away and don't come back."

"No deal," the Dragon said. "If all I wanted was for you to go away, I could simply eat you. Try again."

"How about a ticket to *Peter Pan*," I said. "With the original Tinkerbell."

A low rumble shook the ground like an earthquake. The Dragon was either amused or irritated. "Surely you have something better than that."

I hesitated. "The Magic Magnifying Mirror of the Mermaid Queen," I admitted. "But I'm supposed to give to the Green Lady."

"Tempting," the Dragon said. "But not quite tempting enough. My Scales are very powerful. They weigh the balance of every commercial transaction across at least three levels of reality. The only thing you could bring to the table that would even tempt me would be something like . . . oh, the air rights to Central Park."

"What?" Fleet and I said it at the same time, only she sounded like she understood what he was talking about.

"Air rights," the Dragon boomed impatiently. "Don't you know anything about business at all? Central Park itself is protected from commercial development, but there's no reason the air above it can't be used for something profitable. A mall, perhaps."

"You're out of your mind," I said. "Build over Central Park? No way. What about the birds and flying Folk? What about the trees? They need a lot of room, you know. Plus sun and fresh air. Choose something else."

"The trees would not be disturbed," the Dragon said

smoothly. "And there would still be plenty of flight room. We'll put it in the contract."

I didn't even have to think about it. "No deal."

"It's entirely up to you, of course," the Dragon said genially. "It's your quest. Maybe I can sweeten the deal for you. I'm a bit of gambler, you see—it's my great weakness. There's a little task I've got in mind. I'm willing to stake my Scales against the Central Park air rights that you can't complete it."

I didn't need a Folk lore expert to tell me that I'd lose this bet. The Dragon of Wall Street may be a gambler, but he's not stupid. "No," I said.

"It's not a complicated task."

I wondered what a dragon considered simple. "What is it?"

"Telling you beforehand is not standard operating procedure, but I appreciate that you can't make an informed decision if you don't have all the data. Here it is: very simple, really. I want you to make the Bull cry and the Bear laugh."

I almost laughed myself. The Dragon of Wall Street might be the biggest and most powerful Genius in New York, but he sure didn't know much about Folk lore. His task was nothing but a variant of a common fairy-tale plot. Usually it was a princess you had to make laugh or cry, depending on what kind of spell she was under. If she couldn't laugh, you made a total fool of yourself; if she couldn't cry, you shoved a chopped onion under her nose.

Then she'd laugh or cry, her father would give you her hand in marriage and half his kingdom, and everyone would live happily ever after.

If it worked on a princess, why not a bull and a bear?

"Okay," I said, pretending reluctance. "It's a deal. Your Scales against the Central Park air rights that I can't make the Bull cry and the Bear laugh."

"Done," said the Dragon. His voice boomed through the Treasury like thunder. "DowJones, set this young lady up for an appointment with the Bull and the Bear. Tomorrow evening's relatively clear. I leave the matter of a reward for Fleet's remarkably independent thinking up to you. Polishing coins? Cleaning the coffeemaker in perpetuity? I'm sure you'll think of something appropriate."

CHAPTER
21

WHEN YOU THINK YOU'RE THE COCK OF THE WALK, YOU'RE
PROBABLY ABOUT TO FIND OUT YOU'RE JUST FRIED CHICKEN.

Neef's Rules for Changelings

Fleet had a total hissy. All the way back to Maiden
Lane, I got to hear about how everything was a disaster, how her life was ruined, and how it was *all my fault*.

"If you hadn't pestered me into taking you to the
Dragon," she said as the three of us got out of the elevator
at her apartment, "everything would have been fine."

"Right, like you were having such a nice life before."

Fleet unlocked the door, kicked her high heels across
the room, ripped the tie from her braids, took off her
jacket, and collapsed onto the sofa. "Do you have any
idea how gross that coffeemaker gets?" she wailed. "I
don't know why I listened to you!"

"Because I promised we'd rescue you," I said, settling
into the easy chair. "Don't be such a stick-in-the-mud. I've
got a shot at winning this bet. I'm on a quest, remember?

When's the last time you heard a fairy tale where the hero messed up a quest?"

"I don't know," she said. "The only fairy tales my god-mother told me were the ones with lots of gold in them, like 'Rumplestiltskin.'"

"Trust me, I know this stuff," I said. "I'm an only child *and* a foundling. That's at least as good as being a poor widow's son. Anyway, I'll do my best. Now quit moaning and tell me all about the Bull and the Bear."

Fleet groaned. "You don't know? What kind of fairy godmother did you have anyway?"

"A giant white rat," I said.

"Well, *that* explains a lot."

"Astris is the best Folklorist in New York Between!" I said hotly.

"I'm sure you know every traditional fairy tale in the book. But the Bull and the Bear are Modern Urban Folk lore, which is different. The Bull is like all the optimists in the universe rolled into one. He thinks everything is wonderful and can only get better. He plunges into things without thinking about the consequences or who might get hurt. Kind of like you, Neef."

I decided to ignore her dig. "What does he do when something really bad happens?"

"He morphs into the Bear."

"He what?"

"You deaf or something? When things get tough, the Bull turns into the Bear. The Bear—"

"Let me guess," I interrupted. "The Bear believes everything is terrible and can only get worse. He thinks too much and never takes risks. Like you," I couldn't help adding.

"Jerk," Fleet said, and covered her face with her hands. The tiny braids fell forward like a black curtain. "We're doomed."

Changeling, who had gone back to her self-imposed task of organizing Fleet's books, stopped and looked at her. "What is wrong with Fleet?"

"She's a bear," I said.

"I thought she was a mortal changeling, like you."

"Well, she's *like* a bear, then." I turned to Fleet. "Cheer up. Don't you know that things always look worst right before the happy ending? Don't you know there's no such thing as a totally impossible task?"

Fleet lifted her head and glared at me. "Don't you know that real life isn't like a fairy tale?"

"Hello," I said. "Dragons? Giants? Maidens in doorless towers? In New York Between, fairy tales *are* real life."

"Not on Wall Street, they're not," Fleet said stubbornly. "Wall Street is all about deals and markets and gold. Wall Street is about power."

"So is 'Jack and the Extension Ladder.'"

Changeling said, "Sometimes Mom says Strumble is laughing, but Dad says she is just anthropomorphizing."

Fleet looked at me. "What did she just say?"

I shrugged. "Strumble is Changeling's dog, that's all I know."

"'Anthropomorphize,'" Changeling explained patiently, "is from the Greek. 'Anthropos' means 'man, human being.' 'Morphosis' means 'giving shape to.' 'Anthropomorphize' is when you treat something that is not human as if it were."

"I think she's telling us that Outside animals don't laugh," I told Fleet. "Which is totally beside the point, because we're not Outside. I've seen Astris laugh—the Pooka, too, even when he's being a dog or a horse."

Fleet shook her braids gloomily. "So they laugh. Big deal. Have you ever seen a supernatural cry?"

"Banshees!" I said triumphantly. "Listen to me, Fleet. I may not know anything about brokers and investors, but I know this is going to work. Making things cry is easy. All we need is an onion and a handkerchief."

"Just shut up for a minute and let me think." Fleet started to worry her thumbnail with her teeth.

Changeling put the last book in place, got up and took the Mirror out of Satchel, and carried it back to her corner.

"Okay," said Fleet. "If this works, I'll be out of here; if it doesn't, I'm already cleaning the coffeemaker for life. I suppose he could eat me, but at this point, I don't care. We can buy an onion on Canal, and a handkerchief, too. I'm not letting you stink up one of mine."

I grinned at her. "You're a princess, Fleet," I said. "I'm sorry I called you a bear. Come on, Changeling. We're going back to Chinatown."

Changeling, absorbed in the Mirror, said, "I need more data. It is possible that the Bull lacks tear ducts."

Fleet and I left her to it and went to Canal alone.

Now that we had a plan, Fleet was totally bullish. It was the end of the morning Rush Hour, and the streets were clogged with gold-blind brokers and investors. Fleet taught me this game the younger Wall Street changelings liked, where you had to zigzag through a crowd of brokers as fast as you could. Of course, I kept bumping into Folk, which made them roar and take blind swipes at the ground. Mostly they hit another broker; sometimes they came pretty close to taking my head off. But they didn't catch me, and by the time Fleet and I got to Chinatown, all sweaty and laughing, we were friends.

Our first order of business, as Fleet said, was to find the largest and stinkiest onion in Chinatown. At the third food stand we went to, we found one that made my eyes water from about three feet away. The shinseën shopkeeper wrapped it in some newspaper, gave it to me, smiled, and held out his hand. I smiled back and shook the hand and thanked him for his generosity in my best Mandarin.

This was not the right thing to do. The shinseën jerked his hand away and launched into a long and violent speech about round-eyed tricksters and onion thieves, while Fleet laughed helplessly.

"How do you pay for things in the Park?" Fleet asked when she'd paid him for the onion. "Enchanted leaves and dog poop?"

"Pay for things? You mean with money? We don't. We trade."

Fleet shook her head. "Are you telling me you've never been shopping?"

"What's that?"

For some reason, this made her give me a hug. "Neef girl, shopping is the most fun you can have without magic. Come on, I'll show you."

Shopping turned out to be a little like questing, only safer. Instead of trading for things with fresh meat or favors or songs or magic talismans, Fleet gave the shop-keepers silver coins out of a magic purse. It seemed to work kind of like Satchel, only Fleet said that it would give her only so many coins a day. She called it Budget, and grumbled a lot about how small it was.

Budget seemed pretty generous to me. Besides the onion, it bought us a red silk handkerchief with mysterious-looking signs on it, some poison-green mesh slippers decorated with sparkly flowers, some buns with red bean paste in the middle, and, most wonderful of all, the jade frog with ruby eyes that had winked at me. The shop-keeper knocked down the price when I told him how I'd seen it the day before, and threaded it on a black silk cord so I could hang it around my neck. We also bought four silver hair clips, two for Changeling and two for me.

While we shopped, Fleet talked. She told me about the mortal changelings she knew and how they all hung out at a café called the Wannabe in Midtown, when they were off duty, and traded gossip about the Folk.

"I know mortal changelings from Midtown and the Village and the Upper West Side and even Park Avenue," she said. "But none from Central Park. None of my friends has ever met a Park changeling. I didn't know there were any."

"There's only one at a time," I said. "Usually they get eaten by the Wild Hunt. I managed to escape them, but the Lady got mad and threw me out. I can't go back until I get all this stuff for her."

"It doesn't sound like a lot of fun," Fleet said. "Why do you want to go back?"

"It's home."

"So's my apartment in Maiden Lane," Fleet said. "But I know if I get out of Wall Street—I mean really out, not just on a field trip—I'm not ever coming back."

"It's not the same. You hate Wall Street. I love Central Park. It's not all bright lights and bustle like Broadway or Chinatown, but there's plenty going on. The Folk are fun to be around, mostly, and I've got some good friends."

"Friends!" Fleet rolled her eyes. "I don't believe you,

Park girl. Changelings don't make friends with Folk. They love them, they hate them, they go on dates and get their hearts broken. But they don't hang out."

This sounded very weird to me, but I didn't feel like arguing. "If you say so." I took another bite out of the red bean bun we'd been sharing. "Speaking of places to live, where are you going to go when I've rescued you from the Dragon?"

Fleet snatched the last bit of bun out of my hand. "Someplace where nobody expects me to keep track of appointments and make coffee, that's where. Somewhere I can learn to be an artist. I was thinking the Village— there are lots of artists there. But it's awfully close to the Maze." She sighed and popped the soft dough into her mouth.

"What about the Metropolitan Museum?" I asked.

"I'd do anything to live there," she said passionately. "But they don't take changelings either, or at least that's what I heard."

I didn't know what the Curator's policy on changelings was. As far as I knew, I was the only mortal regular at the Museum, but that didn't mean anything. "Maybe he just forgot to ask for one. The Old Market Woman told me he's horribly absentminded."

Fleet turned to me, her deep brown eyes aglow. "You know the Old Market Woman? Personally?"

"Sure. She teaches me classical languages."

"Wow. She was the docent I got for my field trip to the Museum. I thought she was awesome. Scary, but cool, you know what I mean?"

I didn't. The Old Market Woman was my teacher and my friend, and I'd never thought of her as either scary or particularly cool. But I nodded anyway.

"Do you know Rembrandt's *Self-Portrait*?" she asked shyly.

I did, and she asked me excited questions about it all the way through the Financial Maze. It felt good to be talking about the Museum. The fact that Fleet was jealous of the time I spent there didn't hurt either.

"I wasn't kidding," she said as we approached the tower's invisible door. "I'd do *anything* to be able to live there."

"Help me get through this thing with the Bull and the Bear, and I'll see what I can do."

Up in the apartment, Changeling was still where we'd left her, muttering over the Mirror. Fleet put on her green sparkly slippers and got a cup of tea from Microwave. "I'm pooped," she said. "Wake me if she turns up something useful."

She disappeared into an inner room and closed the door.

I sat down, I got up. I unpacked Satchel. I found a knife and chopped the onion and wrapped it in the handkerchief, I scrubbed my stinky hands with soap, I paced around Fleet's piles of papers, I stroked my jade frog. I thought about how I could make the Bear laugh.

The fact that it was his nature to be gloomy wasn't such a big deal: Kelpies are gloomy, and they laugh—mostly when they're trying to drown somebody. Almost any supernatural will laugh when a mortal falls down, and if the mortal rips their pants or breaks an arm, that's even funnier. I considered tripping Changeling or Fleet, but not for long. I was the hero of this quest—making a fool of myself was *my* job.

I was wondering if Satchel would give me a banana with the peel still on it when Changeling snapped out of her Mirror trance. "I have data," she announced.

"Great. Hang on a minute, so I can call Fleet. She needs to hear this, too."

Waking Fleet almost counted as an extra impossible task, and when she was finally awake, she wasn't exactly happy about it. She was even unhappier when Changeling made her report.

"According to WallStreetLore.nyb, the Bull and the Bear are mutually exclusive," Changeling told us from her nest by the bookcase. "They cannot exist in the same reality. The Bull's reality is all hope, and the Bear's reality is all despair. The Bull cannot cry without becoming the Bear. The Bear cannot laugh without becoming the Bull."

"Impossible," Fleet said bearishly. "I knew it. Can I go back to bed now?"

Changeling and I both glared at her. "Do not interrupt me," Changeling said. "On Magicanimals.nyb, I read that the Brahmin Bulls of East Sixth Street are known to weep whenever a cockroach is exterminated, indicating that some mythical Bulls do indeed have tear ducts. If the Wall Street Bull is similarly equipped, and if the trigger for its transformation into the Bear is genuine grief rather than simple lachrymation, your onion may very well make the Bull weep without calling up the Bear."

"See?" I asked Fleet. "I told you. Changeling, you rock. Now, what's up with the Bear?"

"I thought you might apply nitrous oxide, on the same principle."

Fleet clutched at her braids. "What is she *talking* about?"

Changeling scowled at her. "It is very rude of you to speak about me as if I were not here. Nitrous oxide is a gas used for anesthetic purposes, most commonly by dentists. It causes euphoria and disinhibition. In other words, laughter. Or at least, the appearance of laughter."

"Perfect!" I said. "Where can we get some?"

"I have failed to find a reference to it anywhere online," Changeling said. "I have therefore concluded that nitrous oxide is unknown in New York Between."

I was disappointed, but Fleet pitched something very close to a fairy fit. We had to listen to a lot of ranting before she calmed down enough to listen to my idea about taking a fall and maybe splitting my jeans.

"That's not funny," she said. "Now DowJones falling

off her high heels and splitting her skirt—*that* would be funny."

Changeling agreed, or at least she laughed for the first time since I'd met her. Fleet and I agreed that Changeling laughing was a good sign and settled down with the rest of the buns to plan.

The best idea—it was Fleet's—was to push DowJones over backwards into the Dragon's coffee bowl, but we couldn't figure out how we could get her to take one of us up on the tower with her. For maximum effect, we should time it for when DowJones was carrying the coffeepot. Just talking about it made Fleet and Changeling laugh so hard they cried. I hoped the Bear shared their sense of humor.

Still chuckling, Fleet went back to bed. Changeling curled up by her beloved bookcase with some cushions. I lay on the sofa and tried not to think of all the things that could go wrong. Eventually I fell asleep and dreamed of giants and the Wild Hunt and the Dragon piling gold over Central Park. I was almost glad when Fleet woke me and said I just had time for a shower and breakfast before our appointment with the Dragon.

I'd never had a shower before. It was like being out in a heavy rain, only hot. I liked Honey's bath better. For breakfast, Satchel produced some eggs, and Microwave gave us a warm, sweet, gooey thing called a cheese Danish. Changeling liked it. I was too nervous to eat it, or the eggs either.

After breakfast, Fleet fussed over our clothes. We needed to look professional. Changeling absolutely refused to give up her embroidered jacket or her shabby sandals. She did let Fleet smear her hair with some sticky stuff and pin it back with two of the silver clips we'd bought in Chinatown, but only after Fleet had done mine first.

When we were ready, we stood side by side in front of the bedroom mirror. I thought the black jacket Fleet had lent me made me look taller than Changeling, more DowJones-like. I tried arching my eyebrows and looking down my nose.

"Don't do that, Neef," Fleet said. "And let Changeling carry Satchel. People think you're important if someone else is carrying your stuff. I can't believe I forgot to buy you shoes yesterday, but I guess it's too late. Okay, let's go. We don't want to keep the Dragon waiting."

Park Folk aren't exactly into time. There's daytime and nighttime, Solstice and Equinox, summer and winter. Wall Street Folk, on the other hand, are all about clocks and appointments, and they expect everybody to pay strict attention to them.

Everybody except the Dragon.

After we'd practically killed ourselves getting to the Treasury in time for our appointment, the Dragon made us stand around waiting for just about forever. We weren't the only ones, either. A bunch of security giants and some worried-looking dwarves and a couple of kobolds were gathered at the base of the coffee tower, along with a handful of mortal changelings in Dragon-gray suits who were probably the other Executive Assistants. They were all beautiful and grim and icy, and their mouths twisted into little sneers when they saw us.

Changeling passed the time by watching the Dragon's eyes. Fleet bit her nails. I thought about how hard it was going to be to trip anyone as on the ball as DowJones. Maybe I should just go back to Plan A and do the falling part myself. Taking a dive into the coffee bowl should be good for a laugh. If I could get up to it.

The dwarves went into the dome of the Dragon's claws and came out again, looking more worried than before. The kobolds went next and didn't return. I was ready to jump out of my skin. Finally DowJones clicked over to us, looking even snottier than she had the day before. "The Dragon will speak to you now."

She escorted us to the other side of the coffee tower, near the Dragon's claws, but not in them, which was just fine with me.

"Glad you could make it," the Dragon boomed, sounding horribly cheerful. "I hope you don't mind if we skip the chitchat. I want to put this matter to rest so everybody can get back to work."

This was it. I swallowed. "That's cool with me," I said. "When do we start?"

Sudden as a lightning strike, a huge white Bull materialized on the surface of the Dragon's hoard.

The Bull of Wall Street was medium huge, say about the size of the Central Park Dairy, and blindingly bright. His hooves and horns were paved with diamonds and his eyes were twin diamonds as big as dinner plates. A bull's mouth isn't really made to smile, but he was doing his level best. The result was both goofy and terrifying.

"So that's the Bull," I said. "Cheerful, isn't he? I suppose I have the usual three chances?"

"The number of chances was not addressed in our negotiations," the Dragon said smoothly. "Time is gold, and I've already wasted enough on this nonsense. You get one chance. Take it or leave it."

I wanted to argue with him, but I didn't dare. There's moxie and there's suicide. I turned to Changeling. "The Talisman of Perfect Sorrow, please," I said grandly.

Changeling pulled a red silk package from Satchel and gave it to me. The stink of chopped onion attacked my eyes and nose. Blinking and sniffling, I stepped out onto the hoard. Coins and jewels slid under my bare feet as I walked toward the Bull, the Talisman of Perfect Sorrow balanced on the flat of my hand. When I was close enough, I lifted it toward the Bull's huge, glittering nostrils.

The onion's effect was immediate and dramatic. First the Bull snorted so hard that I flew backwards and landed sprawling at Fleet's feet. The security giants laughed and pointed. I levered myself up and watched the Bull stamping and tossing his head and bellowing. His horns and eyes flashed. Coins and cast-off scales fountained from his hooves. No tears, though, not even a scattering of tearlike diamonds.

"Well," said the Dragon. "It's been nice doing business with you. DowJones will draw up the papers for the Central Park air rights. You can take them to the Lady when you go. On second thought, perhaps DowJones should accompany you and supervise the transaction herself, in case the Lady has any . . . questions."

My heart settled somewhere around the bottom of my stomach. My throat closed up, my chin trembled, my eyes got hot and prickly, and something started jumping up and down in my middle.

I hadn't cried—full-out, openmouthed, nose-running sobbing—in so long it took me a while to realize what was going on. I tried to stop, but I couldn't. I couldn't even stay on my feet.

The thing about a total meltdown is that you don't think about much while you're having it. The world could be coming to an end around you, and you wouldn't even notice. Eventually, however, you stop crying.

When I'd calmed down, I realized that the Treasury had gotten very noisy. The loudest noises I'd heard there before (except for the Dragon's voice) were the clink of gold and the tap of high heels against the scaly walkway. Now my ears rang with howls and screams and deep, breathy hoots. Plus, the air stank, even to my tear-clogged nose, of rotten eggs.

I lifted my head and opened my swollen eyes straight into the depths of a huge scarlet cavern ringed with long, wicked teeth. A hot wind fanned my hair and caught sulfurously in the back of my throat.

The Dragon was laughing.

I sat up and looked around. Down at the foot of the coffee tower, all the Wall Street Folk were holding their sides and leaning against one another or rolling on the ground, helpless with laughter. The Executive Assistants were nowhere in sight. Out on the hoard, where the Bull had been standing, I saw a complicated blur of dark and bright that made my head spin.

I got to my feet and stumbled over to Fleet, who was kneeling with both hands over her face, trembling like a fairy's wings.

"Fleet? It's me, Fleet. Are you okay?"

Fleet lifted her face, ashy with fear. She stared at me wildly, then over my shoulder at the complicated blur. "Will you look at that!" she exclaimed. "You did it, Neef! The Bull and the Bear are laughing and crying at the same time!"

I nearly collapsed again, this time with relief. "Are you sure?"

"Pretty sure," she said. "They're turning into each other so fast I can't actually tell who's doing what."

I stared hard at the blur that was them both. "What you mean is, they're both laughing so hard they're crying. Does that count?"

She looked thoughtful. "Maybe so. But the Bear is laughing, and water is coming out of the Bull's eyes. It's a technicality, but I still think you win."

"Great," I said. "Let's just get the Scales and get out of here."

Fleet shook her head until her ponytail flew. "Bad idea. What if we can't carry them? What if Himself sends giants after us to get them back? Can't we just make a run for it and hope he decides it would be a waste of resources to have us followed?"

With victory in sight, I felt like Super Changeling again. Part of me knew I should reassure Fleet and find Changeling and plan how we were going to get the Scales home. The rest of me didn't care. "No way. I won those Scales fair and square, and I'm taking them. Are you going to help me or not?"

She shot a terrified look at the guffawing Dragon. "I'll help, I guess. But we have to hurry."

I ran toward the Scales just as if I thought I was going to snatch them up as easily as Carlyle had snatched me, and carry them triumphantly out of the Treasury.

DowJones emerged from behind the Scales, brandishing the heavy silver coffeepot in both hands. I skidded to a halt.

"Get out of my way, DowJones," I panted. "I did what the Dragon asked. I made the Bear laugh and the Bull cry. The Scales are mine, fair and square."

"No, they aren't," DowJones said grimly. "The Dragon would say you rendered the deal null and void by exceeding the terms of your bargain. In other words, it took you two tries to succeed, and he only gave you one. If I were you, I'd cut my losses and run."

"What about me?" Fleet wailed, stumbling up behind me. "After this stunt, he's going to have me for breakfast."

"You'd better go with her then, hadn't you?" Dow-Jones lowered the coffeepot. "You're not going to believe this, Fleet, but I'm not your enemy. I feel sorry for you. All the Executive Assistants do. You're completely unsuited to this job. It's not entirely your fault; the Bureau of Changeling Affairs made a bad call. It happens." She sighed. "I'll tell the Dragon that the Bull trampled the three of you to a bloody pulp. He won't care, as long as the Scales are still here."

"What about the Central Park air rights?" I cried.

"I don't know. Nobody's signed anything. The contract's not even drawn up. I may be able to convince him the deal's a no-go."

Fleet and I looked at each other. The storm of supernatural laughter was beginning to subside. We didn't have much time. I knew we didn't really have a choice, but I didn't want to leave with my quest unfinished.

I started to say something, I don't know exactly what, but Fleet interrupted me. "Is anybody going to stop us?"

"Not if you get out of here before Himself sobers up," DowJones said.

"We have to get Changeling!" I cried.

Luckily, she hadn't gone far. Fleet found her by the coffee tower, doing her flowered turtle impersonation, with Satchel clutched tight in her arms. She poked and prodded her to her feet, and then the three of us ran through a narrow gap in the Treasury Wall and down a tiled corridor toward the familiar rumble of the Betweenways.

CHAPTER
22

In the end, it was Changeling who got us back to the Metropolitan Museum. Fleet didn't know where we were going, and I didn't care. When we reached the Betweenways station, I folded up on the platform and put my head in my arms. I could hear Fleet and Changeling talking, but it was like listening to some made-up language. I wished I could turn into something peaceful, like a rock, or go to sleep for a hundred years, like the Sleeping Debutante.

Instead, Fleet grabbed my elbow and hauled me onto the Betweenway. It was like a mirror image of my first trip, where Changeling was totally freaked out and I was—well, calmer than she was, anyway. This struck me as funny, so I laughed and then I cried, around and around like the Bull and the Bear.

When we got off the Betweenway at the Metropolitan

Museum, the Old Market Woman and Bastet were waiting for us.

"The Head of Apollo prophesied that you'd be arriving,"
said the Old Market Woman.

"You look like somebody's been trying to sacrifice
you," said Bastet. "I want to hear all about it."

"Tough," I said. "I'm not in the mood for stories." And
I ran for the Tomb of Perneb, where I could be miserable
in peace.

I guess funerary friezes are used to weeping mortals;
I must have cried gallons of tears, and they never cracked
a smile. Like some stupid eldest brother, I'd flunked
my quest. I couldn't go back to the Park. Since I hadn't
been eaten by the Dragon, neither could the Pooka. And
Changeling couldn't go home. Oh, and I might have lost
Central Park's air rights to the Dragon of Wall Street. My
life was ruined and so was everybody else's and it was *all
my fault*.

Eventually I must have gone to sleep, because I woke
up feeling like I'd been wrestling a wind sprite, and my
face was stiff with dried tears. An apple and a piece of
cheese had appeared beside me, along with a pitcher of
water and my favorite pale green Chinese bowl. I was too
depressed to be hungry, but I drank half the water and
poured the rest into the bowl so I could wash my face.

When I came out of the temple, Bastet was sitting
with her back to me and her bronze tail wrapped primly
around her paws.

"Mew," I said pathetically.

She sneezed in an amused way. "You need to work on your accent," she said severely. "You just gave a kitten call, which is insulting in more ways than I can tell you. Nonetheless, I'm glad you survived your quest. So is the Curator."

"Thanks." I sat down beside her and hugged my knees to my chest. I wondered how the Curator was going to react when he found out that Fleet wanted to become the Museum's official changeling. I wondered if he'd let me live here, too. And Changeling, of course. I wondered what the Pooka would do. My eyes went hot again.

Bastet butted me with her hard bronze head. "That's enough of that," she said. "They're waiting for you."

I scrubbed both hands over my face, hard, and then I got up and followed Bastet out of the Egyptian Wing into the Great Hall.

I wasn't surprised to see the Green Lady hanging out by the Museum Shop, looking at postcards. The Curator had probably sent for her as soon as I got back. She turned when she heard Bastet's bronze feet clicking on the marble floor and planted her green hands on her hips.

Today she was wearing a leafy minidress, and her dreadlocks were stuck with roses. She gave me a disdainful once-over. "If it's not the great hero, home from her big quest. Whassamatter, kid? Ain't you glad to see me?"

I curtsied. "I'm always glad to see you, my Lady Genius of Central Park." Oddly enough, I really meant this. I loved Central Park, after all. Maddening as she was, the Green Lady was Central Park. So I loved her, too.

"Where's my loot?" she said.

Bastet clicked forward. "Neef has been on a quest," she said severely, "not a shopping spree. She'll present the talismans she's collected in the presence of the Genius who witnessed the original bargain."

The Lady's hair gave an irritated twitch. "I want it *now*."

"Then you'd better hurry," Bastet said, and trotted off toward Ancient Greek Sculpture.

Following Bastet and the Lady, I knew for the first time since I started this adventure just what was going to happen next. It was kind of comforting to know that I'd come to the last chapter, that there was nothing I could do or say to change the way things were. The story would end, and somebody would live happily ever after, because that's the way stories in New York Between always end. It just wouldn't be me.

We stepped through the door into the Fountain Court. The cheerful bronze boys raised their pipes to their lips and blew a shrill fanfare.

The Curator had dressed up for the occasion with a red bow tie and a matching handkerchief. He'd pushed his glasses onto his forehead and forgotten them, but with the Assyrian Lion and the Minoan Priestess flanking him, he looked impressive anyway. The other docents and guards were ranged behind them. On one side, I saw an unfamiliar Egyptian princess in a pleated white gown and a hollow-cheeked man in black. Then the Egyptian princess waved at me and I recognized Fleet. The hollow-cheeked man, I realized, was the Pooka.

"Hi," I said weakly.

The Pooka stepped forward and opened his mouth.

"Enjoying your visit to the museum?" The Green Lady's voice was poison sweet. The Pooka shut his mouth, bowed, and stepped back again. The Lady turned to the Curator and gave him a little nod.

"Green Lady of the Parks," he said formally. "Are you prepared to keep your bargain?"

"I am if she is."

"Hero," said the Curator. "Present the magical talismans."

There was an awful moment where everybody was looking at me and I was wondering where Changeling was with Satchel and whether I was going to have to excuse myself to go look for her, and what an anticlimax *that* would be. Then I heard the leathery slap of sandals and turned to see the Old Market Woman herding Changeling into the Fountain Court.

Changeling's hair was springing out of her hair clips, her shirt was untucked, and the flowers on her jacket were hairy with loose threads. But her head was up and her mouth was firm.

I was very glad to see her.

The Lady, however, was not. As soon as Changeling came into the room, the Lady's hair came alive in a tangle of hissing snakes. The docents, who were a pretty tough bunch, weren't fazed, but Fleet put her hands over her ears, and the bronze dolphins dove for the bottom of the pool. The Pooka covered his eyes with one long hand and shook his head. Changeling gave a startled yelp, then retreated into her flowery jacket and shut down.

The Curator beckoned to the Minoan Priestess, who rustled purposefully toward the Lady, her snakes held high. The roses settled back into the Lady's hair.

"Don't get your ruffles in a twist, pipsqueak," the Lady snapped. "I'm not going to turn into anything. I'm just going to take care of that changeling over there."

The Lady turned to Changeling, forefinger cocked. Without thinking, I jumped between them. "Oh, no you don't," I said.

"Butt out, kid," the Lady snarled. "I have to get rid of it."

"Why?"

"It doesn't belong here, that's why. It's a changeling. I made it for the Bureau of Changeling Affairs so they'd have something to leave in your place. If you're here, it has to be there, or nowhere. I'm voting for nowhere." She grinned toothily at me. "Unless you'd rather go Outside and let it take your place with the Hunt."

Now it was my turn to get mad. "What's your problem with Changeling, anyway? She's a lot more fairy than I am. She can do all kinds of magic stuff. She can see things I can't, she can remember anything, she can fix stuff even a Computer Wizard can't fix."

"See now, that's *just* what I'm talking about," the Green Lady said. "Who ever heard of a Park fairy who could fix computers? She's different. She might change things. Change is dangerous. She's got to go."

"Fine," I said. "Send her back Outside, then. Once she's safely home, I'll give you your loot, and everybody will be happy."

The Green Lady bared her teeth in an unfriendly smile. "Loot first," she said.

I turned to Changeling and lifted Satchel off her shoulder, being careful not to touch her. There's nothing like a good blast of fury to kick the mind into gear. I hadn't failed *completely*, after all. I had the Mermaid's Mirror and the ticket to *Peter Pan*. With luck and a little fast talking, I could probably salvage some kind of happy ending out of this mess. Maybe the Pooka could go back to the Park even if I couldn't. Fleet was right: I could live anywhere. All I needed was friends, and I had made enough new ones to know I could make more.

I opened Satchel, pulled out the Mermaid's Mirror, and flourished it. "Behold the Magical Magnifying Mirror of the Mermaid Queen!"

The Green Lady made an unladylike grab for it. "Gimme."

I pulled it out of reach. "In return for the Mirror, I get to stay in New York Between, right?"

"That was the deal," she agreed. "Hand it over."

I gave the Lady the Mirror. She looped the golden chain around her neck and clasped her hands over the silvery disk in a gesture that made me think of the Dragon.

"Next."

I reached into Satchel, picked one of the tickets out of the envelope, and held it up. My hand shook a little.

"One orchestra ticket to *Peter Pan*," I said.

"In return for the freedom of the Park," the Lady said. "Give."

I took a deep breath. "I want to change the deal. In exchange for the ticket, I want you to let the Pooka go back to the Park."

You'd think I'd broken another geas.

"You can't pull the old bait and switch on me!" the Lady screeched.

The Curator held up his hand. "Stop! Stop, both of you. Neef, you can't just go around renegotiating your bargains like that. It just isn't done."

When the Curator says a thing isn't done, he means it. The Lady held out her hand; reluctantly I laid the shimmering disk in it. She checked it over, then narrowed her eyes at me. "With the original Tinkerbell?"

"Yes," I said wearily.

She tucked the ticket away in the neck of her leafy dress. "Best for last," she said. "The Scales of the Dragon of Wall Street."

Everybody leaned forward: the docents, the guards, the Pooka, the dolphins and the cheerful boys, even the Curator was waiting for me to pull this one last rabbit out of my hat.

I took a deep breath. "I don't have them," I said, then went on, very fast. "I do have another ticket for *Peter Pan*. You can have it if you want, but you have to let the Pooka back into the Park."

The Lady's smug little half-moon smile flopped into a snarl. "What?"

"I didn't get the Dragon's Scales. I understand that means you won't restore your protection, so I can't live in the Park anymore. That's okay. It's a big city. I can find another place to live. It won't be as nice as the Park, but I think I'll be able to—"

My words trickled to a stop; the Lady was shaking her head gently. "You don't get it, do you?" she said. "You promise me the Dragon's Scales, you gotta get me the Dragon's Scales, or die trying. You want me to look like a fool?"

There was something about her soft, cold voice that made my mouth go all cottony and my stomach try to fold itself up and disappear.

The Curator cleared his throat. "If I may just remind you, Madame, you cannot take back the boons your hero has already won." The Lady glared at him. "It's just not done," he said firmly.

They glared at each other. The air crackled, and the docents shifted uneasily. Someone tugged at my jacket. I turned around to see Changeling frowning at me.

"Satchel," Changeling said.

I don't know how Satchel works. It doesn't get heavier when I put things in it, and sometimes they're not there next time I look. Besides mortal food, sometimes it produces handkerchiefs and gloves when it thinks I need them. I didn't have any control over it at all. But maybe Changeling did.

I put Satchel in her hands. She lifted the flap and started to rummage inside.

Hope sprang in my chest. It hurt.

Changeling pulled out two familiar-looking iridescent plates. They were roughly fan-shaped and silvery gray, with pale narrow stripes and a sheen like heavy silk.

"Dragon scales," Changeling announced, holding them out triumphantly.

The Lady stared at Changeling with her jaw around her collarbone and her hair lank with shock.

"There you are, Lady," I said. "The Dragon's scales, just as I promised."

The Lady recovered herself. "No way, José," she said briskly. "Those bits of shed horn aren't what I meant, and you know it."

"Madame, you try my patience," the Curator said.

"Those bits of shed horn may not be what you meant, but they are exactly what you asked for."

Thank you, Curator, I thought, but the Lady waved a dismissive hand. "Nuts to that. They're not the same thing at all. In the first place, they're just a couple of pin-striped castoffs. In the second place, they're not good for anything."

"I wouldn't be so sure of that," the Curator said. "You may remember that the teeth of even ordinary dragons are very powerful indeed. The scales of the Dragon of Wall Street are bound to have extraordinary virtue."

"Fuggedaboudit," the Lady said. "The deal's off."

Changeling's mouth settled into a grim line. "That is wrong," she said.

For the second—no, third time, all eyes were on Changeling, but she didn't seem to notice. "The Lady promised to place Neef under her protection in exchange for the Dragon's scales. Neef has kept her promise. If the Lady fails to keep hers, she will be in clear violation of her own rules. And that would be *wrong*."

There was an air-shivering moment when I thought that the Green Lady was going to go totally snaky. Her eyes started to whirl and her dreads lifted and twined, scattering roses everywhere. Then she put her hands over her whirling eyes and took a huge breath. When she lowered her hands, she'd shrunk noticeably and her nails and teeth had lost their Wild Hunt pointiness.

"Uncle," she said. "I give up. You win. On a technicality,

but you win. Give me the scales. I'll take Neef under my protection again. And the Pooka can come back to the Park. The quest is accomplished."

I took the scales from Changeling and gave them to the Lady. With too much to feel at once, I felt pretty much nothing.

The Pooka bounded over to me and whacked me on the back, mouth in a triumphant V.

"I knew you'd do it," he crowed. "I thought I'd die of laughing when the changeling pulled out those scales, the creature. 'The Dragon's scales' indeed! She's the wonder of the world."

"She's pretty cool," I agreed, and then, when I got a better look at him: "Oh, Pooka! You look terrible!"

"I'll thank you to be keeping a civil tongue in your head," he said huffily. But he didn't deny it. He was as white as Carrera marble, and his eyes glittered as if he had a fever. Even his flying eyebrows seemed to have landed. He looked like a trickster who had been in a museum for three days without playing a single prank on anyone.

"A tiny bout of mischief, and I'll be right as rain again," he said. "But it was all worth it, eh? At least we can go home."

"Right," I said, but somehow I wasn't as happy and excited about it as I should have been.

"Can I go home now?" Changeling asked.

"No," said the Green Lady. "The Wild Hunt's going to

give me no end of grief over losing Neef here. I'll just cut my losses and give them the ringer instead."

Now I felt something. Fury. "You can't do that!" I cried. "You promised to send her home!"

"I did not—you just hoped I did. Besides, I made her. I can do anything I like with her."

I looked at the Pooka, who shrugged. I whirled around to the Old Market Woman, who lowered her eyes. I turned to the Curator, who said, "She is within her rights, Neef. When you think about it logically, it's a perfectly reasonable compromise."

"No, it's not," I said, outraged. "It's mean and cruel and totally unfair. Besides, I promised her I'd get her home if she helped me."

The Pooka coughed unhappily. "You shouldn't be promising what you can't deliver."

This wasn't happening. There had to be something else I could trade for Changeling's life, something nobody had thought of yet, something no supernatural would think of.

The Lady laughed. The Mirror glinted at the end of its golden chain.

"Before you give Changeling to the Hunt," I said slowly. "I have three questions for the Green Lady."

She shook her dreads. "You're a real pistol, kid, you know that? I don't know why I put up with you. After all this, you want to ask me questions?"

"They're important questions. For you, not me."

The Lady shrugged. "Okay. Shoot."

I licked my lips. "What are you going to do with the Magical Magnifying Mirror of the Mermaid Queen?"

"Find out stuff, of course. Isn't that what it's for?"

"What kind of stuff?"

"I don't know. Stuff." She frowned. "Watch it, kid. You're getting on my nerves."

"One last question, Lady." I took a deep breath. "Do you know how the Mirror works?"

She shrugged. "I'm a Genius, kid. I'll figure it out. I mean, how hard could it be? The Mermaid Queen has the brain of a flounder."

"Nevertheless," the Curator said in his dryest voice, "it might be as well to find out."

My heart was in my mouth as the Green Lady looked into the Mirror. She tapped it gently, then shook it. It seemed pretty obvious to me that she didn't have a clue what she was doing, but what did I know? Maybe being the Genius of Central Park was enough by itself to make the Mirror work, even without knowing how.

She turned the silver disk over and gave it an impatient thump, then looked up, her eyes glittering angrily. "It's busted," she hissed.

Hope sprang again, less painfully this time. "That's funny," I said casually. "Not very long ago, Changeling was using it to tell her about the Bull and the Bear."

"Then why isn't it telling *me* things? Is there a magic word? A secret button?" The Green Lady shook the Mirror under my nose. "You have to tell me. I may not be able to take back my boons, but believe me when I say I've got plenty of other ways to make you suffer."

"Oh, I believe you," I said honestly. "But still I can't help you. I don't have the first idea how the Mirror works."

There was a stunned silence in the Fountain Court, broken only by the bubbling of the dolphins and the Pooka's low, admiring whistle. The Green Lady ground her teeth. "You think you're pretty smart, don't you?"

I was beginning to enjoy myself. "Yes, I do. But I didn't figure out how to use the Mirror. Changeling did."

"Better start figuring out how to get the secret out of her, then."

"No deal. If you want Changeling to teach you how to use the Mirror, you have to promise to let her go home. Not just any old place Outside, but back to where she was when Carlyle snatched her."

"That's a lot to ask for a little Mirror lesson," the Lady said.

"It's a lot of Mirror. But only when you know how to use it."

"I'll think about it," the Lady said sulkily.

The Curator looked like he was going to say something, but I didn't give him the chance. "You won't think about it," I said. "You'll do it. I bet there's a rule about accepting a treasure without giving a boon in exchange. Knowledge, in this case, is as great a treasure as the Mirror itself."

The Green Lady's hair writhed once and lay still. "You are right, mortal child," she said. "Knowledge is precious. I accept your bargain. Drat."

"Does that mean that Changeling can go home?"

"Yes."

"You promise?"

"Okay, okay. I promise. But she has to bring me up to speed on the Mirror first."

The next part was torture. The Lady was too proud to talk directly to Changeling, and Changeling was too freaked out to talk directly to the Lady. So the Curator put them in separate rooms, and I went back and forth between them, translating. It took forever, but at least I learned how to use the Mirror myself. Which was a good thing, since the Lady couldn't remember how to turn it on from one time to the next and had to send for me to start it whenever she wanted to consult it.

But that was much later. That day, the Lady turned the Mirror on by herself twice in a row, and went off triumphantly to play with it. The Old Market Woman bustled off to make arrangements about getting Changeling back home again, and Fleet reminded me that I'd promised to talk to the Curator. She'd been making friends with the exhibits in European Painting and was very excited about taking painting lessons from Rembrandt's *Self-Portrait.*

I found the Curator, who was cataloging Japanese prints, and gave him all the reasons I could think of that the Museum should have a mortal changeling of its own. He listened for a while, then threw up his hands and said he'd make Fleet a Special Resident Member in exchange for the extra ticket to *Peter Pan.* So Fleet got her happy ending and the Green Lady got a date for the theatre.

Then it was time to say good-bye to Changeling.

She'd disappeared after the Lady's Mirror lesson, looking like she needed a little quiet brick-counting time. I found her in the Temple of Dendur, nibbling cheese and counting softly.

"Changeling," I said. "The Old Market Woman has sent for a Kid-napper from the Bureau of Changeling Affairs to take you home. It will be here soon. I came to say good-bye."

She stopped counting, but she didn't look up. "I want you to come with me."

"I can't, Changeling. I'm going home, too."

She nodded. "Will you visit me?"

"That's against the rules," I said miserably.

She frowned. "I do not like that rule."

"I don't either."

Now that it was time to say good-bye for real, I was getting kind of teary. I had a feeling like there was more

I wanted to say, but I wasn't sure what it was. I hesitated for a moment, then tugged my jade frog over my head and held it out to her. "Take it," I said. "It's a present. So you don't forget New York Between."

She cupped the frog in her hand and, for the first time, looked me straight in the eye. "I will not forget," she told me. "I have an unusually acute memory."

"I know. Good-bye, Jenny Goldhirsch. I'm really glad I met you."

I wanted to seal my gift with a hug, but I knew she'd hate that, so I settled for a wobbly smile and turned to go.

"Wait," Changeling said.

I turned back.

"I have a present for you, too." She held out her hand. When I just looked at it blankly, she made an impatient noise and grabbed my wrist. She reached in her pocket, brought out a pen, and started writing on my palm. The sensation was weird, somewhere between a tickle and a prickle.

"There," she said. "This is my address. I know your memory is poor so I wrote it down for you in case you ever think of a way to circumvent the rule about visiting."

I looked at the blue numbers and words inked on my palm.

"Thank you," I said thickly. And then I went to the Great Hall where the Pooka was waiting for me, and then we went home.

~ ~ ~ ~ ~ ~ ~ ~

The shadows were long and golden over Central Park Central. I trotted over the grass with the Pooka, in dog shape, at my heels. Central Park Central looked smaller than I remembered, and the buildings of the City closer and taller to the east and west. The setting sun glinted from the transparent wings of little flying Folk and scattered golden sequins over the surface of the Turtle Pond.

"Home," said the Pooka. "There's nothing like it. I'll be off now, if I can trust you to be keeping your own hide safe for a day or so. I've a powerful thirst for mischief on me, and a score with the Wild Hunt to settle."

"I'm fine," I said. "Thank you, Pooka."

"Pish-tush," said the Pooka, and loped off toward the North Woods.

I took the long way up to Belvedere Castle, avoiding the Shakespeare Garden and the Turtle Pond. Tomorrow I'd go and apologize to the Water Rat for ignoring his advice. But right now, all I wanted was to see Astris.

She'd lit a lamp in the kitchen. I could see the golden glow through the window as I came up the back steps. The courtyard was still warm from the sun. It had only been a few days since the Solstice Dance, and only a couple of full moons since I'd gone to fetch the Blockhouse brownie on spring cleaning day. But so much had happened since then that the adventure with Peg Powler and Blueberry felt like it had happened to another person.

I pushed on the door and went into the kitchen. Astris was standing at the kitchen table, beating a bowl of cookie dough like she was mad at it.

"I'm home," I said.

The spoon skidded across the floor. Then Astris did something she'd never done before. She dropped down onto all four paws, scampered across the floor, and jumped up into my arms. It was kind of a shock to feel how light she was and how small under her thick white coat of fur. I hugged her, and was about to kiss her twitching pink nose when she wriggled free of my grip and leapt to the floor.

"You needn't squeeze the life out of me," she scolded, smoothing her ruffled sides. But her whiskers quivered like fairies' wings, telling me how worried she'd been and how glad she was that I was home.

Of course she wanted me to go to bed right away, and of course I wanted to talk. To my surprise, I won that argument, and I sat down on my favorite stool to give her the outline of my adventures while she finished up the silvery moon cookies and put them in the oven to bake. Even though I only hit the highlights, I was still talking when they came out.

"That's quite a tale," she said when I had my mouth full of cookie. "The Water Rat is going to love it. What am I saying? Everybody in the Park is going to love it. Does it have a moral?"

"I guess," I said. "'Don't bite off more than you can chew'?"

Astris laughed. "Not all morals begin with 'Don't.'"

"No? You could have fooled me." I yawned. "How about, 'There's no place like home'?"

"True," said Astris, "but not the point. Try again."

I thought for a minute. "'Old stories are important, but sometimes you have to make up new ones.'"

"Very mortal," Astris said. "Very Neef. Say it just that way when you tell the story."

Neef's Guide to
Supernatural Beings

*Arranged in alphabetical order, with country of origin, where known.
All Folk in this list are traditional, except the ones designated "Literary
Characters," "Cyberspace," or "New York Between," who don't appear in
any of the old lists but exist anyway. Astris says it's important to remember that there are Folk all over the world, not just in New York Between,
but the New York ones are the only ones I know personally.*

Bäckahäst (*Scandinavia*): A black horse with a long,
drippy mane, who lives in the water. If you ride him, he'll
drown you, and then he'll eat you.

Banshee (*Ireland*): A spirit who shows up when somebody important is about to die and screams and cries like
nails across a blackboard, only louder.

Blindworm (*New York Between*): Seriously overgrown
worm, related to sewer alligators and wingless dragons.
Toothy, greedy, and icky, but not very bright.

Bogeyman/Bogeywoman/Bogie (*Everywhere*): The one

who will come and get you if you don't do as you're told. Some are traditional, some are made up. They're all bad news.

Boggarts (*England*): Household spirits who like to play painful practical jokes on mortals. Mostly, they're invisible, but sometimes they put on human or animal shapes so they can bug you better.

Bogles (*England*): Little, black, hairy goblins who hate, hate, hate a messy room so much they pinch you and pull your hair until you clean it up.

Brownies (*England*): Household spirits. Small (less than knee high), big ears, long arms. Neat freaks. Cleaning makes them happy. They'll go away if you give them clothes.

~ ~ ~ ~ ~ ~ ~ ~

Chih Nu (*China*): Celestial weaving maid and dressmaker to the Chinese gods and to New York supernaturals of taste and discernment.

Chin Chia (*China*): Spirit in charge of literature and scholarship. If you don't want blisters all over your body, don't ever let him find out you haven't done your homework.

Closet Monsters (*New York Between*): Monsters who live in mortals' closets. No two monsters look exactly alike, but all of them have long claws, big, shining eyes, and lots of teeth. Oddly enough, they only eat cloth or paper: socks and homework, mostly, but occasionally sweaters, shoes, and books as well. But they can hurt you if you poke around in their closets without paying attention.

Corn Spirits (*Europe*): Spirits of the wheat harvest. There's not a lot of wheat grown in Central Park, so the few that got stuck here by accident devote themselves to taking care of the grass.

~ ~ ~ ~ ~ ~ ~ ~ ~

Demons/Devils/Devi (*Everywhere*): Bad guys. They come in many colors, sizes, and shapes, with anywhere from two to twelve arms and one to five heads, all of them fully equipped with sharp teeth. If a named supernatural has the word "demon" in its description, keep away. Very far away.

Djinn (*Middle East*): Wind spirits who can take any form at all, although even in their mortal shape, they can't hide their goat feet and square-pupiled eyes. They can be helpful or nasty, depending on their mood, which changes frequently. They grant wishes, but you have to be very careful what and how you ask.

Dragons, Eastern (*China and Japan*): Long and colorful snakes with lizard legs and horns and long, delicate whiskers. Even though they don't have wings, dragons can fly.

They are basically guardian spirits, and therefore good guys, although kind of difficult to talk to. They read a lot and are very, very smart.

Dragons, Western (*Europe and Great Britain*): Hoarders and guardians of treasure. Some of them have wings; most of the ones left in New York don't. All of them have teeth and claws and like to sleep on beds of gold. The Dragon of Wall Street has eaten the larger immigrant examples, but there are a few left in Madison Avenue and Midtown.

Dryads (*Greece*): Guardian spirits of trees, groves, and woods. They look like wispy girls, and it's hard to get them to talk about anything but tree maintenance. Good dancers, though.

Dwarf (*Everywhere*): Short guy with long beard. Dwarves can be good or not-so-good, but they're almost never bad clear through. They're into metal and technology and gold.

~ ~ ~ ~ ~ ~ ~ ~

Elf (*Europe and Scandinavia*): In the Old Country, a general term for Folk. In New York Between, more commonly a mortal-shaped supernatural who is very beautiful and very stuck-up. They look down on changelings and Folk from other countries—basically, anybody who isn't an elf. They like music and art and breaking mortal hearts.

Eloise (*Fictional Character*): The Genius of the Plaza Hotel, Patroness of Spoiled Brats, and heroine of the series of books by the mortal Kay Thompson.

~ ~ ~ ~ ~ ~ ~ ~

Fairy (*Everywhere*): A general description that covers all kinds of nature spirits. They can be any size, but the most co mmon are small, delicate, and winged.

Fu Dog (*China*): Supernatural watchdog that hangs out in front of houses in Chinatown to protect the Folk who live there against demons and devils. They work in pairs.

~ ~ ~ ~ ~ ~ ~ ~

Garuda (*India*): A bird with a human head and a cool headdress. There's really only supposed to be one at a time, but the New York ones are little and colorful and there are plenty of them.

Genius (*Greece*): Traditionally, the spirit of a sacred mountain or grove or fountain. In New York Between, the spirit of a famous and interesting place.

Ghosts (*Mortal*): The ghosts of mortals who die in New York City are all over New York Between. I don't know much about them except that they mostly don't bother us, and we mostly aren't interested in them.

Ghouls (*Middle East*): Gray, bald, skinny. Flashy dressers. Good at business, the shadier the better. Favorite food: bodies, preferably human, preferably well-rotted, but they'll eat anything. They're not aggressive, but they're sneaky.

Giants (*Everywhere*): Big guys. How big they are and whether they're good-natured or nasty, dangerous or helpful, depends on where they're from. Scottish and Norse giants are pretty bad-tempered. French giants like to eat. English giants like to work in stone—they built a lot of New York Between. Giants are very sensitive to gold fever, which is why there are so many of them on Wall Street.

Gnomes (*Germany*): Short and strong like dwarves, only bald and clean-shaven. Also, they don't have any toes. They're more into guarding metal and treasure than making it.

Griffin (*Europe*): A fabulous monster with the body and tail of a lion and the head, neck, front legs, and wings of an eagle. Over in Europe, griffins have a reputation for being fierce and nasty. In New York Between, a lot of Geniuses keep them as guard dogs because they look impressive and are loyal to their masters.

~ ~ ~ ~ ~ ~ ~ ~

Hamadryad (*Greece*): The spirit of a tree. Not every tree has its own hamadryad, only the important ones, like the mulberry in the Shakespeare Garden. Hamadryads are even more single-minded than dryads and never leave their trees until the tree dies, when they die, too.

Hobgoblin (*England*): A small and ugly fairy who loves tricks, mischief, and bad puns.

Hooraw (*Origin Unknown*): Doesn't appear on any of the lists of traditional Folk, but from what Astris says, I'm guessing it's a big bird with extremely sloppy nesting habits.

Howlaa (*Isle of Man*): A weather spirit. Invisible and very loud.

Hu hsien (*China*): Fox spirits. Like the kitsune of Japan, they can look like foxes or beautiful girls, but they're much nicer. Because they're the patrons of civil servants, they often work as secretaries in Madison Avenue and Wall Street.

~ ~ ~ ~ ~ ~ ~ ~

Incubus *(Europe)*: A kind of demon who likes mortal women. The original boyfriend from Hell. Literally. Do not go out with an incubus, no matter how cute he is or how well he plays the guitar.

Iolanthe (*Fictional Character*): The heroine of *Iolanthe*, an operetta by the mortals Gilbert and Sullivan. Teaches dancing in Central Park. (*See* peri)

~ ~ ~ ~ ~ ~ ~ ~

Kappa (*Japan*): Demon with webbed fingers, a head that is open at the top like a bowl, and really good manners. Hobbies are karate, wrestling, and drowning humans. If you meet a kappa, remember to bow. When it bows back, its strength pours out of its head.

Kazna peri (*Russia*): Demon from the steppes. It's gray, with a nose out to there. It cooks its treasure over a blue fire from around the Spring Equinox to the Summer Solstice, and if you catch it, you get the treasure.

Kelpie (*Scotland*): A water spirit who can shape shift between horse and man shape. Either way, he likes to drown people.

Kid-napper (*New York Between*): An operative of the New York Bureau of Changeling Affairs. Any supernatural that likes stealing mortal children can become a Kid-napper, but pixies seem to be best at it.

Kitsune (*Japan*): Sometimes a fox; sometimes a foxy girl. Kitsune like mortal men. Sometimes they marry one and settle down in New York Outside, but it usually doesn't work out well. The name means "fox maiden."

Kobolds (*Germany*): Small and pointy-headed, like brownies. Miners and metalworkers, they live in the Financial Maze, in the Betweenways, and Grand Central Station.

Kraken (*Scandinavia*): A very, very big sea monster with lots of tentacles, like a giant squid. It's really a deep-sea creature and has no business in New York Harbor, but I'm guessing that even the Mermaid Queen would think twice about telling it to leave.

~ ~ ~ ~ ~ ~ ~ ~

Lamia (*Greece*): Half woman, half snake. She's got a short fuse and a big appetite for mortal men and lost children. You don't want to meet her on a dark night.

Leprechaun (*Ireland*): Little guy, maybe ankle height. Favorite colors: green and gold. Occupation: shoemaking. Hobbies: hoarding gold and drinking beer. If you can catch one and hold on to him, he has to give you all his gold. Hard to catch.

Leshii (*Russia*): Forest spirit, shapeshifter, trickster. Some of his shapes are wolf, old man, and dog. He can be helpful if he's in the mood, but he's got a strange sense of humor. When he plays hide-and-seek, he cheats. He's supposed to have a wife called Lesovikha, but I've never seen her.

Li (*China*): A fire spirit who will help you organize your daily life.

~ ~ ~ ~ ~ ~ ~ ~

Mélusine (*France*): Her top half is woman, her bottom half is snake. Not easy to get along with because of a messy romance in France that no one will tell me about.

Moss women (*Germany*): Wood nymphs, guardian spirits in a small way. They'll grant you a wish if you're sad enough.

~ ~ ~ ~ ~ ~ ~ ~

Nixies (*Germany*): Water nymphs. Like most water spirits, they have a thing about drowning people, so you have to be a little careful when you go swimming with them. But they like changelings and have always been very kind to me.

Nymphs (*Everywhere*): Nature spirits. Really beautiful girls. They live everywhere nature is found. They can be silly or kind or mischievous, but you can always distract them with presents or treats.

~ ~ ~ ~ ~ ~ ~ ~

Peg Powler (*England*): A bogeywoman. If the Lady let her, she'd eat any mortal kid who came near her. As it is, she likes to make them slip and get wet and muddy and scared. A good reason to stay away from boggy places.

Peris (*Fictional Characters*): Originally, peri was the name of a tiny, winged, female fairy in Persia, but that was so long ago that the last one disappeared long before America was even discovered. New York peris are mostly cast members from the comic opera *Iolanthe* by Gilbert and Sullivan, have English accents, and sing and dance a lot.

Piskie/Pixie (*Cornwall*): A wingless fairy, about knee height. Pixies like playing tricks. They steal things from mortals, including children. Their favorite color is green.

Pooka (*Ireland*): A shapeshifter and trickster whose main party trick in the Old Country was turning into a shaggy pony and getting kids to ride on him and throwing them off cliffs. He can also turn into a black dog, a black goat, and a man. My fairy godfather.

Puck (*England*): Puck's kind of complicated. On the one hand, he's a traditional hobgoblin. On the other hand, he's one of the Shakespeare fairies. He likes playing tricks and getting people into trouble, but he can be a good friend if he's in the mood. (*See* hobgoblin; Shakespeare fairies)

~ ~ ~ ~ ~ ~ ~ ~

Red Cap (*Holland*): A household spirit who always wears a red baseball cap and does his best to help poor people pay their heating bills. There's another, English, Red Cap who rides with the Wild Hunt and is pretty much what you'd expect: bloodthirsty, nasty, and very toothy. His cap is dyed red with blood. (See *Wild Hunt*)

~ ~ ~ ~ ~ ~ ~ ~

Selkie (*Ireland*): A man on the land; a seal in the sea. Very strong, very handsome, very gentle—for Folk.

Shakespeare fairy (*Literary Character*): Moth, Peaseblossom, Cobweb, and Puck appear in the play *A Midsummer Night's Dream* by Mr. William Shakespeare and in the Shakespeare Garden in Central Park. They're tiny, they have wings, and they spend most of their time decorating flowers and gathering dewdrops and nuts and things for their queen, Titania. They also sing and dance a lot.

Shinseën (*China*): Fairies who can look like little old men with long beards or beautiful girls. For some reason, in New York Between, they prefer the little-old-man look.

Sidhe (*Ireland*): Kind of like mortals, only lots more beautiful. Famous for red hair, violent tempers, and tragic love affairs. They live in the City, and cross over Outside a lot. (Pronounced "shee.")

Succubus (*Greece*): Girl incubus. A super high-maintenance girlfriend. They only go out with mortals, and the mortals are always really, really, really sorry.

Supernatural (*New York Between*): General term for anything that lives in New York Between that isn't mortal.

Swan maidens (*Northern Europe*): Swans who are girls; girls who are swans. Take your pick. If you can hide their feather cloaks, they have to marry you. My advice? Don't bother. They have bad tempers and they bite.

~ ~ ~ ~ ~ ~ ~ ~

Tanuki (*Japan*): Shapeshifter. Sometimes he's a little fat man; mostly he's a badger. He's always a trickster, with a very basic sense of humor and a weakness for rice wine.

Tech Folk/Machine Folk (*Cyberspace*): Geeks, nerds, bugs, gremlins, spam, worms, hackers, Tech dwarves, and computer wizards. Practically the newest Folk around—except for the gremlins and Tech dwarves, who have been around ever since machines were invented, under one name or another. Bugs, gremlins, worms, and spam are the bad guys. Computer wizards, geeks, nerds, and Tech dwarves are the good guys. Hackers are kind of like tricksters—they'll do whatever amuses them most. Tech Folk come from all over the world and hang out in Cyberspace until they're summoned through a computer.

Tengu (*Japan*): Sometimes he's a crow, sometimes he's a man, sometimes he's a little of each. He's also a bogeyman and a trickster. He particularly hates politicians and members of the clergy and is very sensitive about the length of his nose.

Theatre Folk (*New York Between*): Hoofers dance. Chorus lines sing and dance, mostly at the same time. Gaffers (and their assistants, called best boys) are in charge of lighting. Managers run the theatres. Scalpers (almost all of them ghouls) trade tickets to popular shows for an arm and a leg. Most actors are vampires, but fairies, elves, and other supernaturals sometimes act, too.

Trolls (*Scandinavia*): Big, ugly, hairy, and bad-tempered. They like treasure and solitude and biting people's heads off. They turn to stone in the sun.

~ ~ ~ ~ ~ ~ ~ ~

Undines (*Germany*): Water spirits, shapeshifters, unreliable, but not actively out to drown you. They can turn into snakes or fish, but mostly they don't bother.

~ ~ ~ ~ ~ ~ ~ ~

Vampires (*Europe*): Bloodsuckers. Formerly mortal, now undead. Since they're allergic to fairies, they don't usually bite changelings, but it's better to be safe than sorry. They can't stand the smell of garlic.

Veela (*Eastern Europe*): Nature spirits, guardians of wood and stream and tree. Independent, mischievous, beautiful, not all that interested in talking to mortal girls. They're wonderful dancers, though, and the squirrels like them.

Vodyanoi (*Russia*): Water spirits, shapeshifters. Part of the "lure you into the water and drown you horribly" crowd. When they look like mortals, it's mostly old men with green beards or fur or scales. They can also look like big fish or frogs.

~ ~ ~ ~ ~ ~ ~ ~ ~

Wall Street Folk (*New York Between*): More of a job description than a species of Folk, since almost any kind of supernatural can be infected by gold fever if it hangs out on Wall Street long enough. Folk who are predators turn into brokers. Tricksters and gamblers turn into investors. And that's all I know, even after Fleet explained it all to me.

Water Rat (*Literary Character*): From *The Wind in the Willows*, by the mortal author Kenneth Grahame. He's very English. Personally, I think he's sweet on Astris.

Werebears (*Scandinavia*): Shapeshifters who can look like men or bears. In the Old Country, they were mighty warriors. Here, they're mostly into sports.

Wild Hunt (*Northern Europe*): Traditionally, a host of evil spirits who hunt the souls of the damned on stormy nights. In New York Between, it's more of a mob made up of all the nasty Folk who like fresh meat and scaring people out of their wits.

Will-o'-the-Wisps (*England*): Nature spirits who look like little lights. They enjoy leading travelers astray. Similar spirits appear everywhere in the world under different names.

Wyrm (*Scandinavia*): A kind of dragon, wingless, snake-like, nasty-tempered, greedy. Not all that powerful, which is why the Dragon lets wyrms hang around Wall Street.

Wyvern (*Europe*): A kind of fabulous monster. Body of a snake, head of a dragon, wings of a bat, legs of a bird. It likes fighting better than gold, which makes it an excellent security guard.

ACKNOWLEDGMENTS

Every writer writes to please herself. But a writer who publishes had better please her audience as well, or else what's the point?

I am very grateful to all the people who have been this story's earliest audience. The Genrettes (Laurie R. Marks, Rosemary Kirstein, and Didi Stewart) encouraged me through the difficult early drafts and kept me focused on bringing my beloved New York alive to people who don't live there. The Massachusetts All-Stars (Kelly Link, Gavin Grant, Holly Black, Cassandra Claire, Sarah Smith, and Ellen Kushner) supplied lively critical discussion, useful comments, and some very cool doodles in the margins of the manuscript. Keri MacNair supplied research materials. Helen Pilinovsky and Veronica Schanoes cast a professional eye over my folklore. Mimi Panitch, Deb Manning, Patrick O'Connor, Eve Sweetser, Els Kushner, Tess Baker, Shweta Narayan, and Nathaniel Smith caught inconsistencies, queried motivations, and asked interesting and useful questions. Davey Snyder gave me insights into the speech patterns of Executive Assistants and Dragons. Ellen Klages not only read the manuscript five times (or was it six?), but had something intelligent and kind to say every time. Sara Berg gave me an invaluable education on Asperger's Syndrome and a copy of Dawn Prince-Hughes's wonderful *Songs of the Gorilla Nation*. Holly Black rallied around with moral support, advice, and some very shrewd suggestions during the difficult final draft.

I also want to thank my younger readers: Maya and Rafaela Carlyle-Swedberg, Chiara Azzaretti, and most of all, Liran Bromberg, who honestly, yet kindly, told me what they thought of Neef and her adventures, and the places where things got confusing.

Special thanks to Christopher Schelling, my agent, for taking care of the business end so I don't have to worry about it and being a good friend and perceptive reader as well. And thanks to Sharyn November, whose editorial style is a fine, rich mixture of enthusiastic encouragement and incisive, detailed criticism. Nobody could ask for a better, more attentive editor.

Thank you to Eleanor and Leigh Hoagland and Kelly Link and Gavin Grant, who let me retreat to their houses in the country at the two points when I needed it the most.

And finally, my love and most profound thanks to Ellen Kushner, who named the Eloise Award for Naughty Children, liked Honey when no one else quite understood why she was there (including me), walked all over the North Woods with me looking for the Blockhouse, which wasn't at all where I thought it was, and got us safely home again.